*Sugaring Off*

ALSO BY GILLIAN FRENCH

*The Missing Season*

*The Lies They Tell*

*The Door to January*

*Grit*

# Sugaring Off

## GILLIAN FRENCH

ALGONQUIN   2022

Published by Algonquin Young Readers
an imprint of Workman Publishing Co., Inc.
a subsidiary of Hachette Book Group, Inc.
1290 Avenue of the Americas
New York, New York 10104

LIBRARY OF CONGRESS CATALOGING-IN-PUBLICATION DATA
Names: French, Gillian, author.
Title: Sugaring off / Gillian French.
Description: Chapel Hill, North Carolina : Algonquin, 2022. |
Audience: Ages 12 and up. | Audience: Grades 7-9. | Summary: Partially deaf,
seventeen-year-old Owl feels the most free hiking the forested areas around
her family's New Hampshire farm, but the appearance of Cody, a magnetic
young man hired to help with the sugaring off, forces Owl to make difficult
decisions about their relationship and her relationship with her family.
Identifiers: LCCN 2022018154 | ISBN 9781643752709 (hardcover) |
ISBN 9781643753348 (ebook)
Subjects: CYAC: Sugar maple—Tapping—Fiction. | Family life—Fiction. |
New Hampshire—Fiction. | Love—Fiction. | LCGFT: Novels.
Classification: LCC PZ7.1.F75476 Su 2022 | DDC [Fic]—dc23
LC record available at https://lccn.loc.gov/2022018154

10 9 8 7 6 5 4 3 2 1
First Edition

*For Rhys, who was born during*
*the writing of this book,*
*and for my mom, Jaci, who inspires me.*

# Part I

## MAPLE SYRUP GRADE:
## Golden

*Made from the earliest
sap runs of the season;
light in color, delicate in taste.*

# 1

Owl's first thought is of the foxes, getting to them before the man does, if it isn't already too late. She's sure-footed—Seth always says so—gaining easy purchase on the steep, wooded slope beside the driveway the moment Mrs. Baptiste drops her off at the farm. There's no time to waste; when Owl saw the man out the window of the Suburban, he was almost halfway to the first curve of the access road to the sugarbush. Black ski cap, shoulders hunched against the cold, pack on his back.

Icy crust crunches underfoot, collapses beneath her scant 120 pounds, but Owl rides the skid, grabbing low-hanging branches only long enough to keep her balance, until she bursts out onto the snowshoe trail and pelts off down the gleaming, hard-packed surface to the clearing where the den is.

She slides onto her knees behind the ground blind she built from saplings, balsam bows, and jute twine, peering through, her gaze riveted on the den entrance, a hole dug into the hillside.

There are the usual crisscrossing trails of tracks—four toes, four claws, a chevron-shaped heel—but no way of being sure if the foxes are inside. Mating season is still on—Seth and Holly mentioned waking to the chilling shrieks of a vixen this past week; Owl herself wakes to nothing, save her alarm clock bed shaker beneath her pillow on school days—so the foxes may be out roaming now, about to wander directly into the path of the man.

Owl's gloved hands squeeze into fists; she allows the foxes two, three, four seconds more to show themselves. Then it's time to act. The farm is maybe a five-minute run from here, but there's no guarantee that Holly's home from work yet; Seth will be driving the skidder in Gunnar's woodlot until supper. These trees are Owl's. She'll go it alone.

REACHING THE ACCESS road means a dash across two gullies, ten minutes if she really pushes it up those embankments, digging handholds into the snow to keep from backsliding. Her thighs are burning by the time she reaches level ground again, entering the sugarbush, where the land becomes groomed, looking more like the forest of storybooks, open spaces between maples allowing her to run all out toward the road. Five-gallon galvanized sap buckets fly by like hovering moons, hundreds of them, often two or four to a tree—Owl ought to know; she helped Seth and Holly hang them last week, fitting spouts into holes drilled into the trunks—until the ground hits a sharp downward pitch, and the dirt road lies open ahead.

Owl hustles along the crest of the embankment until she catches up to him; he's only a few minutes ahead, moving at a slow, trudging pace. She lets the noise of her approach alert him to her presence, stopping where she stands, on the high ground, one hand resting against the nearest tree.

The man turns, his gaze traveling, not immediately picking her out of the woods, dressed as she is in a brown weathered Carhartt coat, neutral-colored for blending. He doesn't freeze at the sight of her, but instead slowly rests back on one heel, staring.

"This is private property." She speaks loudly—usually something she cringes from, moderated volume and diction vital to her, a shield—but she's using every tool of intimidation she knows against a man over six feet tall, broad-shouldered, built. She has her folding knife, of course—always has her knife. Searches for any sign that he's already bagged one of the foxes, but the backpack he wears is black nylon, something you'd bring to school, not store a bloody carcass inside. "You can't be out here."

As he moves closer, she sees the youth on him. Unlined face, clean-shaven. No man—perhaps just barely. His heavy, angular bone structure lends him some years, hat pulled down right over his brows, giving his eyes a low, tracking look. Neither is he smiling, doing anything to disarm. He scans the trees behind her, maybe wondering if someone else might step out. "Where'd you come from?" Some of this she picks up with her left ear—hearing loss only mild in that one—and the rest she reads from his lips.

Owl hesitates, shifts, starkly reminded of how seldom she really deals with strangers. "No hunting."

He flashes his open palms at her, concealed in black knit gloves. "See a gun?" First hint of mocking in his expression. He advances further, testing, seeing if she'll back up. "You forest ranger around here?"

"I found Duke traps. Four of them." Last month, baited with dog food and sown around by the very edge of their posted property line along the mountain roadside, gleaming stainless steel, mostly hidden by scattered dead leaves. "Coil spring traps."

Nothing shows in his face. She waits, rocking slightly on the balls of her feet, not sure what she expects, only sure that her heart rate has picked up and suddenly she's not so certain of herself in this role, protector.

"Come down here." He tilts his head toward the packed dirt. "Come on." She watches, held to this spot by only the thinnest resolve. "What, don't you want me to see you?"

He lunges then, hands held out to grab.

She's in flight, bursting through the brush like a grouse before she registers the exaggerated stomp of his boot at her—like scaring off a stray—but the fear of him giving chase still drives her another twenty feet before she spins around.

Glimpses his form through the trees, continuing up the road in the direction he'd been heading, head tipped slightly back now, as if he might be laughing at her.

OUTRAGE FUELS OWL the rest of the way back to the farm, past the red-shingled sugarhouse, the equipment shed, the side-by-side. Holly turns from filling her arms with firewood, which is kept stacked in neat rows along the deck of their A-frame cabin, to watch Owl's approach, her eyes wide and startled.

Owl brakes at the railing, grasping the welded wire fencing panel, using her free hand to sign until she can speak, keeping it simple to make sure Holly gets it. *Man*—open hand, splayed fingers, thumb touching from forehead to chest.

Her aunt sets the stove lengths down. "Where?"

"On the access road."

"Hunter?"

Owl heaves her shoulders up, scanning the open pasture to the tree line. When she turns back, she's missed something Holly's said; Owl recognizes the awkward spooling of seconds well.

"Where's your backpack?" Holly repeats, pulling her phone out of the pocket of her fleece vest, checking to see how the cell signal looks before texting Seth.

"The driveway." Hesitates, torn between embarrassment and wanting Holly to understand the incident on the embankment, no one around but herself and the stranger. "He tried to . . . scare me. Run me off."

Holly's brow creases and she gives up on an immediate response from Seth, tucking her phone away and gathering the wood. "Let's go in, okay?"

In the kitchen—compact, cabinets and half-sized appliances along the left wall, table and chairs against the right—Holly checks on the bread dough she's left to rise, then goes into the small living room space beyond to feed the woodstove, her attention pulled to the front windows by something Owl can't hear. "Speak of the devil."

Outside, Seth's Ford F-350 pickup crawls to a stop beside Holly's Land Rover; he climbs out—too thin these days, walking with a pronounced limp—holding Owl's backpack up by the top loop as he comes through the door. "Forgot something."

"There's a guy in our woods. I told him he was trespassing, but he wouldn't leave." Owl watches Seth's face, waiting for him to register the violation of it. To unlock the gun cabinet and bring out one of the rifles he keeps meticulously cleaned but rarely uses, the last time over a year ago, when he shot a raccoon Owl found behind the house, dragging one hind leg, biting at the air—obvious signs of rabies.

Instead, he pauses, shuts the door behind him, pulling his camo ball cap from his head and tossing it to the tabletop in a way that Holly can't stand, then sets her backpack beside it. "Let me call Wallace." Goes to the CapTel landline phone, speed-dialing Wallace Morley, neighbor, sometimes fishing buddy, the phone automatically connecting to an operator at a distant captioning service Owl regards with some superstitious misgiving, even though she's the entire reason they applied for it.

The conversation is brief, words scrolling hesitantly across the caption screen as they speak, a hoarse laugh on Seth's end before hanging up. "It's Wall's grandson. He sent him up." His gaze on Owl is steady. "Boy's early. Wasn't expecting him for over a week."

Holly folds her arms. "First I've heard of it."

"Haven't had a chance to tell you. I hired him on to help with the sugaring."

Holly's response is shocked relief, stance slackening. She's been after Seth to get some help other than Owl for a couple years now, a suggestion he's staunchly refused, no matter how badly his knee aches at the end of a long day; but nobody can miss how often he uses the side-by-side and the tractor now, anything to cut down on walking around the sugarbush. "Wallace told me the kid's been looking for work, something to get him out of Manchester."

Holly pauses. "Owl said he scared her."

"I said he tried. It was stupid." Owl's tone is steely, looking to Seth. "I thought he was after the foxes."

Uncertainty passes between the grown-ups, but Seth scoops his cap back onto his head, earning a wry, half-amused look from his wife. "Nah. City kid. Doubt he knows his ass from his elbow when it comes to trapping."

"Or sugaring." Holly's smiling now, an expression not unlike the sun hitting full across the face of their cabin in late morning, blasting the interior with light. Broad cheekbones, teeth white against her brown skin, about four shades darker than Seth and Owl's Scotch Irish peasant stock: She's Passamaquoddy, though Holly's heritage and past are something Owl treads around carefully, a patchwork of impressions pulled from offhand comments or stories told to Owl when she was little. Owl knows how it is to hold privacy close as an infant, to nurse a hurt that others wouldn't understand, even family. "Why didn't he come to the house first? Does he think you pick syrup bottles off the trees?"

"Well, I told Wall that I'd start Cody out tapping the last half acre we didn't get to yet. Guess they must've figured I'd be

9

out there today." Owl's nose wrinkles at anyone granting the stranger a name. "I'll load up the wagon, show him around, get him situated. Sounds like maybe you two got off on the wrong foot." Seth grasps the doorknob as he turns back to Owl, switching to the unspoken wavelength they share, cultivated from the day he and Holly brought her home to Waits Mountain, a seven-year-old with a four-inch fracture in her skull and a stunned terror of her brave new world without sound: *Want to come along?* his expression says.

She takes a deliberate step back, jaw set.

He nods slowly. "Okay." Opens the door to the chill day. "Plenty of time to start fresh tomorrow."

# 2

The morning Suburban ride is always quiet, a reprieve for Owl; afternoons, the little kids are rowdy, talking to the back of her head, poking her shoulder in frustration before remembering she can't hear them over the background noise of three different conversations and the radio. Plus, Aida Frankel acknowledges no one in the morning, not even Owl. Again, relief.

Mrs. Baptiste has to leave the house by five thirty in order to pick up all six of the Waits Mountain kids and get them down to the schoolhouse in the valley before the first bell rings, and everyone is logy with sleep, even nine-year-old knot of energy Micah Streeter, who slumps in his insulated parka, head lolled toward the window, watching the trees stream by with unfocused acceptance.

Griffin Baptiste, eighteen, rides in the passenger seat beside his mother, his earbuds in place; the middle row is claimed by Aida and Owl—the Seventeens, as Mrs. Baptiste calls them—the center seat between them reserved for Aida's huge keychain-jangling purple glitter bag, mostly so none of the little kids get the wild idea they might be welcome between the older girls. But sisters Lulu and Tegan Boulier, six and eight, know their place—beside Micah in the third row.

Aida sits with the heel of one sneaker dug into the edge of the seat, the hood of her silver cropped puffer coat flipped up, a few strands of her hair visible, streaked a shade of teal Owl would never admit reminds her of rocks at the bottom of an aquarium (knowing in full detail what a triumph it was for her best friend to badger her mother into allowing her to dye it at all). Aida swipes doggedly at a phone that probably isn't even connected right now, not this high up the mountain, meaning she's cycling through screenshots she's saved on her camera roll: boys with artificially tanned skin, molded abs flexed above low-riding jeans, hair blown out or buzzed into fades, usually posed as if cramming themselves into some sort of invisible box. Owl's seen them before, while leaning against Aida's shoulder at recess as her friend debates the hotness of each, demanding Owl's affirmation, barely waiting for her reply before swiping on to the next.

Now, Owl is agitated, distracted, but Aida notices nothing, doesn't even look over, her eyes puffy, one brow cocked in warning to all, intent upon the Hotness Reel.

Owl's dreading not just having to face Cody again when she gets home, but working with him in her woods. *Her* trees, her sacred place. Seth made no mention of having fired Cody on the spot when he came back from the sugarbush yesterday; in fact, he didn't speak about the boy at all over supper, answering Holly's "Get everything smoothed out?" with only an affirmative grunt, intent upon his chili and bread, refusing to acknowledge Owl's insistent stare.

Denying Owl eye contact is soaping over her window into your soul—nobody knows that better than Seth—and it was a clear message told through body language: *Simmer down.* Eventually, grudgingly, she'd dropped her attention to her own meal.

IT'S A FORTY-FIVE-MINUTE drive to the valley down the switchbacking mountain road—lengthened by waiting for a group of six whitetail deer to finish a scrambling dash from one side to the other—where the North Plover Schoolhouse stands in the barren township center. No businesses last in remote North Plover, this far into the Great North Woods region, except for ones like Seth's, existing from what the mountain provides. The school's more like a church, with its white clapboards and bell tower. There's a slate placard with the year 1854, another sign marking the building as being on the National Register of Historic Places. The old entrances, one for boys and one for girls, flanking the top of the broad front steps, now filter the K–6 students into one half of the two-room school—formerly one room before the remodel in the 1960s—the 7–12 students into the other.

Mrs. Baptiste parks in the side lot, reaching back between the seats as the kids unbuckle, winking at Owl with her usual brash cheerfulness as she holds her hand out for the knife. With a flicker of inner mutiny, Owl deposits it in the woman's palm, and Mrs. Baptiste locks it into the glove compartment, not to be returned until the school day is over.

THURSDAYS ARE A Ms. Z day for Owl, and Owl alone.

They sit together in the cloakroom, a broad entryway where coats are hung; there's literally nowhere else for private work in the schoolhouse, unless they want to go outside on school property, which they did in warmer months. They'd sit beneath one of the huge heritage oaks on a quilt Ms. Z—short for Zaborowski ("Call me Ms. Z, if you like; saves time")—carries from the trunk of her car, exposed roots protruding from the earth around them like the tentacles of some deep-sea creature, attempting an undulating escape to a distant coastal home.

But today, it's twenty-eight degrees outside, typical late February temps, so they sit in the long passageway—preserved much as it was when Seth went here, and at the turn of the nineteenth century—dark wooden wainscoting, rows of metal coat hooks, and shelves for boots lining the walls. There's a student desk between Owl and Ms. Z. The inner classroom door is closed on the study hall happening inside. On the wall hangs a sign beneath glass, a list of rules for pupils from over a hundred years ago, meant to be humorous in its antiquated-ness: TELLING TALES OUT OF SCHOOL—8 LASHES, CLIMBING OVER 3 FEET UP A TREE—I LASH.

Ms. Z brings an orange to their sessions—it's been her custom since she replaced Mr. Weir as Owl's itinerant teacher of the Deaf last May, when the old man retired—gradually peeling it with her strong, limber fingers during their frequent physical silences, so much more forceful than a verbal pause. Last spring, during one of their tête-à-têtes beneath the oak trees, Micah apparently watched them out a window and, on the Suburban ride home, demanded to know why Owl got picnics when everybody else was doing boring stuff. Owl laughed out loud—Ms. Z wasn't somebody Owl could picture gadding about with a wicker basket and pink lemonade—but Mrs. Baptiste hushed him with startling sharpness. No one spoke for a long time, not even Aida, leaving Owl with the sense that it was she, not Micah, who'd let something unpleasant loose to roam the cab.

How could she explain to him that the orange isn't really food? It's about order, somehow, correctness, a metaphor Owl senses but hasn't fully figured out. If the orange is some sort of test, maybe Owl's lack of understanding adds to the frustration gleaming from her teacher's motionless black eyes during their twice-weekly standoffs. But self-control runs in such a broad, cool stream through this woman that even Owl, who can freeze people out better than almost anyone she knows, often finds her stomach twisted with uncertainty about ten minutes into their meetings.

*How is everything?* Ms. Z signs, whisking one hand up the center of her chest, middle finger depressed. She's sitting with her back to a window that's set into the wall at the end of the cubby section for the little kids, all of whom are currently outside enjoying recess, puffing around the windswept yard in snow pants and pom-pom hats, tightrope-walking the crusty jetties of snow. The gray light streaming through the thick bubbled antique glass casts shadows on her teacher's face, making it difficult for Owl to read her lips; Owl is convinced Ms. Z knows it, that this is the reason why they always set the desk and chairs up at this end of the cloakroom. To deliberately *handicap* her, a word she hates, but what else should you call it? Sabotage?

"Okay." Owl speaks aloud as she bumps the tip of her thumb to her chest twice.

It always begins this way, Ms. Z signing a flurry at her the second they sit down, as if Owl will be bursting for this chance to talk with anyone ASL-fluent, while Owl watches, incredulous, pulse accelerating, grabbing meaning here and there, the rest lost in her inability to keep pace. Compared to Seth and Holly, who learned the ASL alphabet with Owl years ago but still recognize only basic phrases, Owl is a master—here, she's shrunken to child size again, trying to navigate real-time conversation and dreading a look of awkward pity or, worse, are-you-stupid-or-what frustration when she has no choice but to admit she didn't understand.

Outside, the kids now run circles around the old three-seater privy, which used to service the student body, a source of sheer delight to the littles. Micah plays Pied Piper, as usual, and Owl watches through the front window as he skids to a stop in front of the privy door, throwing his arms out as he belts something operatically at the girls, which Owl lip-reads—*Will you peeee with meeee?*—and she fights an impulsive smile as Lulu and Tegan double over, shrieking laughter.

"Rochelle." Ms. Z's voice is level—a ruler edge slapping the desktop—and Owl pulls her attention back to the only person who ever calls her by the given name she'd rather forget. They lock eyes a moment, then Ms. Z clears her throat. "Please get your assignment folders out."

While Owl opens her backpack, Ms. Z takes the navel orange and two rectangles of paper towel from her leather satchel, waiting until she and Owl are facing each other again to say, "Do you feel confident in your understanding of Mr. Duquette's lectures this week?" She's not signing anymore, but peeling the orange, digging her short-trimmed thumbnail into the pocked skin, exposing ten flawless segments, which aren't the least bit appetizing to Owl; oranges haven't looked good to her in months. "Did you get your quadratic equations back from Tuesday?"

"I got an eighty-four." The air between them cools another few degrees; Ms. Z went over each practice problem with her on Monday before the test, reinforcing the instructions with one-on-one speech and sign, which is the whole purpose of these meetings. This is School Administrative Unit 203 doing the best it can by Owl, the only designated special needs student in the North Plover district, having a teacher of the Deaf drive well over an hour from the other, larger district school in Stokely, just like it does with art and music education for the whole student body.

Ms. Z lines up five segments on Owl's paper towel. "Let's see if we can't improve upon a low B, shall we." The words grow frost. "If we try our very hardest."

A few minutes into their work, Owl gives in and bites into a slice of orange. It may not be food, but you *can* eat it.


"—SO THEN MY mom said she was going to take my phone, which is just stupid anyway, since she's the one always making me call her basically every time I need to fart." Aida snuffs, swipes her nose upward with the heel of her stretchy-gloved palm, huddling close to Owl as they walk around the flagpole, the best way they've found of keeping their circulation flowing during lunch. Aida always says she *has* to get out, so they mostly eat from Ziploc bags poking from their coat pockets, sandwich halves and pretzel sticks, as they follow their circuit, heads bowed into the cold.

"Were you really going to meet him?" Owl studies her friend's profile. They walk with their arms locked together, not just to conserve body heat, but because it's vital to Aida that Owl never miss a word of hers. Ever.

"No! I told you I wasn't." Feels Owl's scrutiny and huffs, cheeks flushed with pleasure and windburn. "*He* DMed *me.* How is that my fault? I didn't even have a chance to decide before my mom went snooping in my accounts. And I was going to tell him no." Gives Owl a sidelong look and bursts out laughing. "I was!"

"Mm-hmm." Aida's usually deep into one online relationship or another, boys from Nashua or Concord, somewhere close enough that they could potentially meet in person if things got serious—which they never have. There was always some spat via text, clearly proving the boy of the moment unworthy. How you could find anything major to fight about with someone who existed only as a profile pic was a mystery to Owl, but at least it kept Aida from hopping a bus south.

"No, seriously. I was." Aida's getting earnest and offended, so Owl stops teasing. Isn't worth enduring the silent treatment for the rest of the afternoon, especially since they sit next to each other in class, and partner in absolutely everything.

Aida requires very little of Owl—she's already so convinced of everything—and maybe that's why their companionship has worked since childhood. Owl checks in, checks out, while Aida expounds upon, well, the world, Owl wedging in a question here and there when there's a pause for breath, and then it's goodbye until tomorrow. They used to go over to each other's houses, have sleepovers, but most of that has petered off over the last couple years. Owl supposes they're drifting. It doesn't really hurt. Never had much in common but age and proximity, and in a school with a grand total of eleven kids, the additional five pulled from the surrounding valley area, proximity is everything. Eventually, after graduation, Aida will move to attend a community college in Portsmouth or the Lakes Region, and Owl will stay here, on the mountain, where she belongs.

The older students' door bangs open, and both girls look over to see Griffin Baptiste amble down the steps. He's husky, with shaggy, dark hair, hands in the pockets of his drab olive parka, hood up, features lost in the fluttering gray ruff, the wire of his earbuds mostly zipped into his coat, where his phone is stashed. Owl says, "Wonder what he listens to?" as they watch him walk to the playground equipment on the little-kid side.

Aida snorts. "Probably French verb conjugation. Brat got a ninety-nine on the last quiz, tu savais ça?"

Owl shakes her head as Griffin sinks onto one of the swings, hangs his arms around the chains, and pushes off slightly with his boots, body bent against the chill. Technically, they're not supposed to go over there during lunch, because it could distract the little kids from their lessons, but for Griffin, Mrs. Montrose-Perlman will close the shades. Since moving down from the Houlton Maliseet tribal lands with his parents five years ago, Griffin's earned the highest GPA of any of them; he's probably one of the only students who can be trusted to stick to the independent-study structure of senior year without a teacher on top of him all the time, and everyone knows he's applied to MIT to major in chemical engineering.

"Must be weird being the only senior." Aida's tone is musing, unconcerned.

Owl glances over sharply, unbelieving, in the same instant Aida seems to realize what she's blundered into. As if either of them needed a reminder of the other would-be senior who'd been a schoolhouse kid until last year, the mere thought of him enough to bring wounded resentment bubbling up in Owl's core.

Aida sniffs again in the silence, shoves her tangled curls back. Now's her chance—some apology, any acknowledgment from Aida, anything to dispel the ghosts—but instead: "These corn chips taste nasty." Her fist strikes the bag through her pocket, making a small crunch, and Owl's hot gaze finds nowhere to land but the pavement. "Mom went cheap again."

# 3

Owl visits the foxes on the way to the sugarbush—an excellent way to stall before she has no choice but to deal with Cody again.

She wears her snowshoes this time, unfastening them as she sits on the layer of balsam branches inside the blind, meant to keep her butt dry and cover her human scent while waiting for a sighting. On weekends, she brings her art pad, and sketches until her fingers go numb.

Today, her timing is near-perfect: The faintest rustle from a cluster of chokecherry bushes along the tree line, and then the male emerges, clutching something in his jaws. A white-footed mouse, crushed and shaken to death, naked tail dangling.

Taut with excitement, Owl leans slowly forward on her knees, cursing every slight crunch of the snow beneath her weight as she reaches for her phone, not wanting to take her eyes off the fox for even a second.

He threads his way along the trees toward the den, coat rusty and sleek, tail a magnificent white-tipped plume, one of the healthiest she's sighted anywhere on the mountain in the past few years. She manages to snap three pictures before he reaches the den opening, slipping down into the hole, where perhaps the vixen is waiting, about to share in the small feast her mate has caught.

Owl watches the screen as the male's small, keen face materializes at the shadowy opening, not emerging, simply watching and listening—sensing her, hidden. Wondering what her next move will be, maybe. She taps the Shutter button repeatedly, wishing there was some way to project the understanding into his brain that she can be trusted, would never harm, never violate.

In time, he recedes, vanishing back, and Owl steps into her snowshoes again, eager now to reach the sugarbush, where Seth is already working, so she can show him her pics, the best she's captured so far.

Her rapid footsteps disappear over the rise, surrendering the clearing to stillness.


ON THE WAY:

Raccoon tracks, barely discernible in the dusting of powder that fell on the hardened snow during the night; some scat.

The call of a chickadee, right above Owl in a cedar tree, near enough for her to hear. She stops, closing her eyes, appreciating it.

A kill spot; something got a large bird, leaving a spray of blood and some scattered feathers Owl can't identify. She snaps a pic, then pockets one of the feathers.

SHE FINDS SETH and Cody toward the edge of the property, which is marked with orange plastic ribbons tied around every fifth or sixth tree. They're nearly done tapping—a small mercy—only about twenty trees left without buckets. Guiltily relieved that her heel dragging paid off, Owl walks down the slope to meet her uncle, who doesn't look away from angling his cordless drill bit into the south side of a trunk to bore a shallow hole. Pulling a stainless-steel spile from the drawstring bag dangling from his tool belt, he reaches for his hammer, then glances over, watching her pull off her snowshoes, the frames too cumbersome for navigating around the trees. "Just in time" is his only comment before nodding to where he's left her drill and tool belt in the topmost of a stack of sap buckets.

She gets right to it; as heavily as the fox pics weigh in her pocket, she knows Seth values hard work above almost all else, even if it's not in his nature to nag—his sole dry comment packs more punch than any lecture.

Cody kneels a few trees over, drill running. She narrows her eyes at his back as she chooses an untapped row for herself. He wears the same wool peacoat as yesterday, dark ombre plaid, ski cap pulled low, jeans, engineer boots. He acts as if he doesn't know she's there. She, for one, feels his presence like the tip of a nail scraped furiously against glass—but she follows suit, keeping her head turned from him as she hangs three buckets to a tree; these maples are old, woods run, thick enough to handle multiple taps.

Between the three of them, it doesn't take long to tap the remaining trees. Owl keeps track of Cody's progress from the corner of her eye, but he never seems to hesitate or fumble. When the last lid has been hung in place, only then does Seth walk over to Cody, who straightens up from hanging a final bucket.

Using his gloved forefinger to nudge the bucket aside on its hook, Seth checks out the placement of the spile, clear sap already trickling from a vein in the tree. "Nice work. Didn't go too deep." He won't make a show of checking the others. Seth's not one to micromanage, either, even when you want him to, always giving you enough rope to tie your own knot— or hang yourself with, as the case may be. Cody says nothing, shows nothing, eyelids heavy, mouth set in a line.

"We already emptied the full buckets into the horizontal tank." Seth speaks to Owl, who stands with her arms folded, drill dangling. "Figured we'd show Cody how to store the sap and all that. Uh . . ." Seth scratches the side of his neck, glances at Cody. "This is my niece, Owl. Guess you two already ran into each other." Neither Cody nor Owl speak. "She'll be helping with the sugaring. Always does." Seth clears his throat in the silence, digging the side-by-side keys out of his coat chest pocket. "Well. Who's riding shotgun?"

"I've got my snowshoes," Owl says, then ignores Seth's look; they both know her shoes fit fine in the space behind the seats.

Seth tosses Cody the keys, and he catches them, a flicker of something—surprise, maybe—passing over his face, then gone. "You know how to get back?" Seth says. "Driveway's on the left. There's a sign if you—"

"I know where it's at." Not gruff; blunt. Cody turns and starts through the trees toward the access road, stopping to gather the unused buckets and lids without being asked.

THEY WALK THROUGH the woods together, Seth keeping on Owl's left side to make himself heard. The day working in the bush has hobbled him, his bad knee barely able to support weight, even with the flexible brace on, and he's sweating lightly along his hairline and upper lip.

Owl pulls out her phone and opens her camera roll. "Look."

Seth takes the phone, angling it up to ease the glare on the screen as he checks out the fox. "What a beaut. You got lucky. Big ol' guy, isn't he?"

"Tail adds about three feet." Their smiles are reflections of each other, satisfaction found in a passion even Holly doesn't quite share. "I think the vixen's going to have kits soon."

"She showing?"

"I haven't seen her in a while. Just a feeling I got near the den today. Like she's nesting." Seth hands her the phone, and she trades him for the mystery feather. "Couldn't ID it."

Seth sucks his teeth, checking out the brown-and-gray pattern with a speckling of white. "Give you three hints. You find them sitting in pines, eating needles off." Counts off a second finger. "Male struts around like a damn fool, ruffling his

25

wings to get the ladies interested. Looks like a chicken and about as bright."

"Spruce grouse. Fool hen." Owl's lips move sardonically, remembering her own flight through the bushes yesterday. "Something big must've gotten it. Fisher?"

"Could be. Maybe coyote. They're back." He doesn't say how he knows; Owl assumes he's heard the pack howling in the night from somewhere on the 3,196-foot summit. "Your grandpa used to say they were vermin, shoot 'em whenever he got the chance. Had some skulls hanging on the side of the shed for the longest time."

Owl searches his face, guessing those skulls were one of the things Seth changed as soon as her grandfather died and the farm became his. It's not the kind of thing he'd keep on display. She never met the old man; he passed from cancer when she was three and still living in the tiny apartment over the convenience store in Dover, a stranger to her family. But she gathers that maple sugaring and a love of the woods was about the only thing Grandpa Dotrice and his eldest son, Seth, had in common.

As they walk through the backyard, the sugarhouse—Seth's pride—with its vented cupola, comes into view, firewood stacked neatly about six feet high beneath the attached shed roof. In the circular drive, Cody leans against the side-by-side, hands in his jeans pockets, watching their approach. It's never occurred to Owl how easy it is to hide your thoughts just by covering your eyebrows. He doesn't look at her, and she pretends there's something interesting on the horizon.

"Pull right up to the door here, and we'll hook the hose to the horizontal tank." Seth props the double doors open with the granite chunks he keeps for this purpose, waiting without a word as Cody reverses the trailer and drops the tailgate to give access to the big poly tank. Owl's been waiting for some city-boy screwups, but so far, he hasn't obliged. She moves around Cody stiffly as he follows Seth, determined to do her part without getting too close, especially in the squeeze through the doorway. Cody is tall, long-legged, dwarfing Owl, at five foot four in boots.

Inside the sugarhouse—storage tanks to the north, huge evaporator arch in the center, sugar kitchen behind a closed door, dense odor of decades' worth of remaindered woodsmoke—Seth grabs the storage tank hose, speaking generally into the charged silence: "Still too cold to really get the sap running, but it's supposed to warm up tomorrow. Sunny days and cold nights are what we need to get the big runs. Pretty soon we'll be checking the taps twice a day so they don't overflow."

Seth nods over at the evaporator, a massive metal cooker with a stainless-steel pan system and a stovepipe straight up through the cupola in the roof. "We'll start boiling off probably early next week. Sap goes bad fast, so we can't leave it sitting more than a few days. That's where I'm really going to need you." Catches Cody's eye, who stops almost reluctantly to listen, as if pulled by autopilot to continue the mule work. "We've got about seven hundred gallons of syrup to make in little over a month's time. We boil late, sometimes 'round the clock."

Owl's gaze snaps to Seth, stiffening as she realizes where he's headed with this. "I need somebody in here feeding that evaporator arch—that's your firebox—every half hour or so, watching the pans, keeping the process moving. I'll show you all the ins and outs." Gestures toward a folded metal cot leaned up against the wall near the workbench. "You're welcome to sleep out here on the late nights. That's what I used to do. Holly will load you up on blankets, not that you'll need 'em. Gets hotter'n hell with that evaporator cranking."

"Okay." As if none of this information touches him at all.

"Good deal."

Once Cody has gone back outside, Owl catches Seth's arm before he can drag the hose out of the sugarhouse. "He gets to sleep here?" Her whisper is scathing.

"Well, I'm not sending him back down to Wallace's at one a.m." He studies her. "What's the problem?"

She fidgets, darts a look out the window to make sure Cody's still over by the side-by-side. "I don't like him."

"What'd he say yesterday that was so bad?" Waits. "Did he touch you or something?"

"*No.*" Now she's turning crimson on top of it all. "He's not family. We always did it ourselves before."

"Well, this year's different. Has to be." Gives her shoulder a solid shake, but she can see the strain beneath his set features. "And he's Wallace's family. He's vouched for. It'll work itself out, Owl."

Owl signs, *Whatever,* an alternating flash of her hands before her chest, fingertips brushing each other—then she pushes past him through the doorway, heading for the cabin. If Seth needs Cody so badly, they can fill the tanks without her.

As she passes the trailer, she feels Cody looking straight at her for the first time today; she glares, and he breaks into a smile, a faint chuckle she can't hear as he ducks his chin. Laughing at her again.

She waits until she rounds the hood of the Land Rover before taking the steps at a run, savoring slamming the door on him before she focuses in on her aunt standing at the end of the counter, a stack of mail and flyers sitting before her, looking down at a letter in her hand.

"I'd appreciate it if you left a hinge or two on that thing." Holly refolds the letter and returns it to the envelope, tucking it into the cupboard with the other bills, kept neatly propped by vitamin bottles, glucosamine chondroitin, Seth's prescription bottle of Percocet. Watches Owl sign *Sorry*, circling a right-fisted A twice on her chest, too angry to feel like using her voice for anyone yet. "Any fires I should be putting out?"

Shaking her head, Owl pulls her boots off, paws through the baking tin, then carries two molasses cookies toward the slanted flight of stairs that lead to her loft. Halfway up, it occurs to her that Holly never asked how the taps did today, or if Owl had much homework, their usual patter. When Owl looks back, her aunt now leans on the counter, resting on her elbows, head slightly bowed over the remaining mail.

Owl's loft is enclosed by a wooden railing and curtains hung on a cord suspended from wall to wall, which are decorated with Owl's wildlife drawings. The half story isn't used for anything but her bedroom. Owl drops onto her bed—familiar squeak of springs and sleep smell rising from her quilts—and gets her phone out to look at the pics of the fox again. She finally settles on one in which he seems to hover above the snow, his light, hopping gait frozen in time.

Owl pulls her eighteen-by-twenty-four art pad, charcoal pencil, and eraser from the cluttered surface of her bedside table, left out since she was putting finishing touches on her northern saw-whet owl, shading in primary feathers to the point where she'll probably have to go back and gingerly lighten with the eraser. Overperfecting again. Her uncle used to compare her to the saw-whets because of how she would sometimes hold still on their earliest wilderness hikes and turn her head, trying to catch as many sounds of the woods as she could with her stronger ear. A nickname—Owl—started casually enough, but within days, became her rechristening. Rochelle died in Dover, at the bottom of those stairs; that was how Owl saw it. And she never once had to explain it to Holly or Seth.

Now, she turns to a fresh page, begins her fox, the initial fluid lines of his skull, jaw ajar to accommodate the indistinct shape of the mouse. But Cody invades her focus, narrowed eyes of some shade she hasn't gotten close enough to distinguish, watching, smirking, finding some hilarity in her that she can't help but try to guess at: her upside-down coloring, maybe—hair so pale it's almost embarrassing, usually worn in two braids, "pigtails" if you wanted to be cute about it (she doesn't)—paired with coffee-brown eyes like Seth's; her plain, practical hoodies and jeans; or was it her voice, her *voice*, the dreaded conclusion waiting at the root of it all that makes her squeeze her eyes shut, clenching her pencil so tightly she feels it bend in her grip and immediately lets go. It's the only charcoal she has, and mail order could take at least a week. Too long to go without sketching.

Owl gets out the spruce grouse feather. Fool hen. A quick kill, nothing but a puff of blood, a short scuffle in the snow, bird too stunned by this sudden change of events to even fight the teeth sinking into its throat. Let it be a reminder, much like the meandering scar mostly covered beneath the side part of her hair, while this particular coyote plans on hanging around.

Won't be fooled again.

# 4

Owl wakes to a sense of wrongness some hours after she's turned out the light, opening her eyes to elongated shadows stretching tremulous fingers toward the slanted peak of the eaves above.

There's a lamp on downstairs. A glance at her alarm clock shows that it's nearly midnight—late for Seth and Holly to still be up.

All through supper, hardly any of them spoke. Holly was grim and distracted, Seth up before he even finished chewing his last bite, saying he had some cleaning to do in the sugarhouse before heading out the door into the near dark on one hobbled leg, Owl watching him go with some aching mix of resentment and longing. The sugarhouse is their place; normally she'd join him, pushing the broom over the floorboards or packaging up shipments of pints or gallons of syrup for stores around the state, but they're both feeling wounded, unaccustomed to being upset with each other.

Now, an elongated human shadow moves across the eaves, and she picks up on a rise in conversation, though at this distance it's noise without meaning.

Sliding out of bed, Owl parts the curtains and kneels at the wooden balustrades of the railing, allowing her a familiar childhood peephole into the living room below.

The hammered-brass moose lamp on the side table casts a burnished glow, and firelight shifts behind the woodstove's glass door. The well-worn leather armchair and couch are mostly visible, and Holly sits directly below—not stretched out with her ankles crossed on the couch arm and a book in her hands, as usual—but in the corner, head slightly lowered, hands resting on her thighs. A surrender. The letter is back, lying open on the cushion beside her.

Seth stands by the gun cabinet, fists jammed into the pockets of his sweatshirt; he's speaking rapidly, occasionally jerking his head toward Holly, and for a rare moment Owl wishes she'd found a way to make hearing aids work for her, even just for the slightest boost at a time like this. A brief attempt when she was nine ended with her shoving them into a drawer in frustration and refusing to wear them, unable to stand the squealing feedback, the unnatural fit, the way they managed to amplify without actually clarifying anything, merely creating a louder, equally confusing maelstrom.

Holly says something, picking up the letter and bringing it with her as she touches his arm, inclining her head. Then the two disappear down the short hallway that leads to their bedroom.

Owl draws out of sight, waiting until one of them returns to shut off the lamp, putting the downstairs to sleep for the night. Did they return the letter to the cupboard?

She walks carefully down the stairs, her stockinged feet landing on the rug with total soundlessness.

No light but the microwave clock and the nightlight plugged in by the baseboard, a strip of cold, starry sky gazing between the muslin curtains.

She checks the cupboard, but the letter isn't there. Chances are, they still have it with them behind their closed bedroom door.

Momentarily at a loss, she tries the trash can, examining what she can see of the contents. A tight ball of paper, mostly buried in one corner, catches her eye, and she fishes it out, unwrapping gingerly.

It's not the letter itself, but the envelope it came in, hand-addressed to Seth and Holly.

His full name heads the return address—it's been so long since she's seen it, let alone heard it spoken—followed by an eight-digit number and a PO box in Concord. The New Hampshire State Prison for Men. The truth of it clings to the paper, to that overcareful writing, more like a boy's than a man of thirty-eight. And faced with this, the first and only time Joel Dotrice has ever reached out to them since his arrest ten years ago, all Owl can hear is the echo of her child self, damning him to hell—twelve years of it—with one understated phrase:

*Daddy hit me, and I fell.*


## THOUGHT IS IMPOSSIBLE.

The next day scrolls past Owl on a panoramic screen—Suburban ride, holding down her desk at the exact center point of the horseshoe formation arranged to make it easier for her to read Mr. Duquette's lips, the ring tighter this year now that the other senior boy is gone, his family moved south, to the Berlin area, last summer. Aida's wide-eyed emphatics inches away, nothing but white noise, which Owl doesn't bother to decipher, Griffin adding something, his expectant smile fading as Owl makes a noncommittal sound, shakes her head, letting them believe she couldn't hear. At least it isn't a Ms. Z day. Her teacher would pick up on a dozen cues that something was wrong, coolly demanding Owl's total engagement, and Owl honestly thinks if that had happened, she might have gone up like August brush in a lightning strike.

No thought, all sensation—radiant waves of it spreading through her again and again as the hours go by, exposing tissue, bone, burning away the layers of Owl down to the scorched remainder of Rochelle, Baby Girl, giddy and small, caught in the wildly exhilarating whirlwind of Daddy until it finally snatched her beneath the arms and hurled her away. There was no *fall*; even in her brutal truth, she softened the edges, fogged the lens. One breath-stealing moment of unreality, and then she was beyond the precipice, into space.


"*QUIT IT!*" AIDA swats over the seat at Micah, who has the third row to himself now that they've dropped off the Boulier sisters. She drops heavily back into place, jostling Owl harder than Micah has with all his seat kicking, saying, "He won't stop," to Mrs. Baptiste at the wheel of the Suburban.

"Micah, I'm going to pull over, and you're going to wipe every single boot print off this car," Mrs. Baptiste calls, unperturbed, the familiar rectangular section of her face visible in the rearview mirror, dark eyes fanned with smile lines, brows black dashes.

Micah stops swinging his feet for a beat of three seconds, still wearing a piratical grin, delighted with the hard-won attention from Aida, queen of the Seventeens—then begins low-level pummeling her seat with the toe of his boot.

Griffin turns in the passenger seat, pulling his earbuds free, looking past Owl to the younger boy. "Hey, Micah? Did I tell you I brought Dante in the car with me this morning?" Micah glances up at the name of Griffin's corn snake, who he's brought into school as part of a biology project before. "Yep. I was going to show him to Mr. Duquette. Only took him out of his case for a second, but . . . he got away from me. Mom hasn't been able to find him." He sighs, fitting his earbuds in. "Last place I saw him was back there. Hope he didn't find a way to get into your seat. Or Aida's. Crazy the places snakes wriggle into." Griffin's gaze slides to Owl for a second, deadpan, and she smirks a little, distractedly, shaking her head.

Micah sits absolutely still, then slowly lifts his boot heels up onto the edge of his seat. Aida spins to face front, triumphant, and Mrs. Baptiste gives her son's knee a smack as she shakes with silent laughter.

They slow to a stop in front of Aida's house, a modular with an off-kilter front yard, all boulders, stumps, and stump holes pooling stagnant water, a work in progress, which may never be cleared and filled at the rate her dad's going. "Have fun with the troll," Aida says to Owl as she shoulders her backpack, making one last grab for Micah's hat, who dodges— "Too slow!"—before she hops out onto the dirt, sunlight turning her metallic coat into sheer glare while she slouches up the driveway, her family's beagles racing to meet her in howling cacophony.

As Mrs. Baptiste pulls back onto the road, Owl's phone vibrates; she peers into her coat pocket at the preview on the glowing screen. Text from Aida, managing to make it through now that they're in range of her parents' signal booster: *Van's Sunday?*

Their usual, meeting up at Holly's work, where Owl helps out; Owl sends back a thumbs-up. Weekends mean little this time of year; with sugaring begun, her free time will have to be stolen in pieces from now through March, when the season wraps up with Maple Weekend, when sugarhouses all over the state open up to visitors for demonstrations and tastings and tire sur la neige.

They reach the farm's driveway, and Owl exhales slowly through her nose as the part of the day she's been dreading most—returning home—looms. She envisions the cabin, all comfort, all familiarity scraped away by the existence of a letter, crammed with words she can't begin to fathom after a whole decade of silence. Thank god Seth and Holly hadn't given it to her, searching for a reaction; she has no anger about them keeping it to themselves. Always, her aunt and uncle's first instincts are to protect, shelter.

"Owl, hon?" Mrs. Baptiste turns in her seat, stopping Owl as she unfastens her seat belt; the knife has already been returned, their daily business finished, so Owl stares, waiting. "I wanted to tell you . . . It's still a ways off, but we're making plans to go to the Wesget Sipu Powwow in Fort Kent this year. If Holly wants to come along, she's more than welcome. I mean, you all are. She should give me a call sometime."

Her expression holds a rare hesitance; Winnie Baptiste, always ready with a grin in the coldest morning, often dressed in T-shirts that say STRONG INDIGENOUS WOMAN and HOMELAND SECURITY (above a vintage photo of braves holding rifles), FIGHTING TERRORISM SINCE 1492; who makes cupcakes wrapped in cellophane on the birthdays of each of the kids on her route; who once steered them out of a 360-degree spin in a blizzard, which ended with their front passenger wheel hanging over the ditch in the oncoming lane, then sang "Greasy, Grimy Gopher Guts" all the way home to get a laugh out of the Boulier girls, who were nearly in tears over the scare. "We're all one nation, right?"

Meaning the Wabanaki Confederacy, which includes both Passamaquoddy and Maliseet tribes. Owl glances at Griffin, whom she finds already looking at her, a slight smile, a kind of mild curiosity in his eyes, and for the first time it strikes her that maybe he's listening to nothing at all through those earbuds, opting for the kind of noise cancellation she spends her days struggling against.

"I'll tell her." Owl's smile is a strained flash, reflecting the storm inside her more than the fact that this is hardly the first time Mrs. Baptiste has tried to reach out to her aunt. Holly will never call the other woman; never has, to Owl's knowledge, not even with Mrs. Baptiste coming over to say hello during school functions, pulling up a chair beside Holly at the occasional community suppers the Dotrices stop into down in the valley, Griffin usually sticking with his dad, especially after Greg Baptiste was diagnosed with MS and used a wheelchair in the final years of his life.

Owl climbs the steep driveway to the farm, passing the simple wooden sign, carved with DOTRICE MAPLE FARM—SYRUP FOR SALE, swinging from a metal post bolted to a big ash. Practically no one drives all the way up the mountainside to buy some, since the road is seldom traveled by anyone but locals and hikers searching for trailheads; most of their family's money is made from the long-standing deals Grandpa Dotrice made with Hannaford grocery stores, and gift shops around the state, but also Holly's many innovations, like designing an online store and getting them on the New Hampshire Maple Sugar Association's sugarhouse map.

The cabin waits, windows dark while everyone's still out for the day; Owl pauses only long enough to swap her backpack for her snowshoes, then heads for the sugarbush at a good clip, head lowered, hands in her pockets. Hates having Seth upset with her, if he still is—she never apologized last night, went to bed before he came back in from the sugarhouse—but she needs to swathe herself in layers of Owl again, starve those Rochelle memories of oxygen until they smolder out. Foxes will wait.

SETH'S PREDICTION OF a heat wave—forty degrees in the sun—has panned out, and Owl finds her uncle and Cody halfway into the second tap check of the day.

She gets right to work, pouring partially full sap buckets into a five-gallon collection pail, which she lugs over to dump into the top of the horizontal tank on the trailer, keeping her head down until she feels the familiar tug on the end of one braid as she passes Seth. They're okay. Immediately, she settles deeper into herself, like a well-loved cotton sweater stretched to shape.

They work in silence a few minutes, until Seth says, "Well. Guess you two can handle the rest of this?" Cody and Owl both stop where they stand. "I'll be getting back." His stance is uncertain, rubbing his chin with one hand as his gaze sharpens on Owl's disbelieving face. "You need me, I'll be right in the cabin. Okay?"

He limps through the trees toward the farm, each step rigidly controlled as he leaves them.

Owl looks immediately to the snow, walking down the slope to the access road, where the side-by-side is parked. Cody's close behind her, and she moves to the left, trying to shake him, not realizing he's done the same and now is nearly on her heels. With a frustrated exhalation, Owl steps to the right, pretending to ignore him as he holds his hands up in a *Hey, sorry* motion, dangling a five-gallon pail in each.

More trips, her shoulder muscles twitching with tension, and she strains to hear his footsteps, to divine where exactly he is behind her, fighting to resist the urge to whirl around and check. She never expected Seth to leave—nobody said anything to her about working one-on-one with Cody like this—and at once she can't catch her breath, can't remember how to fill her lungs, until she's found the cool oblong shape of the knife in her pocket. Pulls out the blade, just for a moment, pretending to clean around the spile and making sure he sees.

When she turns, he's hunkered down by a low tap three trees away, his gaze on the knife, sudden animation in his face, wryness playing around his mouth. "You gonna use that on me?"

She's hot, half humiliation, half bravado. "Maybe."

He starts laughing again, dismissing her.

Owl drops her pail in the snow and forces herself straight over to him, stopping with the blade clenched in her fist, directed down. "Keys." He looks at her; his eyes are a shade of slate blue, more gray than not; who-blinks-first turning into more of a challenge than Owl expected, and it shakes her: "Now. You don't drive. I drive. Give them." Sticks her palm out.

He takes his time, mouth moving as if turning over a loz-enge, then reaches into his wool coat and dangles them out in front of her. She refuses the bait; he drops them into her palm. "Do you even have a license?"

"I'm seventeen." Owl paces away, relieved to find her pail still standing upright—no sap spilled—grabs it, and heads off down the hill. In truth, she doesn't have her license, hasn't even taken driver's ed, although Aida begged her to come with her to classes in Stokely last year. Owl doesn't see the purpose of driving, not for her—all a car can do is take her away from here—and, anyway, Seth had her trained on the side-by-side and the Kubota tractor before she was ten.

A sudden crunch of snow crust and he's alongside her, looking down into her face, and she guesses that he probably said something to her back that she couldn't hear. He contin-ues staring with an insulting intensity, finally prodding her into saying, "What?"

"Gave you shit the other day." He smiles—not a bad smile, even scraped of all sincerity—and he laughs again. "You come out of the woods, screaming about traps and hunting—" Shrugs, a faintly cocky adjustment of shoulders and neck. "How was I supposed to know they had some little niece run-ning around the place."

"So if you'd known, you wouldn't have done it?" She sets her pail on the trailer, needing to climb onto the edge of the bed in order to pour it into the top opening, watching as he's able to dump both his pails in flat-footed. "Nobody knew you were coming. You should've stopped by the farm first."

"I *did.*" Slams his pails into the back, beside hers. "Nobody was home."

The sound of the engine drowns out everything for Owl on the drive back, and she never looks away from the road; if he's talking, she doesn't have to know about it.

Pulling up to the sugarhouse doors, she kills the ignition and gets out, wondering if Seth is keeping watch from one of the cabin windows.

"Wild ride." Cody unfolds his long legs from the passenger seat with some difficulty, holding on to the top bar to swing out. "Pretty sure I saw roadkill pass us."

"You don't floor it with a hundred gallons of sap in the back." Not used to feeling agitated for so long on the average day, she mentally calculates how long it will take them to check all the maples left in the acreage, times how many trips from sugarbush to house . . . Approximately the rest of her life before she can escape him.

She rushes in for the storage tank hose, just wanting to empty the horizontal tank as quickly as possible, sloppily hooking up the hose in a way she never would've risked in years past—spilled sap was money wasted; she learned that early on—and she makes herself slow down, heading into the sugarhouse to switch on the suction, raising her brows expectantly as Cody follows her in. "Let me see your knife again," he says.

Exhaling through her nose, she takes her knife out—an Applegate combat folder—and shows it to him before stuffing it into her pocket.

He snorts. "Where'd you find that? Army surplus store?"

"No. Army vet."

He looks in the direction of the cabin. "Seth?" Cocks his head. "You're shitting me." Tone incredulous enough to be insulting.

"Two deployments to Afghanistan," she says, hitting the switch with some relish and going outside. Regret is instantaneous—Seth wouldn't want her using his service to show somebody up. He'd say taking that shot just now was about her, not him.

What she knows about Seth's time in the army is through Holly, who gave her some details when they came across the old basic-training graduation photo of Seth, American flag displayed behind him, a hollow-eyed boy worked and bellowed down to a razor's edge. And she knows Seth's knee problems stem from a botched surgery after being wounded in action, shrapnel from an IED. Owl's one certainty is that a few years ago after mentioning maybe asking for a Leatherman for Christmas so she didn't have to keep borrowing his, he'd produced the folding knife at breakfast the next morning.

"Found it in a drawer," he'd said. "Yours if you want it."

She'd had it out of his hands before he even finished his sentence.


THEY'VE REACHED THE sugarhouse with their last full tank when a familiar rust-pocked white Dodge Ram Heavy Duty lumbers up the drive, bouncing to a stop on bad shocks—Wallace. He's a big man, barrel-chested, with shaggy hair showing beneath his ball cap and a round, good-natured face prickly with graying stubble.

He honks the horn once and climbs out, hitching up his jeans, raising a hand as Seth appears in the doorway, gripping the frame before endeavoring down the steps to meet him.

Owl looks at Cody, who glances Wallace's way, but keeps on his route to the sugarhouse, apparently thinking he's already qualified to run the hose. The work has gone fast, once Cody finally stopped talking; it took Owl and Seth until dusk to finish this last season.

Seth and Wallace walk over to them at a slow bullshitting pace, and Owl catches the shape of Wallace's words on his lips:
—*beautiful wife of yours?*

Seth: *Pretending she doesn't know you're here.*

Both laugh.

"Thought I'd swing by, see how he's doing," Wallace says, sound filling in for Owl as they reach the side-by-side, the words for Cody's benefit, who stops in that barely tolerant way he'd used with Seth, doglike, basic command-following the absolute most he'll give the older men. "Make sure he's minding his manners." Undercurrent there, beneath the bright wrapping. Owl's willing to bet Wallace and his grandson have already butted heads.

"He's doing good," Seth says, nodding. Faint sheen of sweat on his brow again, which he runs his knuckles over distractedly. "Picks things up quick."

"'Course he does. He's related to me, ain't he?" Another big laugh, a hard shake of Cody's shoulder. Owl's skin seems to tighten with the tension, the steely, sidelong flick of Cody's eyes. Can't Wallace tell that Cody doesn't want his touch?

Wallace releases, hand finding his own hip pocket again. "Break your heart, Code, knowing that Seth here could be sucking all that damn sap straight down into the tank with a flip of a switch, no hauling required. Wouldn't even need you. Most spreads this size use vacuum power these days. Got everything streamlined through tubing."

It's an old gibe, one Seth deflects with his usual "Too hard on the trees," but his tone is flat, gaze unfocused. "Not natural, doing that to them."

"Ahh." Wallace waves him off, rocking back on his heels, taking in the sugarhouse and surrounding trees. "Backyard sugaring is all you're doing here. Still looking at things how your old man did. You update your system, bet you could pump another hundred gallons out of these woods every season. Really put yourselves on the map."

Seth smiles, finally. "Christ, Wall, we wanted to be on the map, we wouldn't be living out here, right?" Claps his hand on Wallace's back, steering him toward the cabin. "Coffee's on."

Cody watches them, as if making sure nobody's coming back for one last hearty laugh, then goes into the sugarhouse, Owl not far behind.

"Why's your uncle take that?" When she lifts her incredulous gaze to him: "Fuckin' old Wall." Cody jerks his head toward the road as he drags the hose out the door. "That's all he does. Goes around, stopping in and giving advice nobody wants, drinking up all their coffee."

Owl doesn't speak; even Aida's worst tirades about her mom never come close to this harshness: the knot in his jaw, the total lack of understanding for know-it-all, basically well-meaning Wallace, whose pop-in visits were a part of life—and who'd stuck his neck out for Cody to get this job in the first place, never mind giving him a place to stay. "He's our neighbor." Pauses again, piecing the words together, not sure she's captured even half her meaning. "Everybody needs each other out here. That's the kind of place it is."

"Yeah?" Jams the nozzle onto the bulkhead. "'Cause it seems like a place people come to get buried."

# 5

Early evening, in the warm hibernation cave of the living room, Owl, Seth, and Holly gather around the woodstove and TV. Seth sits in the armchair with the footrest up, two ice packs around his knee, bottle of Sam Adams beading sweat on the end table within reach. "What you think about maybe hiking up to the Notch tomorrow?" he says, keeping his attention on the screen, volume low, subtitles on.

Owl sits up straight, surprised out of the doze she'd been sinking into at one end of the couch, covered up to her chin in a fleece blanket. Her gaze immediately goes to Holly, at the opposite end of the couch. But her aunt nods, smiling faintly, not lifting her attention from the crossword puzzle she's doing while saying, "Sounds good to me. Haven't been there in a while."

Long while. Over a year and a half, since Seth's knee really got bad, but he holds his hand up as Owl looks at the ice packs.

"I'll take it easy, stick to the path." Sips from the bottle. "Rocks will be too icy for climbing, anyway."

"But you bring your helmet." Holly gently swats her folded puzzle magazine down on Owl's foot. Owl's never given them trouble about the helmet—she appreciates what a head injury can do to a person—but Holly lives in wait for the day Owl does, same as she did when Owl used to ride her bike thirty minutes down the road to Aida's house, then home again. "How's this. You protect your noggin, I'll pack us lunch."

"Deal." Owl sinks deliciously into the thought of skating on the basin below the falls at the Notch, something they used to do throughout the winter, the deft motion of her blades skimming the ice, air so cold it sears her throat and steals her breath in columns of steam, surrounded by a cathedral of stone.

She'd come so close to bringing up Seth's desertion this afternoon, demanding that he never, ever leave her alone with Cody again, but it would only spark more embarrassing questions, opening up the chance of Cody telling somebody that she'd shown off her knife earlier. She didn't want to picture Seth's face if he found out—disbelief, disgust, after all the talks they'd had about the proper handling of weapons, respect for the damage they can do—much less the shame of him maybe taking the blade back.

But if they're planning a hike to the Notch tomorrow, Seth must trust Cody to do the first tap check of the day by himself already. At least she'll get a reprieve from Cody, maybe figure out a different way to make Seth see that he shouldn't turn his back on him, Wall's grandson or not.

It's only as her eyelids grow heavy again that the timing of this trip to one of her favorite places—and Holly's lack of protest over Seth pushing himself too hard, a battle of wills that's been on the forefront of their lives for months now—syncs, and instantly, Owl knows.

Tomorrow, they're going to tell her about the letter.

THEY SET OUT at midmorning, waiting so Seth can check in with Cody when he arrives, let him know he'll be on his own until the afternoon.

Owl stays on the deck, swollen-eyed from a restless night, adjusting the straps on her hiking pack, which contains her climbing helmet, skates, and water bottle, keeping Cody always on her periphery, noting the insolent tilt of his head as Seth speaks to him down by the sugarhouse. He walked to their place again. No man she knows except for Seth would be caught on foot when he could drive his truck, or one of the motley collection of ATVs and other motorized toys they were constantly posting on the online swap 'n' sell groups or trading in for something newer to bomb around on the trails 365 days a year. Supposes if Cody lives right in the city, maybe he doesn't even need a car.

*The kid's been looking for something to get him out of Manchester,* her uncle had said. And for the first time, she wonders why.

THE THREE OF them don't speak much on the hike up the Notch trail, walking single file in their snowshoes as sunlight winks through the lacework of branches above. They stop briefly to check on the foxes—no activity visible outside the den—but Seth points to a curled imprint some thirty yards away, where a fox—maybe one of the mates, maybe not—has slept right in the snow. Owl snaps a pic for later, although right now, *later* feels like the hard and sudden stop waiting at the bottom of a cliff.

The Notch is just under an hour's hike away, in that no-man's-land beyond their property, which borders a national preserve and a piece of massive acreage that's been for sale as long as Owl's lived here. Other hikers come this way occasionally, but for the most part, it's unclaimed. Easy to think of as theirs.

They stop and check for moose at a couple marshes on the way—for a spellbound twenty minutes one spring, they watched a cow and her two calves grazing among the water reeds here. The land grows rockier as they continue, talus cropping up as the elevation steepens and they begin the true climb into the natural fissure where a waterfall, in the warm months, makes its 150-foot surge into a basin below. Even now, the warm spell hasn't melted the falls free of their final moment of violent release, the ice yellowish and gleaming in the daylight.

Holly, her hair in a ponytail, red bandanna tied as a headband, glances at Owl, tapping her temple, and Owl stops to put her climbing helmet on, even though she'd need a death wish to go bouldering today, with pockets of sheer ice hidden in every potential handhold and foothold across the rock face. Holly's concern is an accidental fall, anything that might send Owl tumbling down toward the talus.

First, they hike all the way to the huge plateaued ledge—hundreds of feet wide—for the view. Miles of sloping, winter-ravaged forest, icy, opaque ponds and lakes inlaid like shards of frosted glass, accessible only by foot or ATV. Owl and Holly leave their packs on the ledge, Owl pausing only long enough to sling her skates around her neck before hustling back down the path at a near run, Holly not far behind.

Seth holds on to a nearby boulder, lowering himself by painstaking inches into a sitting position, right leg held out stiffly, releasing controlled breaths until his back is supported against the rock. Rattles in an inner pocket for the bottle of Percocet, washes two down with water.


THE ICE ON the basin is softening but still solid enough to hold Owl's weight. "Stay away from the middle," Holly calls out from the perch she's chosen, giving a frustrated, musical whistle through her teeth when she sees Owl can't hear her. Of course the girl knows the rule of thumb; she'll be eighteen in August.

Owl strikes out on her blades faster than she should, forgetting the awkward period where you have to relearn balance, how to push with your quads and let your feet glide, sailing across a surface that should make any creature slip, flail, and skid away in a heap.

The basin is as near-perfect a circle as nature creates, and Owl skates the circumference, adding more and more speed until she's flying, pulse accelerating, breath coming hard, wishing her dread could peel and blow away behind her like an unwanted cloak, knowing what's waiting for her at the end of all this.

WHEN THEY MEET back up with Seth, he's gotten lunch out—plastic-wrapped peanut butter and peach jam sandwiches, chips, cheddar cheese and apple slices—all things Owl loves, yet she sits with her knees drawn up to her chest, never feeling less like eating. She pushed herself too hard down there, intended to from the beginning, and now her legs are throbbing. The silence is dense in a way it never is between them, and she hunts for anything to say to delay what's coming, seizing on, "Mrs. Baptiste asked if you wanted to go to a powwow with them." Probably the worst choice of a diversion.

Holly nods, taking her time unwrapping her sandwich. "That's nice of her." Her tone modulated, uninvolved.

Owl knows she overstepped and wishes she could stuff the words back down. She knows that Holly doesn't speak to much of her family, save her younger sister, who emails sometimes. The most intimate part of being Passamaquoddy that Holly has shared with Owl was the stories—"Glooscap Fights the Water Monster" being a particular favorite—told late at night when Owl was younger and suffered bouts of insomnia and nightmares. Holly would come to her, sit on the edge of the bed—*Sleep can be a hard thing*, she'd say—and then her quiet, night-hoarsened voice, with tales of Lox, the wolverine spirit who learned from Bear how to start a fire by jumping over maple bark, or Kwimu, the spying loon, would gradually swirl around Owl like a weighted net, catching her, carrying her to rest on the bottom with only the slightest disturbance of silt. Never once did Holly push Owl to talk about her dreams, promising it would somehow help, that naming the terror could defeat it. There was only one terror, one voice, which cut through the anxious chaos of Owl's sleeping memories, not with roaring intensity but with weak, horrified pleading: *Oh god, Ro, oh shit, nononono, I'm so sorry.* And one childishly pure emotion dragged her into waking world every time, leaving her staring into the dark of the loft, tearful, guilt-stricken, nauseated: *Daddy, please don't hate me.*

Now, her voice feels like all she has, so she uses it, speaking down into her knees. "I know about the letter."

Holly and Seth turn to her in one motion, Holly then flicking her gaze to Seth, who shifts on the rock, knee still held rigidly.

After a beat, Seth says, "You go snooping for it?"

Owl's shoulders flinch in a reflexive shrug. "I don't mean I read it. I saw the envelope." Falls quiet. "It wasn't addressed to me."

"That's right. It wasn't." Seth brushes roughly at some crumbs on his coat, none of them quite sure why this has turned into a question of Owl breaking the rules, but his brusqueness passes, leaving Seth merely tired. "We weren't going to keep it from you forever—"

"I don't want to see it."

"We were just figuring out how to bring it up," he finishes slowly, watching her, digesting her response. "You should know what it says." Owl's shaking her head, mouth and nose pressed to her knees, gaze on the rock. "And there were phone calls. Two. Before this. From Victim Services, at the prison."

"They wanted to let us know that your dad was up for parole again," Holly says, her tone low. "And then they let us know when he got it."

Owl breathes warm moisture into the fabric of her jeans. "It was supposed to be twelve years."

"Guess some board of jackasses decided ten was enough." Seth's anger is coiled and contained, stuffed down deep for Owl's sake, but she wishes he wouldn't bother; he's usually so patient with her that she forgets how severe he can be, able to cut someone out of his life for good if he decides they're not worthy of trust. "I gave them an earful on the phone, but it doesn't matter now. It's done. That's mostly what he—your dad—was writing to say." He hasn't spoken his younger brother's name in Owl's presence in a decade. "At this point, I guess he's already been released."

"But . . ." The denim feels hot and wet against her skin, and she straightens, words coming hard and fast. "I'm yours now. You guys went through the courts."

"Owl, nobody is taking you away." Holly's hand finds the center of Owl's back, gentle pressure. "The adoption's been final for a long time. He has no rights." A moment's brittle comfort.

"He can come here, though. He knows where to find us." He grew up on the farm, after all.

It's sobering, bringing back every cringing, sickening sensation from that early time when they were all adjusting, finding their way to each other through an atrocity other people only spoke about in whispers.

Holly nods slowly. "You're right. He can, and he does."

55

"The hell you say." Seth's response is sharp, immediate, scaring Owl more than anything has yet, because it's obvious they've already argued about the possibility, that it's real. "Not even he could be that stupid."

"Well, don't bark at me about it. You saw what he wrote." Holly takes a breath. "Owl, I think you should take a look at the letter."

"No." At their silence: "I don't *want* to."

"And we don't blame you. Seth wanted to tear it up when he saw it. But I wouldn't let him, because this is about you, not your dad. Does that make sense? About your right to know what's going on and help decide how we respond to him."

"We don't," Seth says. "Problem solved."

Holly puts her hand up, her gaze firm on Owl. "He asked for permission to write to you. Just you."

Owl's body suffuses with heat, nerves afire at the thought of reading the name Rochelle Dotrice written in that boyish script, his hand—that of nightmares—bearing down earnestly with a ballpoint somewhere out here in the free world. "I don't give it." Arms locked so tightly around her own legs that her shoulders are shaking, feeling the weight of their stares, sure that Holly is about to speak again. "I said *no*."

Owl's voice slaps back at them, echoing out over the winter-starched expanse. And so the three of them sit, gazing out, at an impasse.

# 6

Seth's coloring is chalky, eyes sunken, by the time they get home. Owl knows it's the pain but feels responsible anyway, wishing she'd talked them out of going. Maybe they would've changed their mind about the letter, destroyed it, allowing her own secret knowledge to fade beneath the passing days until even she might believe she'd forgotten.

Holly shrugs her pack off in the kitchen—"I'll get ice"—following Seth's labored progress toward the bedroom, while Owl stands, sweating beneath her coat and hat from the hike, watching them go.

As it is, there's no way Seth can help with the second tap check. Owl knows her responsibility to the trees; making Holly roust her out of the loft to do her chores after what happened at the Notch would be inexcusable. Already, she's wishing she could retrieve the shout over the mountain, her *no* in the face of granite ledges carved by thousands of years of glacial movement, birth and growth and death churning in the woods all around them while she beat her fists like a toddler. She goes back outside, head down. Fool hen.

Of course, the timing couldn't line up with Cody coming or going from the sugarhouse in the side-by-side, so it's another hike through the woods to the sugarbush.

She spots him from afar, collection pails hanging from his arms as he carries them to the horizontal tank, then heaves the sap in roughly, thoughtlessly. She nearly calls out a warning—he's going to spill—but somehow, hardly anything sloshes over the rim, achieving the same result as all her practiced care.

Owl starts emptying sap buckets into her pail, the two of them eyeing each other from a distance, seeming to agree, for once, that silence is best. Her mind feels exhausted, outmoded, like the old cider mill at Gunnar's place, belts squealing, wheels hurtling, struggling to process concepts instead of gallons of water and pulp: Joel Dotrice out of prison, wanting contact, maybe moving closer all the time. What if a strange car pulls into their driveway, tomorrow or the next day, a man's silhouette behind the windshield? How quickly could she lose herself in the woods, find a place where not even someone who grew up on this land could hunt her down?

Distracted, she thinks nothing of Cody's nearby footsteps. Then she jumps at the sudden clicking beside her left ear.

His hand, inches away, thumb working the button of a silver lighter.

He's setting her hair on fire. With a choked sound, she jerks back, shoulder banging into the trunk. Incredibly, he smiles, nodding as he holds up the knockoff Zippo and turning it between thumb and forefinger. "Chill. It's empty." Smile spreads to a grin. "You know? No lighter fluid." Flips it, catches it, hides it in his coat pocket. "You didn't even blink when I tried it on the other side."

It hits then, what he was doing. Testing her.

Outrage drives her into him, her palms slamming his chest. Then twice more, using all her strength to push him—solid, immobile, another granite wall—while he holds his hands up in mock surrender, laughing. "Holy Christ, spaz, don't hurt yourself."

An animal's growl in her throat, she dashes her fist across his front—he's an uninvited letter, a clueless parole board, a request for permission so brazen and terrifying—raking her knuckles raw with the teeth of his coat zipper, strength spent almost as quickly as it overtook her.

She spins unsteadily away, breathless, barely seeing, thinking only of reaching the side-by-side.

"You leaving?" Two tugs on the hem of her coat—unconscious mimic of Seth's affectionate braid tweak. "All pissed off again?"

She spins, swinging at him, intending to slap his face, but, diverted by a last-second craven fear of being hit back harder, lands it across his shoulder instead. *"Don't ever do that!"* Her chest heaving, daring him to laugh at her just one more time.

Mockery has faded to a kind of cockeyed fascination, but he says nothing, watching as she wavers, then walks to the tree she was tending with stiff deliberation, her winter layers hiding the fact that she's shaking.

He chooses the tree beside her to pull buckets from, looking over a few times before he says, "So. Guess you're the child."

"*What?*"

"'Slow Deaf Child.'" Already moving on to the next tree, unhooking more buckets. "I walk past that sign every time I come here."

Leave it to him to bring up a source of embarrassment to her ever since Holly contacted the DMV to get one of the yellow metal road signs placed about halfway between here and Aida's house, the only way she would let Owl bike by herself, in addition to getting her a helmet and handlebar mirrors and two blinking lights—as if there were a constant stream of traffic coming up from the pass instead of just the occasional trundling John Deere, which Owl's Deafness would somehow make her swerve into like a panicking squirrel. "It means *drive* slow."

He takes this in. "They put up a whole sign just for you?"

He doesn't say it meanly, so she stays quiet, not completely sure how to respond. "You shouldn't start a lighter right next to someone's head."

"I told you. Nothing in it." He walks past her with two armloads, leans close to her good ear, saying, overloud, "No fuel, no flame."

"And you've never been wrong before." Raising her voice to match his as he follows the trampled path to the access road.

If he answers, she can't hear it, but even with his back to her, she reads his body language clear enough: *Never once.*

SUNDAY, AIDA COMES through the door of Van Johnson's Wilderness Outfitters in St. Beatrice, sagging against the handle with all eyes on her, leaving no doubt that she barely made it over the threshold alive.

Owl is a part-time employee, only working one day a week, using the pricing gun or putting out stock, straightening the footwear section with its jumbled shelves of Red Wing and Timberland boots, waiting for Aida to show. Aida's mom, Trini, drops her off on her way to do the weekly grocery shopping, supposedly so Aida can hang out with Owl instead of moping through the aisles of Market Basket, but the real draw for Aida is having the password to the high-speed Wi-Fi connection at Van's.

Owl's presence here is more about socialization than anything—they all know it—Holly and Seth concerned that her world is too small, and that helping someone find game spray or hand-warmer packs will keep her from pulling too deeply inside herself.

Aida crosses to her usual spot, the big wooden chair carved and painted like a black bear, which holds a place of honor at the end of the counter. "It is *freezing* out there."

"It's almost fifty," Holly says from behind the counter, emptying a paper roll of quarters into the cash register tray.

Aida balls herself into the deep seat of the bear, bracing the heels of her high-tops against the edge, staring out at Main Street with hunted eyes before glancing around for Owl; satisfied that she's where she ought to be, Aida gets her phone out.

Holly takes in Aida's outfit. "Snazzy pants, Aid."

"Thanks." Pink leopard-print leggings, T-shirt too short to cover her butt. Already deep into her feed, grinding gum in her molars with the rhythm of scrolling.

Holly shares a look with Owl, who lip-read the whole thing and hides a smile by returning a stray muck boot to its box. Things have felt strained at home since the Notch yesterday; nobody's fault—at least, nobody present—just the result of being pulled and stretched out of their usual roles.

It's been a long time since Owl was a traumatized little kid needing her aunt and uncle to run damage control for her, nobody knowing how much—if any of it—she could be expected to overcome. At least the adoption process had gone smoothly, begun after Owl had lived with them for a year; Child Protection Services' investigation into their household was swift, and Joel Dotrice never fought it. The papers simply came back from his lawyer's office, signed.

Owl and Holly were much more about collaboration now, indulgently poking holes in Aida's drama, working together as equals at the farm and Van's.

A customer dumps an armload of clearance ice-fishing gear onto the counter in front of Holly, who scoops it closer with both hands, making some remark Owl almost reads from her vantage point: —*right time?* Time of year, probably, to buy a new reel.

Holly already has the guy laughing. She's good—efficient and businesslike but also speaking the language of the men who'd been buying their ammo and blaze orange at Van's for twenty years and weren't expecting to find a woman at the helm now. "Maybe they think being Native buys me some cred. Has to be a first time for everything," Holly once said to Owl sardonically. "Like I must've been born knowing how to hunt and gather. It's all a game, anyway—you know, female, move back three spaces. Indian, jump ahead three. Get nowhere." Shook her head. "All just a game." What had started as a cashier and stock-person position for Holly became a managerial position within a year, and then old Van himself decided to take his long-overdue semiretirement, now only coming in once a week to sit in the office, do the ordering, and essentially rest his eyes.

Owl and Aida walk to Community Drug on Owl's break, as they always do, clutched tightly arm in arm down the wind tunnel of Main Street, filled with mostly dusty, empty storefronts, hollow-looking apartment windows, and one blinking yellow light swinging lethargically on a wire above the asphalt.

The drugstore is only two buildings down from Van's, but Aida swings Owl into the narrow alleyway between a former furniture store and a real estate office, her face ecstatic. "Look what Tyson sent me last night. My mom would shit."

"Who?"

"*Ty-son.* I told you about him. Didn't I? I know I did." Aida's swiping and tapping her phone screen, holding it up close to Owl's face.

It takes Owl a second to process what's she's seeing in the dark selfie, probably taken in some dimly lit bedroom—then the impression of bare flesh hits, exactly what part of the male anatomy she's looking at, and Owl claps her hand over her mouth, shoving Aida's wrist down with the other, eyes blazing.

Aida cackles, stomping her foot and bouncing in a half circle, two-tone curls jouncing out from beneath her hood. "Okay, I can delete now. Just wanted to see your face."

"That's—!" Owl chokes off with a sound of disgust, caught somewhere between indignance and giving in to Aida's contagious mad giggles. "You could've warned me." Her cheeks feel scorched.

"Warned you?" Aida swivels at her with the phone out. "'Penis comin' atcha'—like that?"

Owl yells and spins away, breaking for the sidewalk, and Aida chases her, soon both of them laughing as Aida catches Owl's coat sleeve and they swing together through the doors of Community Drug, stopping in midshove under the bored eye of the clerk. Aida snakes her arm through Owl's and leads her with great dignity to the cosmetics aisle, where they go off again, Owl wiping tears from her eyes. "You blocked him?"

"Not yet." When Owl stares at her: "I will. Probably. I don't think he's a real perv or anything. He just . . . wanted me to see." She gives Owl a look from beneath her brows. "Guys love their things. They're like obsessed with them. It's the law of the jungle."

"The law is about guys' things?" Owl hiccups more incredulous laughter, resting her forehead against the edge of the shelf. "You can't let your mom find that."

"Duh. I told him he can't send any more or he'll get me in trouble." She pulls a tinted lip gloss out of a rack, comparing the shade sticker on the tube to her skin tone in the tiny, smudged mirror set into the display. "Ugh. This place has nothing." Looks wistful, defeated. "Do you think Walgreens will ever come here?"

They walk the aisles through the racks of eye shadow, foundation, lipstick, Aida debating the possible merit of false eyelashes before deciding her mom would shit again, looping around to the next aisle, of shampoos and body washes, popping every top, sniffing scents they've tested a hundred times before, until they're loopy on huffs of agave and humectant.

Aida grabs herself a Diet Pepsi and starts pushing through the chips, saying, "I've got ten bucks," which is Owl's prompt to follow suit. Trini keeps them well fed on snack food, always tucking a folded bill into her daughter's pocket before peeling off for her two-hour Sunday escape.

Owl's reaching for a bag of kettle chips when Aida says, "Whoa. Hell-o."

Owl follows her gaze to the plate glass windows, revealing the strip of storefronts on the opposite side of the street and the lime-green glow of Houlihan's neon shamrock sign, the only bar within a thirty-minute drive of North Plover. It's notorious for making the police blotter of the local paper nearly every week, as well as for the legendary tale of one drunk supposedly biting another man's ear off during a brawl years ago, the ear only found much later, sunken into the depths of a whiskey glass.

Both girls recognize Wallace's pickup, parked along the curb, the lot itself mostly empty this early in the afternoon on a Sunday, when even the most dedicated drinkers don't show up until around four p.m.

Wallace swings by Aida's place as often as Owl's, though with Aida's dad, shooting the shit turns into a can-you-top-this competition, resulting in ruffled feathers and both men crabbing about each other to anyone who'll listen for the rest of the week.

Wallace is on the sidewalk now, moseying toward Houlihan's while speaking back to the man trailing him, who's stopped to finish his cigarette.

Ski cap, dark plaid coat, shoulders hunched as he takes a final drag, releasing the smoke from the corner of his mouth so that the wind whips it away, before pitching the butt, sweeping the street with squinted eyes as he turns to follow Wallace into the bar.

"Who is *that*?" Aida's gaze is riveted.

Owl watches Cody disappear through the dusty glass door as it closes on the gloom inside. "I'm not sure."

# 7

Ms. Z wears a corona of light as she sits in front of the cloakroom window, the glass running with ice melt from the schoolhouse roof, the little kids outside smeared to colorful whirling dots.

*Mr. Duquette told me you have a big project coming up for County Founding Day. We should discuss.* The side of Ms. Z's right forefinger taps her left palm, lingers as Owl watches—the equivalent of sounding out words for a child just learning to read—her gaze following the momentary play of confusion across Owl's face before Owl has the sense to harden her expression.

Ms. Z slowly rests her hands on the desktop. "You weren't aware of this?" Turning to verbal speech, stage one of Owl's dressing-down. Ms. Z's on the younger side for a teacher, maybe thirty, given to wearing clothes with a vintage look to them, though Owl's not sure of the era—high-waisted slacks, cardigans over short-sleeved small-patterned blouses, oxford shoes, everything in demure shades of khaki or navy or maroon. Not an ounce of makeup, the same seed-pearl studs in her lobes whenever Owl sees her. "He spoke to everyone about it on Friday and passed out an information sheet for you to look at over the weekend so you could think about what topic to choose. Were you absent?" As Owl's gaze flicks away, Ms. Z's hands fold carefully, one over the other. "Perhaps only mentally."

Owl's memory of Friday is obscured by the discovery of the envelope. There is the impression of Aida's face at one point, leaning close to Owl in her chair, adamant about something, to which Owl made noncommittal noises, returning to the storm inside. "A group project," Owl says. She tries to keep the interrogative out of her voice, but Ms. Z picks up on the question mark at the end.

"Look in your assignment folder. You're as capable of reading the details as I am." She reaches down and brings the orange out of her bag, gouging the pocked flesh with a well-placed thumb. "I have other students I work with throughout the week. Did you know that? Three of them. Two at the larger district high school, and one at an elementary school in North Conway." The peel comes hard, and Owl watches with discomfort as her teacher rakes her thumbnail through the white flesh between the fruit and peel, pulling a piece free and dropping it to the paper towel. "This younger girl is profoundly Deaf. I've never seen anyone, of any age, work so hard to become an expert at signing. Her need to communicate is something I don't think either of us can fully appreciate." Drops another peeling. "We have it easy."

Owl's head comes up—she must've misunderstood, her focus misdirected from Ms. Z's lips by the orange ritual—but she can tell in an instant by Ms. Z's placid expression that she'd heard perfectly. Owl's fists close, nails dig in.

"These other students are members of classrooms with three to five times as many kids as you have here in North Plover. They're contending with more background noise, much less teacher attention, a heightened pace. Their time with me is to ensure that they receive an educational experience equal to that of a hearing student." The orange, denuded, is set whole on the paper towel, center eye gazing up at Owl. "But in your case, what I feel we're contending with is a lack of effort from a student used to having the earth moved for her."

Owl's mouth hangs ajar, lips making shapes uselessly a couple times before she at least manages to shake her head.

"Have you ever considered cochlear implants?" Ms. Z gathers her things, swinging her cardigan from the back of her chair and shrugging it on, reaching for the long strap of her bag, face still controlled, but hardened through the eyes. "You might be a good candidate. Eliminate the need to sign completely, which I suspect would be a relief for you. It would also eliminate the need for me to come here twice a week to be treated like the enemy." She takes her coat from one of the hooks, hesitating by Owl's chair. "Deafness isn't the enemy, Rochelle."

She leaves, passing through the dripping curtain of runoff from the roof's edge, leaving Owl sitting in the sun-washed entryway, speechless.

STEAM GOUTS FROM the vents of the sugarhouse cupola, engulfing the roof before it furls into a blue cloudless sky. Boiling off's begun.

Owl lets herself into the dense, moist heat of the sugarhouse and shuts the door softly behind her, surveying the scene.

Seth and Cody stand beside the evaporator, the vents in the arch door seething with flame, steam rising from the open steel pans on top. Seth's fingers run down the rubber tubing attached to the wall, which connects to the storage tanks. "Here's where your gravity plays in again. Open the valve, sap gets pulled down from the tanks into this warming pan, then lets off into the big flue pan to cook. Lots of water in sap, so basically, we need to boil the hell out of it, evaporate the water from the sugar to get our syrup. Pan segments aren't separated, so the sap can flow down here to the draw-off as it thickens up."

Standing next to Seth, Cody is rendered unrecognizable, with his coat off, ski cap tucked into the back pocket of his jeans, revealing a wholly unexpected head of hair: thick, dark reddish gold, trimmed short over the ears and collar, longer on top, enough that it shags over his brow as he watches the motion of the bubbling sap. His brows are burnished, too, lightening his entire face, not at all what she'd imagined above those narrowed blue-gray eyes.

"All comes down to keeping a close eye on things. Undercook, consistency will be too thin—can't use it. Overcook, it'll burn to the bottom. This model's an oldie—been here since my dad ran the place—and it's not heating real efficiently anymore, but I got a new one on order. You don't ever want to let the sap level get too low, like not less than a couple inches in the pan at a time. Thermometer here in the finishing pan will let you know when it's hit boiling point for syrup." Seth lifts his gaze to Owl, making it clear he knew she was there the whole time. "And that temp is . . . ?"

"Two hundred nineteen Fahrenheit," Owl says.

Cody looks over at her, a bit slowly, as if he's reluctant to look away from the sweet, bubbling vapor. Owl's done her share of watching the hypnotizing bubbles rise as the sap darkens and thickens into its next stage of life, her face bathed in dew until the heat becomes too much to take. Cody's eyes still give her nothing, and she raises her brows at him indifferently. Definitely the same boy, hat or not.

Seth leans down to open the arch door. "Time to feed the beast. Every half hour, sometimes every hour if you've got a good blaze going. I usually lay in a row of firewood right along the wall here so I'm not going in and out the door fifty times a day." He shoves some stove lengths into the firebox, sparks whizzing into the air, looking back over his shoulder at Owl. "I'll keep an eye on things here if you two want to go check the taps."

Owl's stomach sinks—she'd harbored a small hope that maybe they'd already done the second check before they started boiling—and she watches Cody move past her out of the sugarhouse without giving her another glance. She lingers, protests welling up behind her lips, but Seth gives a universal sign: two heaves of his thumb toward the door. *Get a move on.*

Once outside, she finds Cody sitting in the driver's seat of the side-by-side, the keys dangling from the ignition. Even with his head turned mostly away, she can see his smile.

She stands stiffly, debating a fight—Ms. Z's words return then—*used to having the earth moved for her*—and, inflamed by the sheer unfairness of it all, gets into the passenger seat, sitting with her arms crossed.

He makes a point of driving too fast, the empty tank shimmying in the trailer hard enough for Owl to feel the vibrations through her seat, but she won't give him the satisfaction of complaining.

Surrounded by nothing but trees and the gravel shoulder ahead, the scene with Ms. Z is inescapable. What started out as the pure shock of having a teacher walk out on her, leaving her to return to the rest of the class almost twenty minutes early with no explanation for Mr. Duquette and all the kids staring, has built into resentment, as the things Ms. Z said really hit their mark. *We have it easy . . . Deafness isn't the enemy, Rochelle.* She wishes so much that she'd fired *something* back at the woman. *We,* as if their lives have the slightest thing in common. There was also the dreaded possibility of the school calling Seth and Holly to tell them Ms. Z made a complaint about her once she had reached civilization.

They've been on the access road maybe thirty seconds

when a shadowed motion between the trees—so swift she nearly misses it—makes Owl sit forward. "Stop!"

He glances over, not braking, then curses, stomping the pedal as whitetail deer scatter out in front of them, down the embankment from the maples—two does and a buck that hasn't dropped its antlers yet, scrambling from the sound of the engine in gangling leaps, which take them up the opposite slope and through the brush.

Owl's out of the side-by-side before they've fully disappeared, quick but careful, counting to five before scaling the embankment and stealing through a sparse area of brush as she enters the woods. Seth taught her how to still-hunt. Leading with the ball of her foot, letting her weight settle onto her heel as she chooses her steps carefully, scanning 180 degrees ahead of her in search of those white flags.

It's not a sound but a sense—being watched—that makes her look around, not wanting to move her feet again unless she has to, since another crunch of snow could spook the deer.

Cody stands behind her, keys in hand. "What are you doing?"

"Following them." At a whisper.

His gaze is wary, incredulous, flicking to the woods beyond. "Why?"

"To see where they go." She turns away from him again. "You don't need to wait."

She continues her slow pace down a slope that's partially clear of snow, exposing a bed of old leaves and dried pine needles.

The buck is in the gully some twenty feet below, standing decoy-still as it looks at her. Maybe three years old, with

73

a muscular neck and flared nostrils. His almond-shaped eyes hold a guarded directness. Judging her.

Rewarded, Owl sinks into a crouch until she rests on her heels, not even noticing the dampness soaking into the seat of her jeans and the hem of her coat. It's the nature of deer: Mortal terror of the growling, hurtling machine on the road will only drive them so far before the shelter of the trees causes tunnel vision, their short memories fading, thinking it safe again to watch, listen. Trusting the woods.

*Split the landscape into quarters. Don't try to see everything at once.* Seth's advice, engrained from growing up hunting with his father, passed on to Owl for spotting wildlife. Sectionalized, it's easy to pinpoint the things that make the woods asymmetrical to her eye—a big, abandoned-looking nest sagging in branches overhead, a rotten, broken birch leaning against a stand of ash, and the motion of the does' slender legs beyond a bayberry bush. Grazing.

Granules of crusty snow trickle past Owl's boot, and she gradually turns her head. Cody stands above her, one shoulder braced against a trunk, looking at the buck, his own eyes unnarrowed for once, fixed with a dark conflict of emotion she doesn't understand.

Below, the buck's black nose twitches, scenting their humanness, which Owl always tries to imagine: meaty, fetid, maybe, not belonging. Then he veers, galloping down the gully bed, out of view, the hoofbeats of the does joining him.

"Let's go." Cody's voice is abrupt in the new silence, carrying down into the ditch. At first, she thinks he's overcompensating for her hearing, but when she turns to him, he's already taken backward steps, eyes riveted on the place where the deer vanished. "Come on."

"Are you scared of them?" At once, she knows she's hit on it, as he ducks his head and swings around, striding through the trees with his hands in his coat pockets. "They're *deer.*"

If he answers, she doesn't hear. She stands, brushes off her jeans, and follows, assessing him curiously once they get into the side-by-side. "You didn't have to follow me."

He jams the keys into the ignition. "Yeah. You get lost out there, they'll blame my ass."

She laughs. "I'm not getting lost in my own woods."

He spits into the dirt, then, and launches them forward with a jolt, spraying gravel.


THEY SPLIT OFF in the sugarbush, occasionally spotting each other as they lug their pails, Owl now looking at Cody intently, trying to conceive of being frightened of the quiet, watchful grace of that buck, the liquid eyes, the sleek tawny form. Cody keeps his eyes averted.

After fifteen minutes or so, their trips to the horizontal tank collide, and Owl finds herself venturing a question as he empties his bucket, her tone guarded: "Have you always lived in the city?"

"Yeah." Steps away from the trailer. "Well. And Natick, Bow. Got dumped there for a while." Sees her uncomprehending look. "Foster families."

She's not sure what to say—hadn't seen that coming—and nods, setting her full pail on the trailer, ready to boost herself up when he grabs the wire handle and dumps it into the tank in one motion, holding it out for her to take with an impatient shake.

"Was just now the closest you've ever seen a deer?" she says. He doesn't move. "They can't hurt you, you know."

"Think I'm scared of getting hurt?" He won't let go of the handle when she pulls, not until she's off-balance and stumbles a little when he releases. He smiles. "I'm never scared. Don't get scared. My scared bone broke and stayed that way."

"Good for you." Owl sidesteps him.

Raises his voice: "Who dumped you?"

When Owl turns back to him, he's getting his cigarettes out of his chest pocket, a crushed-looking half pack of Newports. He taps one out in a practiced way before parking it in the corner of his mouth, where it wags as he speaks, and pats his other pockets, searching. "Seth's not your dad. So who didn't want you?"

She stands, holding her bucket with both hands, a dark tracery of sap stains soaking into her gloved fingers from the handle after he'd dumped the contents so roughly into the tank. Nobody's ever asked her this directly; the answer takes thought.

"Lots of people." Her gaze loses focus on the trees across the road, a double exposure of leafless limbs, humps of sap buckets at staggered levels. "That's how it works. You must know. Your parents lose you first . . . then they work their way down the list. Hoping somebody says yes." Turns her attention to him expectantly, as if having pulled free the delicate caul of some dream.

He's standing, hands resting on the pockets they last touched, cigarette motionless. He works it to the opposite corner. "You mean DHHS?" Nods, finds the silver lighter in his hip pocket. "Like to play God, huh? Kids don't got any rights. Yup. Been there." Chuffs laughter. "Hey, look at it this way. At least they got you away from the geniuses who named you after a bird, right?"

Her jaw tightens. "Nobody named me that. I chose it."

More laughter. "*Chose* it? Jesus, that's even worse."

The moment is crushed. "Shut up."

He lights his cigarette then, a jet of flame shooting out of the knockoff Zippo.

Owl's eyes widen. "You said it was empty."

Cody stalls, filling his lungs before pinching the cigarette out of his lips between thumb and forefinger. He grins. "Guess I bought a refill."

His smoke-filled breath clouds her face as she reaches him in three strides, knocking the cigarette down with her fist before he can react.

"*Hey.*" His voice is scary—loud, rough—but she plants her feet.

"You can't smoke."

He snorts, gesturing to the nothing around them. "Why the hell not?"

"You'll get ash in the sap. It's food. People eat it." She wheels around, heading for the bush. "Keep your cancer to yourself."

When he's sure her back is turned, he lunges for the butt in the snow, licks his fingertips to pinch off the glowing tip, hissing as he tucks the Newport behind his ear for safekeeping.

# 8

Owl's foul mood trails her into the cabin later, where she yanks off her sticky gloves. Holly looks up from tasting the marinara sauce simmering on the range. Her laptop is open on the table; she'd been updating the Van's site while she cooks.

"Mm—don't take off your boots yet." Holly slides a plate down the countertop toward her, heaped with spaghetti and garlic bread and salad. "Do me a favor and run that out to the Syrup King." A nickname taken from the packaging of a rival Canadian syrup maker, featuring an illustration of a strapping, crown-wearing lumberjack bursting out of his flannel shirt. "He'll be out there till eight, probably." Holds up a finger. "Wait. Give me a second. I forgot Cody."

"He's not out there."

"Where'd he go?"

"I don't know. Home." Last Owl saw of him, he was heading away from the sugarhouse after finishing some discussion with Seth. Owl had deliberately stayed outside, busying herself by gassing up the side-by-side and stacking freshly washed pails for tomorrow, stalling until she was sure Cody was leaving, his figure stretched long and lean in the growing dusk shadows on the driveway.

"Really? I thought Seth would teach him how to filter tonight." Holly goes to the glass pane in the door, peering out at the dusk, as if Cody might've changed his mind and was now sitting on their front steps like a lost puppy. "Well, next time he's heading out right at suppertime, invite him to eat with us, okay? A meal at Wallace's place probably adds up to a can of Spam and a fork." Shakes her head. "Don't ask me why Wallace doesn't at least lend him one of his vehicles to come up here. Like his own grandson can't be trusted with one of the four-wheelers. It's cold out there."

Owl drags her hat off. "Why can't Seth and I work together and leave Cody at the evaporator?" Her sudden vehemence makes Holly turn. "He's getting trained on boiling. And Seth can take breaks if he needs to—"

"What he needs is"—Holly's voice is a whip's crack—"a knee replacement. About three years ago."

In the awkward silence that follows, Holly paces over to the stove, where the saucepan is bubbling, splattering the range; she stirs swiftly. "Then we wouldn't be living like this, him in agony half the time, on the pills and the rest of it. Of course, if the surgeon at the VA hospital hadn't screwed up so completely in the first place, we wouldn't even be having this conversation. He's got an appointment coming up with an orthopedic surgeon in Berlin, and it's way the hell overdue." Releases a tense breath, sets the spatula down, keeping her gaze fixed on the backsplash. "I know you miss it being just you guys out there. But your uncle can't keep doing this to his body. It's killing Seth not to run the sugaring himself, and you complaining because you don't like Cody isn't helping."

Owl shifts, knuckles curled on the edge of the countertop. "I didn't know Seth needed a new knee."

"Because he doesn't tell you things like that, hon. When does he ever?" The letter lies beneath the surface of Holly's words, unmentioned in days; now she studies Owl's small, tense face with less frustration. "Better take him his food before it gets cold."

"Can I bring mine, too?" Owl's voice is quiet, humbled, lifting her aunt's gaze. "I want to check on the den after I eat."

Holly smiles a little. "Good thing I don't mind dining alone."

SETH'S IN THE sugar kitchen, lit brightly against the fading daylight beyond the windows, chair pulled up in front of the steam bottler, which he's unhooked from the evaporator now that the sap's all boiled for the day. From the valve, he's filling plastic half-gallon and pint containers, labeled with DOTRICE MAPLE SYRUP, a picture of a farmer driving a team of Belgians up to a steaming sugarhouse, and gold foil stickers reading GRADE A: GOLDEN. The refractometer, nearby, is used

80

to grade the syrup by how much light passes through sample drops from each batch.

"Lifesaver," Seth says as Owl sets his plate, loosely covered in a sheet of paper towel, beside his elbow. "I was about to pour some of this stuff on a piece of cordwood and start chewing."

Smiling, she pulls another folding chair out and sits beside him, taking over the bottling for a while so he can eat. It's her favorite stage of the process, seeing the hot, finished, filtered syrup streaming straight down into the bottle neck, so pale and golden at the kickoff of the season that it reminds her of the word *gossamer*; she isn't totally sure of the definition and, for once, isn't motivated to look it up, choosing to believe this sheer, sweet reward at the end of all the hauling and cooking and monitoring is just that: gossamer.

His knee—not just damaged but beyond saving—hasn't left her mind, and she says, "You didn't want to teach Cody this?" as she twists on a plastic cap until the safety seal locks together, standing the bottle up with the other ten Seth has done.

"Not tonight. Learning his way around the evaporator is going to be enough for a while. I don't think the kid's ever even started a woodstove before—didn't know the first thing about how to stack the wood or add kindling or anything. Not that he came out and said so. Can't get much more than a yup or nope out of him."

*Lucky.* Owl's glad her hands are full so they can't project her thoughts without her permission, which happens from time to time, a sign popping up like a dropped bar of soap in bathwater. She wouldn't mind trading the honor of being the only one Cody seems to want to talk to. "How old is he?"

Seth pauses with his fork. "Nineteen, Wall said."

Another full bottle, another cap locked. Not for the first time, Owl almost tells him that she and Aida saw Cody going into Houlihan's on Sunday—but it would only make Wallace look bad, maybe get him in trouble; not worth the fleeting satisfaction of knowing she'd made life as difficult for Cody as he does for her on a daily basis. "What do you know about him?"

"Not a ton. Wall said he'd had a rough time growing up, got into some trouble. But he's earned his GED, and now he's trying to save money, get some legit work experience under his belt."

"What was so bad about Manchester?" She glances over. "You said he needed to get out."

"I don't know. Bad friends, bad choices, I guess. Needed a break from the place, get some perspective." Seth slides a cardboard box over to her—it's the glass maple-leaf bottles, eight- and three-ounce sizes, big sellers as gifts and souvenirs. They were always a point of fascination for Owl; she likes to hold them up to a window just to watch the light stream through. He watches Owl fill the first maple leaf, cutting the valve at the right moment—almost too full, compensating for the syrup shrinkage that happens after a bottle is sealed—nodding as she lays it on its side, where the hot syrup will sanitize the mouth and inner cap. "Huh. Perspective. We could all use a little of that."

SETH GOES WITH her to the fox den afterward, even though kneeling is almost impossible for him at this point. He edges down onto the balsam branches at an angle that makes Owl cringe, wanting to hold her hand out to him but not wanting to shame him, either—this isn't how it works, her steadying him—instead, holding her arm at a useless level a few inches from her body, where he probably doesn't even notice it in the near darkness.

She's missed this, pairing up for outdoor projects, hiking deeper into the woods than they've ever gone before, Seth pointing out signs of wildlife like deer rub or holes where yellow jackets have made a ground nest. They'd lost it a scrap at a time, Seth begging off when he never would've before, Owl spending more and more time alone with the trees. "This is a good time to see her," Owl says. "She'll be coming out to hunt soon, I bet."

It happens, but not until night comes down, the sky twilight blue with a sprinkling of stars, when it's gotten so cold they're ready to pack it in.

Seth seems to hear the vixen first, breaking off their quiet conversation as he looks over, and Owl sits forward, phone in hand, ready to take video.

A flash of white chin and throat in the dark as she emerges and skitters across the crusty snow toward the trees. Owl tries to follow what she can barely see with the eye of her camera, the seconds cycling onscreen until Seth puts his hand on her shoulder. "I think she's gone."

"Hope I got enough to tell if she's really going to have kits."

"Ah, she must be. The way she's sticking to this den. She's probably got a couple more dug around here as backups. They usually do that, in case the first one gets disturbed by some other animal." He falls silent a second. "Now, if you don't help me up, I'm going to have to spend the night curled up in there with her."

With an anxious laugh, Owl leans in with both arms, a relief to be able to help without worry of pride, providing a brace for him to heave himself up onto his good leg.

They walk back with Owl's phone flashlight glowing, even though they don't really need it; both have walked this path enough times to have the topography memorized, every exposed root and dip in the ground, Seth holding a heavy, low-hanging cedar branch aside so Owl can go first down the slope that ends beside the sugarhouse.

It takes her a moment to realize he isn't following. Turns the light on him, sees him standing, looking back, branch still in hand. "What?"

When she looks in that direction, an inky shape takes off into the sky, some sort of bird spooked into flight. Seth's face is still, listening. "I don't know. Something prowling 'round." But his tension makes her think he has a very definite idea. She scans the thin beam through the darkness. "Come on," he says. "You must have homework. Don't want to be up too late."

She continues, her spine straightening, shoulders prickling with the pins-and-needles sensation of something very wrong on the edge of her perception, but no matter how she strains to hear, she can't discern any motion in the underbrush around them. Whatever Seth hears is out of her reach; she hates the vulnerability.

...

IN HER LOFT, secure in the presence of her aunt and uncle below, Owl skims her way through her assignments, slapping the folder shut on the handout about the County Founding Day group project, stomach acidic and uneasy in the knowledge that in just a couple days, Ms. Z may choose to drop the guillotine on her, hacking into Owl for everyone to see—Mr. Duquette, Seth, and Holly. The attack Ms. Z waged on her today in that low, modulated voice still hums, hivelike, in her mind, and she finally shoves away her school papers and grabs her art pad and pencils, ready to lose herself in forming her fox.

She falls asleep on top of the covers, art pad resting on her chest, fist curled beside her head. Maybe an hour passes, possibly two, before she wakes, groggily noticing a glow outside her curtains, like when the deck light is left on, which never happens once all three of them are in for the night.

She goes to the glass, peering down. Seth is partially visible from her vantage point, sitting directly below her window in one of the Adirondack chairs that flank the front door.

A rifle lies across his lap, gripped with both hands, his head turned in the direction of the woods beyond the sugarhouse. His posture is rigid, maintaining alertness. Standing sentry.

# Part II

## MAPLE SYRUP GRADE:
### Amber

*Darkening a shade as sugar levels
change midway through the season;
rich, full-bodied taste.*

# 9

Thursday takes an eon to arrive, yet still comes too soon, Owl bound with nerves and anticipation, having rehearsed a hundred dreaded scenarios in her mind since Tuesday. And there's every chance that Ms. Z may not show for their session at all, simply abandoning Owl to explain the situation to everyone on her own: that she essentially drove her teacher away, that she's impossible, incorrigible, the sort-of-Deaf girl who bit the only hands that speak to her.

Owl doesn't set up the desk and chairs, instead closing the classroom door softly behind her and perching on the front steps of the school, elbows on knees, face resting in hands, backpack on the floor beside her—so Mr. Duquette doesn't ask questions before absolutely necessary.

The little kids at recess hesitate in their play, watching as Ms. Z's hybrid car pulls into the lot at its usual time and parks in the spot nearest the school, before they return to whatever game has them turning dizzying pirouettes, arms outstretched, Micah the Instigator calling out orders that Owl can't quite get a fix on.

Ms. Z crosses to the front steps with her arms folded. A beat passes, neither of their expressions yielding. Ms. Z says, "Let's go for a walk."


IT'S SUNNY, BUT the wind has teeth, hardly the kind of weather in which they've taken their past sessions outside, but exactly the kind where Owl can almost feel the sap gushing from the maples' veins, the rapid faucet drip of it into the buckets pattering throughout the bush, keeping them boiling all week just to stay on top of their good fortune before March— the true cruelest month—turns frigid again.

Owl walks with her hood flipped up over her hat, in step with her teacher, along the hard-packed trail around school property, beaten down by child-sized boots. Micah stares as they go, no doubt wondering where Ms. Z is hiding the picnic basket.

"Rochelle," Ms. Z says, the name carefully weighted, as if reaching out to test ice gone yellow and mealy with thaw.

"I think I should talk first." Owl walks swiftly; her words feel thick, clumsy with emotion. "You got to say a lot last time, and I didn't get to say anything." Checks on her teacher sideways, seeing if the woman's going to cut her off, but Ms. Z's profile is sculpted alabaster. Owl can't seem to take a full breath or steady her voice. "You called me spoiled and lazy. I think what you really don't like about me is that I'm not Deaf enough for you."

Ms. Z's gaze is trained on the snow; Owl swallows, plunges forward: "You act like having some hearing is the same as having all of it, and I'm nothing like the real Deaf kids you teach. You said it's *easy*. Being half in the world and half out of it, missing things all the time, trying to figure stuff out after everybody else is already laughing?" Her teacher's lips part, but Owl's words come fast. "No, I don't sign a lot. Because nobody understands. At home, they try, but they know I can hear and talk, too, and they think I should use those things. I do both because I *am* both. But being both feels the same as being nothing. Nowhere." Having met a mental wall, Owl looks down. Said her piece. All she could do.

Ms. Z remains quiet for a beat, perhaps waiting to make sure that Owl's done. "First, let me say that I shouldn't have left the way I did last time. It was unprofessional, and reactionary, and I regret it."

She stops, facing Owl, her eyes narrowed against the glare, strands of dark hair blowing in front of her face. It strikes Owl that maybe she wasn't the only one waiting for a phone call from the school administration over the past two days. "But in my defense, these past months with you have been an exercise in frustration that I wasn't prepared for. I've never had a student hold me at arm's length like this. I'm here twice a week, giving you a chance to sign and maybe not feel quite so isolated or reliant on lip-reading, but all you want to do is vocally tell me that you've got three questions left at the end of your American history chapter. Yes, I function as a tutor, but also as a support person, who has at least some grasp of what it is to be Deaf in a hearing world. And you're giving me nothing."

"That's all I ever did with Mr. Weir. Talk about homework," Owl says sharply. "He didn't think I was bad."

"Rochelle." A pained finality to her words. "I don't think you're bad."

They stare at each other, Owl's hard expression gradually fading to wary expectance.

Ms. Z exhales slowly, pushes her hair behind her ears. "I've completely mishandled this. We should've talked— really talked—a long time ago." The corner of her mouth quirks slightly. "Pity it took an argument to open the lines of communication."

Owl shifts, glancing at the school, wondering who can see them out here, surrounded by bare oaks. "So . . . what do we do?"

"I'm not sure. We don't want to keep going the way we have been every week, correct?" Owl shakes her head vigorously; Ms. Z's wry expression deepens, emphasizing a never-before-seen dimple in her right cheek. "Agreed. How about this. I give you an assignment during our time today. Don't look like that—it's not challenging. In fact, we'll both do it. Each of us will come up with a list of what we want these sessions to be about. What we each need to get out of them in order to make it worthwhile." She holds up a hand. "Then we'll discuss on Tuesday."

Owl considers—Ms. Z's gaze is sharp—but then she sets her jaw, nods once. Ms. Z begins to turn toward the schoolhouse, but Owl stops her with a question: "You said Deafness isn't the enemy. Who is?"

Her teacher blinks against the cutting dryness of the wind. "Maybe there isn't one."

Owl digests this, rejects it, her gaze turning inward as she scans the dark, dappled facade of the woods. "Yes, there is."

SUGARHOUSE HEAVING STEAM, sweet sauna of maple and woodsmoke, gush of sap from hose to tank, from tank to evaporator pans. Cody's shape moves through it all, around Owl, behind, stripped to a black quilted down vest over a flannel shirt to accommodate for the near-seventy-degree temperatures inside. Seth present, but peripheral, making sure the sap never boils too low, showing Cody when to scoop impurities off the foaming surface of the pans, while Owl gives the storage tanks their weekly scrubbing with hot water and a nylon brush.

The sap is boiled down and filtered by five o'clock, ready for bottling. Lights glow in the cabin windows, Holly's shape visible, moving between counter and stove. Seth watches Cody poke at the fire with the tongs, then shut the arch door and close the dampers to let the flames burn down on their own. "Dinner break," Seth says to him. "Might as well take a load off inside, get something to eat. Syrup will keep till after— then I can show you how to use the bottler."

It's the right tack to take, not an invitation but a practical matter. Cody watches him a moment, shrugs, walks silently behind Owl and Seth toward the house, coat under his arm. Owl looks back at him once, hoping to impart an entire meal's worth of warnings with a single frown, that he'd better be damned delicate with her family, but he's watching the ground, not noticing.

Holly looks up as they come in. "Hey, Cody. I've been telling Owl that meals are included in this gig, but I wasn't sure if the message was passed on. Take a seat." She drags the chairs out from the table, missing the glance Owl shoots at Cody, who returns it with a steady, benign look, a mask over the pointing-and-laughing mockery he'd be showing if they were out in the sugarbush right now instead of penned in by adults.

A quick rattle of pills as Seth pops his Percocet, Holly cursing softly, stirring a pot of rice rapidly sticking to the bottom. "Self-serve tonight, guys, but everything's ready. Cody, Coke okay?"

"Yeah." Momentary mental speed bump, then politeness occurs to him: "Thanks."

Owl bugs her eyes at him, mock impressed; he pops the top, holding her gaze while taking his sweet time adding the soda to the glass Holly set beside him, waiting for the fizz to die down over the ice cubes. Owl notices Seth watching them, bemused, and looks down at her plate, redness creeping into her cheeks.

Owl is last to go fill her plate, in line behind Cody, and she watches with disbelief as he loads it with four drumsticks and fills in the rest of the space with a mountain of rice, peas ignored. Places a glob of butter on the mountain, adds another when he seems to realize it's real, not margarine.

Next couple minutes, everyone tries not to watch Cody eat, a high-speed inhalation of everything in front of him, never touching his napkin, not even a pause for a drink until

94

the plate is clean, after which he drains his glass in two swallows, sitting back with his hands on his thighs as his system processes the caloric shock wave. Owl picks at her food, unsure whether she's fascinated or disgusted, then glances over as Seth clears his throat, speaking to Cody.

"I won't keep you much longer tonight. Bottling's pretty straightforward. Bet you're probably ready to get home." Cody's gaze flicks over at the word *home*, says nothing. "You want a ride later, say the word. Not a lot of fun walking down that road in the dark. No streetlights around here."

Mention of the coming night makes Owl bow over her plate and tuck in, burying the thought of Seth on the deck, gun in hand, staring at the blackness beyond the sugarhouse. Her uncle, who hasn't raised his scope to a whitetail or turkey in almost two decades, but who, she knows this, gut-level, would not hesitate to put a bullet in anyone who threatened their family. Least of all the silhouette she pictured standing between the trees the other night, same as the one behind the windshield of the strange car that pulls into their driveway in her worst imaginings, sending her bolting into the forest of her father's own childhood. No one in the house has spoken the possibility, but last night, she saw the outside light go on again, and saw Seth sitting below, no gun this time, simply keeping vigil.

"So, Cody, we're going to have a little crowd here on Saturday," Holly says. "Kind of a sugaring party. It's mostly work. Wallace probably said." Holly pauses in her chewing when Cody looks back, brows drawn, obviously knowing nothing about it. "Well. We usually end up having a few neighbors come help one or two weekends out of the season, let them take as much syrup home as they want in payment. Fair warning, it'll probably turn into a full-on mountain-man jamboree later in the evening. Gunnar brings his cider, and they hang around gossiping until midnight."

"Wouldn't call it that." Seth is deadpan, tossing down a chicken bone.

"Sorry. Gossiping about your tractors." To Cody: "Anyway, you're more than welcome to stay if you want."

Owl looks hard at him, daring him to freeze Holly out the way he does the men, thereby giving Owl reason to let her foot swing freely into his shin, but he nods once, gaze on Owl's untouched second drumstick. "Sounds lit." Leaving everyone off-balance, searching for signs of sarcasm.

ABOUT AN HOUR later, Owl sees them leave—she's been checking out her window every now and then, knowing her ears can't alert her to the sound of Seth's truck starting—but the stray headlights reflecting off her wall are warning enough to see them pull down the driveway in the direction of Wallace's place.

"That kid makes your uncle look chatty," Holly had said while she and Owl washed dishes, Cody and Seth out in the sugarhouse again, filling bottles and packing them into shipping boxes for some of the automatic orders. "Never thought I'd say that about anyone."

Owl grunted. "Until you're alone with him. Then he won't shut up. Even when you tell him to."

"Hmm." Holly kept her focus on the plate she was drying. "What does he talk about?"

"Nothing. Everything. I don't know." Owl, seized by a conviction that she'd said too much—and that her aunt was hiding a smile as she turned toward the cupboard—took to scrubbing the baking sheet so hard it left a fresh scratch mark on the battle-scarred aluminum.

Now, once the pickup headlights flash Seth's return, Owl is surprised by his knock—rapping on top of the balustrade hard enough to make sure she hears—not just because of the hour but because he rarely ever ascends to her loft. "Come in."

The concept of the loft as her territory, to keep as clean or messy, private or open, as she likes, was put in place her first day here, Seth and Holly showing her upstairs and then leaving her alone to check things out. She remembers running her small hand over the bedroom furniture, junk-store pieces sanded and refinished to match, still smelling faintly of polyurethane; the patchwork quilt on the bed; the walls left blank, space for her to fill; and how thankful she'd been for the curtains—Holly actually apologizing for the material, lavender and seagrass-colored checks with a silver thread woven through, saying it had been on sale, but Rochelle could choose something else the next time they went into Stokely, if she wanted—never guessing that privacy was water to her aching thirst, antidote to the hospital rooms with nurses popping in the door every hour to test every system, every function of the eggshell girl who the doctors managed to mostly piece back together again. It was a lifetime away from the closet-sized bedroom in Daddy's apartment, window leaking endless traffic noise and streetlight pollution, floor covered with her piles of toys, chewed stuffed animals, dirty clothes, used tissues, lollipop sticks, and stickers she'd plastered everywhere.

Seth parts the curtains gingerly, peeking in at Owl sitting on the bed, doing her reading for English, *Invisible Man* by Ralph Ellison. He doesn't smile, instead looking at her a moment before stepping through. "Sorry to bust in."

"You're not." Resting the paperback open on her bed, she waits, uneasiness growing as he lowers himself into her desk chair, gazing around at her drawings, still unsmiling, distracted. "Get the bottling done?"

"Boxed, labeled, ready to go." Said in a breath of laughter, shaking his head. "Kid's a machine. Just wants to get this crap done and get out of here." Owl laughs, too, but the look around her uncle's eyes keeps her from relaxing. "Listen." Seth shifts, moving his hands down to grip his knees, massaging the bad one. "I know it's the end of the night. Bad time for this. But Holly says there is no good time, and I'm starting to think she's right."

Owl watches him reach into the chest pocket of his chamois shirt and pull out a folded envelope, flattening it roughly. "I've been carrying this around since yesterday. If Holly wasn't the one who checks the mail, you probably never would've seen it."

Her gaze skims the boyish handwriting, a water skipper over a pond, flying to any other place to land. "I don't want that."

"You've got no idea how many times I almost fed it to the fire. The last time was just now, out in the sugarhouse, when

Cody was working in the kitchen. But Holly would've known, and I would've known, and—shit." Rubs his face. "I still want to torch it. And if that's what you want to do, go ahead. But Holly's real big on it being your call, and she thought that it should be me who gives it to you."

Owl's throat is dry. "Why?"

"So you know that it's your decision, not mine. She's afraid that you'll just side with me and not really figure out how you feel about all this. Him." Strain in Seth's voice; he's laying his shoulder into the massive boulder blocking the way to his feelings about Joel Dotrice. "I think you're a kid who knows her own mind. At the Notch the other day . . . well, you didn't leave me with any doubts, and I don't like doing this to you. But it's your letter." When he holds it out, she pushes back with her heels, pressing herself into the headboard. "Owl."

Stares at him, refusing to budge.

He exhales through his nose, sets the envelope on the desk. "See you in the morning."

She wants to leap from the bed as he leaves, stuff the envelope back into his hands, demand to know how she could ever sleep with that thing in here shredding her peace, make him toss it into the woodstove now, because she'll never read it. Instead, she watches him go, her gaze tracking with its own trajectory, landing on the envelope, slightly humped from being folded in half for a day, the line down the center splitting the name of the addressee in two: *Rochelle Dotrice.*

# 10

Saturday, everyone arrives by nine a.m., the driveway as full of vehicles as it ever is, many of the Waits Mountain kids coming with their parents, the Baptistes a notable exception. Wallace's truck, the Streeters' Hummer with a plush suction-cupped Darth Vader marking Micah's window, the Boulier sisters riding along with them, and Gunnar's snowmobile parked off to the side, which he guided down the woods trail from his yurt to their place, ski goggles in place, wildly curling white hair flying out from beneath his stocking cap. He grins as he climbs off, opening the pack on his back to flash the half-gallon jug of his home brew for Seth to see, who lifts his coffee mug in a cheers from where he and Owl sit on the front steps.

"Like the way you think," Wallace calls, hauling a suitcase of Coors Light from the floor of his truck cab.

Cody climbs out the passenger door and heads toward the side-by-side, his eyes inaccessible beneath the low edge of his hat. He ignores his grandfather and the rest of them greeting each other, the offers of coffee and muffins inside, and the mothers carrying Crockpots of casseroles and Rubbermaid containers of sandwiches and brownies. When he reaches the vehicle, he drops heavily into the driver's seat, head tipped back. Owl gets the distinct impression that he's waiting for her, and she just looks at him, holding her spot.

The moment Owl has dreaded—Aida's mother's Jeep Wrangler pulling in—happens next, Aida sliding out of the passenger seat like tiredness has reduced her bones to sand. She rounds the front of the car as her mother, Trini, a small, plump woman with a cap of curls identical to Aida's and a perpetually apologetic brow, waves hello to Holly. Aida spots Owl without surfacing from her sullen shell—she's been helping once a season since they were kids, and the excitement has faded as sleeping until eleven on Saturday became more precious than earning enough real syrup to grace her pancakes for the rest of the year—but when her gaze finds Cody, her mouth falls open and stays that way.

"Thanks for coming out again this year," Seth says to the small group. "It's supposed to get up near sixty by midday, so the sap's going to be running like a river. You've all done this enough times now to know which parts you like helping with and which you don't, so feel free to jump on whatever, helping Owl and Cody with the first tap check or getting the evaporator ready to roll for the day."

"Tap check," Aida pipes up, running over to hug Owl's arm while staring openly across the yard at Cody.

Seth hesitates, distracted. "All righty. Plenty of coffee, tea, breakfast inside—help yourselves. Appreciate it."

Owl walks to the side-by-side with Aida attached; she'd planned on making Cody slide over into the passenger seat, but now it's all she can do to shake her friend loose into the back seat and climb in beside him, her face hot from Aida's theatrics, unable to meet his eyes. At the last second, she notices Trini watching them, alarm so obvious in her posture that Owl says, "Buckle up," with so much authority even Cody fastens his belt before jamming the accelerator down and taking them off down the driveway with the trailer rocking behind them.

IN THE SUGARBUSH, Cody climbs out first, grabbing two collection pails out of the stack and taking off for the opposite side of the access road without a look at the girls. Aida waits about three seconds before lambasting Owl's shoulder with slaps. "Oh my god! What the hell! How could you not tell me that guy works for you?"

Owl flinches away, coloring deeply. "He hadn't started yet when we saw him. I didn't know who he was." The lie comes easily, without much guilt or worry of getting caught, if it would shut the door on Aida's interrogation for the time being. Owl's thoughts on Cody are a knot of hard, constricted layers, capable of wounding, nothing she wants to deal with right now.

"Yeah, but what about after? Like you didn't recognize the only hot guy we've seen around here ever." Owl shrugs defensively, but Aida's already moving on, clambering out of the side-by-side to grab a collection pail, gaze raking the trees where Cody disappeared. "I know where I'm going."

"No." Owl watches her friend dash for the embankment. *"Aida."* But there's no way to pull her back, nothing to do but follow.

She finds Aida standing alongside a maple, swinging her pail by the handle, only partially hidden as she stares at Cody, some twenty paces away, working with his back mostly turned to them. Owl brushes by, shooting her a grim, imploring look as she begins collecting sap, caught between relief and annoyance when Aida starts lackadaisically checking taps on the same tree she is, never looking away from Cody and forcing Owl to move on to the next tree and the next, because she hates the inefficiency of Aida standing on her heels.

Another party of tap checkers arrives on snowshoe on the opposite side of the road: all three of the little kids, plus parents, and, not surprisingly, Trini, who appears behind a thin screen of bramble bushes, craning her neck, looking cautiously satisfied once she places her daughter with Owl, Cody too far off to be seen from her vantage point.

"Who is he?" Aida hisses in her ear, a suppressed giggle like plucked ukulele strings.

"Wallace's grandson." Owl's voice rises in frustration, and she bites it down, knowing he must've heard. Hefts up her pail. "Help me."

The other girl doesn't seem to mind becoming Owl's assistant, even as she glances back repeatedly in hopes of catching Cody checking them out. He never is.

The horizontal tank level rises quickly with so many hands pitching in, parents helping kids. Inevitably, during one trip to the tank, Owl and Aida arrive at the same time as Cody, doing an awkward box step thanks to the heavy pail between them, sap sloshing dangerously. Aida stops short, nearly bumping Cody's chest, face turned up into his.

He holds her gaze expressionlessly for a few hard seconds as they turn a half circle around each other, allowing the magnetism to stretch, until he breaks it by turning his back on her to dump his pail into the mouth of the tank, then pivoting and doing another up-close pass of her hopeful, grinning face. He turns once on the embankment, taking a few backward steps, this time his eyes full on Owl, his free hand pulling a cigarette from the pack in his pocket, flicking the tip of his tongue along the paper before tucking it behind his ear and heading off.

Owl sets her jaw, barely noticing Aida's smothered giggles and whispers, trying to get a glimpse of rising smoke as she climbs up to dump the bucket in.

She leads the way back into the trees, not waiting for Aida, working up a good head of steam by the time she sees Cody, cigarette in his teeth. She opens her mouth to rip into him this time, maybe even tell Seth—not seeing until he turns to her that the tip is unlit.

He smiles around it, bites down, takes another sap bucket off the hook; Owl deflates, giving him a narrow look before walking away, brushing by Aida, who watches without comprehension, then hurries after.

AT LUNCH, PAPER plates and plastic forks, food heaped on every countertop and spreading over onto the cleared-off coffee table, people grabbing whatever seats they can find: the living room rug, the stairs to the loft. Owl catches glimpses of Holly threading through, constantly moving, never landing long; she always seems more comfortable facilitating than settling in with a group this size. Little kids, red-cheeked from the heat and sweating in the overkill turtlenecks and fleece jackets their parents forced them into before they came. The men, for the most part, take their plates out to the sugarhouse, where steam tumbles from the cupola so fast it looks like a house fire in the final moments before collapse.

Trini manages to wrangle Aida into sitting beside her on the couch, both of them eating while letting their gazes roam the hectic room, Owl seated on the floor beside them with her plate on the corner of the coffee table, turning when Aida's head suddenly jerks up.

Cody comes through the front door, the first they've seen of him since lunch break began. He stops and looks at the crocks full of Swedish meatballs and macaroni and cheese, a room full of flushed faces turning to stare—then impassively slides sideways through the melee, heading for the bathroom.

Aida does a slow neck roll to watch him walk behind the couch, ending up eye to eye with her mother's furrowed, consternated gaze.

Owl eats as she watches Cody try the knob, rest back on his heels when it won't turn, then get barreled into by Lulu a second later, a cannonball at waist level as she tries to escape from Micah, who's got his ambrosia-salad-coated fork pulled back in classic catapult style. Lulu coughs on a giggle, looking up into the face of a stranger—Owl stops midchew, riveted—as Cody's hands right the little girl's bird-bone frame like you would a crooked cane chair, barely even glancing at her. Then he gives her a light push between the shoulder blades to launch her off again in her dash right out the front door and down the steps, where she's already forgotten him. Owl relaxes, not realizing how far she's lifted herself off the rug until it takes a second to touch down again.

When Cody's done in the john, he goes straight back outside, not talking to anyone or stopping for a plate, but Owl sees him palm two mini ham-and-Swiss sandwiches into a paper napkin on his way.

THE DAY FOLLOWS the same comfortable pattern it has in previous years: some friends leaving right after lunch, Holly sending them off with a gallon jug of syrup; the rest spreading out around the farm, some watching the cooking process in the sugarhouse, others bottling, the little kids mostly playing and chasing each other around the snowy center of the circular driveway. Micah unearths an old Nerf football of Owl's and plays keep-away with the Boulier sisters.

Aida's bound for disappointment—Owl knows Cody's taken over the evaporator by the time the afternoon tap check rolls around—but Trini's ready, anyway, telling her daughter, "Aid, walk with us," when it's time to head out to the sugarbush, tone leaving zero room for argument. For anyone but Aida, that is.

"Why can't I ride with Owl?"

"Because it's a beautiful day and I want you with me." Thigh pat, head nod. "C'mon." With a disgusted look, Aida follows.

Later, when Owl drives the final tankful back, Aida's on the spot, making some show of helping drag the storage tank hose over before drifting toward the sugarhouse door, propped partially open, first putting her face in the gap, then easing her entire body in like a cat.

Owl turns on the suction and goes in after her. Aida's found a spot on the outer edge of the small cluster of men, her gaze on Cody's back as he checks the pans of bubbling sap. The background noise of the vacuum suction cancels out Owl's hearing, but when Wallace stands from a chair and leans over his grandson's shoulder, she reads: —*want to add some more.*

*Nope. I don't.*

*Gonna burn down to nothing in a minute, bub.*

Cody doesn't speak. Wallace's stare, leaden.

Seth's lips move: *He's got this, Wall. Cooked up the last two batches by himself. I just sat around being worthless.*

*We're used to that,* Gunnar says, and people laugh. Not Cody. His hard, detached expression remains unchanged.

Owl doesn't know Trini's there until Aida jerks around. Her mother stands in the open doorway. "Aida. Time to go." Crooks her finger, lips pursed, gaze going to Cody. "Right now, please."

107

Holly emerges from the sugar kitchen, a cardboard box under her arm. "Wait, Trini—syrup? And I've got two gallons of the dark stuff from last season if you can use it."

"Oh—yes. Definitely." Aida's mom is one of the few who wants the intensely flavored, extra dark end-of-season syrup, using it in her baking throughout the year.

By the time Owl's shut off the hose and gone to park the side-by-side next to the sugarhouse until tomorrow, the Jeep Wrangler is crawling down the driveway, Trini straining forward to watch for scrambling children, Aida staring back out the passenger window. Owl raises a hand, but her friend doesn't see, her searching gaze meant for someone else entirely.


AS HOLLY PREDICTED, by six o'clock everyone has gone home but Wallace and Gunnar, now sitting around the kitchen table with glasses of hard cider or cans of Coors, Seth with the ice pack on his knee, as usual, Celtics versus Lakers on the small camping radio they keep on the windowsill. Cody's finishing up the bottling on his own, quitting time coming a couple hours early thanks to the help with the tap checks.

Owl and Holly are on the couch together, Owl picking at leftovers, Holly alternately reading and resting her eyes with her feet propped on Owl's lap. Above the silhouetted trees, daylight is a fiery pastel border, thumb-smudged, when Cody makes his way inside, the vibration of the closing door making Owl look over.

*Take your coat off and stay awhile,* Seth says, Owl reading the words from his lips for accuracy at this distance as Seth swirls a bit of sediment at the bottom of his glass, in the reflective haze Owl associates with the time after he's taken his evening Percocet. *Plenty to eat in the fridge.*

*Brewskis,* Wallace puts in.

Cody goes straight over and pulls a can out, popping it and sipping as he pulls up the last empty chair, not seeming to notice Owl watching him over the corner of the couch's back cushion.

*Christ, you want to try something rugged?* Wallace slides the bottle of cider over. *Pour yourself a slug.*

Gunnar flicks a look at Seth, neither man speaking, but Holly's paying close attention as Cody turns the bottle, one corner of his mouth going up. *Rotten apple juice. Right?*

*Don't believe me, give it a go.*

Cody fills his glass and downs it like he did the Coke the other night, two swallows. Seth straightens slightly in his seat but keeps his mouth shut. By the time the bottom of Cody's glass touches the tabletop, the 12 percent ABV hits, and he sucks wind on a scalded throat, leaning forward to keep from coughing.

The older men laugh, Seth starting to get up—*Let me grab you some coffee*—but Wallace claps Cody on the back, the usual hard jostle, and nudges his Coors over.

*Here's your chaser. You'll be okay.*

Holly stands, unrolling the fleece blanket she'd had under her head to lay over the couch arm. "Too much excitement for me. Think I'll turn in," she says loud enough for the men to hear.

Wallace leans back. *Nah, already? Pull up a seat with us, have a drink—we were just about to talk sense into Seth about how he ought to bid on that acreage next door.*

Holly makes a sound in her throat. "We had an extra million to spare, I'm sure he would."

*Nah, it can't be that much. Half of it's marshland. Ain't worth nothin'.*

*What's he want it for, then?* Gunnar's smiling, familiar routine of winding Wallace up.

*Well, shit, he don't have to buy the whole thing! They'd probably be willing to sell you just the piece you border on. Plant yourself some more trees, expand your operation.*

*It takes something like sixty years for a maple to start producing well.* Owl follows the motion of Seth's lips. *I don't got that kind of time.*

*Yeah, but your girl does.* Wallace heaves a hand in Owl's direction. *You're always saying she wants to run the place after you hang it up. You'd be leaving her twice the legacy.*

"O-kay, and I'm done. 'Night, gentlemen. Owlie." Holly's warm hand cups Owl's cheek for a moment, a rare touch, and Owl leans into it, eyes closed, before her aunt draws off down the shadowed hallway to the bedroom.

Owl eases into the cushions, miming relaxation, when having Cody in her house has her senses on high alert. There was a time when Owl hid in the loft when Seth's friends—inherited from Grandpa Dotrice, more his generation—came over, having learned to make herself scarce whenever men gathered and conversation grew overloud with drink. But those lessons came from her old life, Daddy's best friends—until they weren't, and some neighbor called the police because their fighting could be heard on the street. A sickening slice of memory strikes her: Daddy out of the room, and a man she only ever knew as Junior coming up behind her in the kitchen, grabbing her right butt cheek with a squeeze, and a shake so hard she'd struck the counter. For years, she thought it was some inexplicable spanking; now, she understands, and her mouth sours. Never told Daddy. He would've gone crazy on Junior, and the cops might've taken him away. Daddy had been put in lockup twice before, that Owl could remember, and she'd had to stay with the downstairs neighbor lady and her sons, where the bed Owl shared with the three-year-old smelled like dried pee, and it was made clear that she was a burden, until Daddy made bail and came back for her.

Owl both hears and feels the front door shut hard and glances over again, seeing all three older men watching where Cody just exited, the curtain panels over the glass panes in the door still swaying with force.

*Kid hates me.* Wallace's lips.

*We were smart-asses at that age, too.* Gunnar pours another finger of cider.

*No. That ain't it. He blames me for his mother.* Wallace sips. *I should've done better.*

Seth shifts in his seat, flipping the ice pack over to absorb the last of its coldness. His gaze trails to Owl peeking over the couch, knows she's reading all this. *Long time ago, Wall. Sounds like you did what you could.*

*Christ. She was always such a mess, Evie. Don't know what the hell Rhetta and I did wrong. Worked my ass off at that concrete plant, thirty years, so we could get by. Rhetta tried to make things nice for her, do the stuff a mother does. Girl still got into drugs before she was sixteen.*

Gunnar nods slowly; Owl gets the sense he's heard this before. *It's a disease for some people. Just like booze.*

*We tried talking to her, getting her help. She ran off to Mass. Finally got herself knocked up with Cody, wouldn't even let us see him. She got charged with possession, kid got dumped into the system. They crossed their wires somewhere, and nobody contacted us. I guess Evie jumped through hoops to prove she was getting clean, went through rehab like the court said so she wouldn't lose custody for good. Rhetta met up with them at a playground once, wanted to at least see her grandbaby. Boy was something like six years old then. Rhetta really thought she was getting her daughter back. Then Evie and the boy fall off the face of the earth again, and we don't hear nothing for like three years. Turned out she'd moved to Manchester, didn't even let us know she was back in the state.*

Seth eases out of his seat, goes to put the pack in the freezer, pour coffee. Wallace's gaze, moist and faraway, drifts to Owl, and she lets her eyes go to the flickering TV screen, knowing he believes she can't understand them from this distance. When she looks again, she picks up on the flow:

*—bad. DHHS had to pull him out of one of those homes 'cause things got so ugly.* Gives his glass a rough half turn, staring into it. *I got no excuse for the second time. DHHS called us, told me the situation. Evie got caught with enough to be charged with intent to sell, Cody needed a place again. At that point, I'd never even met the kid, Rhetta just the once, and she was smack in the middle of her first round of chemo. Sick as a dog. She couldn't have been taking care of a ten-year-old. I never told her they called us. She would've bent over*

*backward for him and ended up killing herself. And I . . .* Presses his lips together a moment, tight and dry. *Couldn't do it on my own. Didn't want to try. So I didn't take him.*

Seth sets a mug in front of him. *Times were hard. You got to let that go.*

*Well, the boy hasn't. When I heard from Evie this time, looking for help with him, saying he needed work, a new start, I was all over it. Sweet Jesus. You should see her. Clean three years now, so she says, but she looks like an old woman. My little girl. Only thirty-nine, and she shakes like this.* Holds up a tremoring hand. *Destroyed herself with that poison. And she still says she's doing her best just to hang on.*

Lips stop. Wallace and Gunnar look at the table. Seth stands at the window above the sink, looking out as night deepens, flame ends.

OWL SLIPS OUT the back door, the blanket from the couch wrapped around her shoulders, not wanting to tip off the men by grabbing her coat.

She circles the house, the only sound her chukkas in the snow. The ember of his cigarette hovers in the dimness of the deck, his faintly backlit shape only visible once her eyes have time to adjust.

"See? Keeping it to myself." Ember lowers as he taps ash off the railing. "Just like you said."

She goes up the front steps, looking into the kitchen from the outside, something she's seldom done. Seth's back in his seat, but Wallace is laughing now, conversation deliberately moved on to lighter things.

"What did you mean when you said this seems like a place people come to get buried?" She goes to the railing, close—reliant, in the dark, on hearing alone and not wanting to miss his answer.

Cody blows smoke, a cryptic spectral shape unfurling in the scant light. "I mean . . . it's so dead here. Nothing to do. Everything's a million miles away." Drives his words home with a gesture of the Coors Light he's brought out with him. "Everybody here's hiding. Nobody would stay if they weren't scared shitless of the world."

"But not you."

"Fuck no. Soon as I get my money, I'm gone. Get myself some cheap-ass car and start driving, see where it takes me. Stop any place that looks cool, take a thousand pictures nobody wants to see but me. Piss on a grizzly bear and share a brew with Abe Lincoln's head, up on whatever mountain that is."

"The Black Hills."

"That's not it."

"Yes, it is. It's sacred to the Lakota Sioux. White people stole it to carve the presidents' heads into."

"Sounds like something we'd do." Fast gleam of his teeth as he nods. "What I'm saying is I'm going to blow my cash on what I want, go all the places I never thought I'd get a chance to. Till the money runs out or the car breaks down, whatever comes first."

She smiles. "Don't know if we can pay you enough to get all the way to South Dakota."

"Yeah, well. That's only one place I'm thinking about." Leans forward on his elbows, gazing over at the woods to their left.

Owl glances at the house, making sure they don't have an audience at the window, but no one seems to realize she's out here instead of up in the loft. "You're wrong about the mountain." Her voice is low. "It can be a place to heal. That's what it was for me."

"Yeah?" He turns back, putting the cigarette in his lips. "You all better now?"

She tries to absorb the sarcasm, watches the ember devour itself, not willing to let this pass without a real answer. "Some things don't get better. They change, turn into something else. And that's the best you get."

He says nothing, just looking at her, seconds sliding past.

"I can show you the stuff you don't see about this place. What makes it special." She shrugs. "Helps to have a guide. I did."

Cody grips the post with one hand, leaning around it. "When are you thinking?"

"It's supposed to snow overnight, get cold again. Sap won't be running like it has been, so we'll have more time." He's close enough now that she smells him beneath the smoke— some basic bar soap, Dial, maybe; heat from the concealed places of him, underarms, his core—imprinting him bodily in her senses in a way he hasn't yet been. "We'll go tomorrow."

# 11

The letter is still where she stuffed it, between her bureau and the wall, crumpled from her fist.

Early morning Sunday, Owl pulls the ball of paper out, flattening it on the floor and resting back on her heels.

The idea of checking the postmark hadn't occurred to her until the first cloudy moments of wakefulness, more a notion from books and TV than experience, since she'd never received much mail. But—she's fairly certain—the stamp from the post office would tell her where he was when he mailed it. If he was moving closer to them. If it was possible he'd already been on the land. Watching.

A return address:

> *J. Dotrice*
> *24 Market Street, Apt. B*
> *Dover, NH 03820*

So he was back there, had an apartment now. The post-mark, a digital stamp across the top, reads only NORTHERN NH. But it was stamped with Monday's date, didn't reach them until Wednesday, and Seth hadn't put it in her hands until the day after that. Plenty of time for Daddy to drive here. For him to be the presence in the woods, the reason Seth got his gun. Just like him, asking her permission to write, but unable—unwilling, even after a decade of not speaking—to wait for her to give it. The overwhelming, suffocating energy of him, it still lashes in her veins, sentient.

For an instant, the potential inside the envelope builds electrically, Owl's fingers curling, mind's eye coursing down the rows of words within (*What could he say? How could he even begin?*) before she crushes it again in her fist, slamming it into the bottom drawer, and dropping against the bureau, squeezing her eyes against the lightning flash afterimage of Daddy's smiling face, so young, younger than anyone else's dad she knew, and handsome—viewed through a child's blind love, the most beautiful man in the world.

If there's any justice, ten years in prison have at least stripped him of that.


FIVE INCHES OF fresh powder fell during the night, coating the roofs and driveway in white again. Owl heads out after breakfast to do her usual chore of shoveling walkways and entrances while Holly warms up her car. Hopefully, she'll be able to make it down to the valley. Owl's already told her she won't be helping out at the store today, saying she's got stuff she should do here; Holly doesn't question it, and Owl hopes her aunt will tell Aida what's going on, since Owl really doesn't want to call her friend this morning. Later. Maybe. No reason why Owl should have to be at Van's for Aida to use the wireless while Trini gets a much-needed break.

Cody shows. Part of Owl had hoped maybe he'd beg off today, fake sick or something, and they'd both know he was avoiding her and could pretend the invitation never happened—but he walks up the driveway at the usual time, hood up over his cap, chin nestled into his collar. Since Cody drove Wallace home last night, the older man needing to be poured into the passenger side, it seems like Wallace would at least let his grandson borrow the truck this morning rather than making him troop through the snowbanks. Then again, Wallace might still be passed out in bed.

When Cody sees her scraping snow from the sugarhouse step, he comes over and bangs the side of his boots against the doorframe; his jeans are soaked to midcalf. "You people ever heard of plows?"

"Town plows leave the mountain for last. During a bad storm, they can't even make it past Knee." Cody's look is blank. "The pass a mile up from the base. Shaped like a bent knee." The information only leaves him looking incredulous, borderline belligerent; Wallace might not be the only one nursing a hangover this morning. It helps, his attitude, leaves her free to give it right back, grinding the wings of her anxious butterflies underfoot after what she ventured last night. "Don't try taking the keys. I know more about winter driving up here than you." Drops the shovel against the shingles.

He lets her navigate the snowy road at a slow and determined pace, and doesn't tease her with the cigarettes at all while they check the taps, possibly because the work is much more strenuous this morning with new drifts to wade through, covering the crust. Breathless, she sees him moving through the trees, his cheeks flushed crimson in the cold, giving him an almost wholesome Christmas caroler look, incongruous with his smoker's cough.

The sap has slowed, as she knew it would, and they only need to make one trip from the sugarbush, not putting enough in the storage tank to justify running the evaporator. What's left is packaging, boxing up the glass maple-leaf bottles, sealed and waiting in a row, now wearing foil GRADE A: AMBER stickers, as the syrup has darkened with the changing sugar levels as they moved into March. It's nearly noon when Owl realizes that Seth has never come out to join them.

Once they've carried more firewood inside and swept the floors, Owl leaves without a word, too self-conscious to look directly at Cody yet, heartbeat and pulse high as she walks to the cabin, wondering why she had to open her mouth last night, why she let Wallace's confession spur her into going anywhere with Cody. This is rare free time she could use to check on the foxes, hike alone, work on her sketches, the usual. Yet here she goes, in search of Seth.

The living room is lit only by the gray poststorm sky above the ruffle of the curtains, and it takes her a second to pick her uncle out in the recliner, legs propped up, ice pack in place. His face is turned away, and she hesitates, never having seen him like this so early in the day. The words feel so foreign being passed from her to him instead of the other way around: "Everything okay?"

He turns drowsily, and the pallor of his skin surprises her, more dark stubble along his jawline than he usually allows. "I'm good. Just taking a breather."

She shifts, her air sealing off before asking—because, god, what if he says no? "We're all done."

"Oh, yeah? Okay, Cody can head—"

"We"—she rushes to speak, bumping into his words, and the first spark of alertness shows in his eyes—"I thought I'd show him Tillman's Lament. Just so . . . he can see." Her gaze won't settle, ticks around like a liar's, and each second of Seth's silence drags nail marks through her resolve. "If you don't need us."

"Oh." He boosts himself with his elbows, catches the ice pack before it slides to the floor, focuses on adjusting it. "If you're done, it's your time." Hesitates. "How're you planning on getting there? Hiking in or—?"

"Two-up. If that's okay."

"Yup, yup." Nodding, but this is unprecedented, no getting around it; they both struggle, unsure where to place their next steps. "Helmets, yeah? Both of you."

"Okay." She bolts, snagging her hiking pack from one of the Adirondacks on the deck and bringing it with her, already stashed before he and Holly got up this morning.

She drags the tarp off the Ski-Doo Grand Touring, their two-seater snowmobile, grabs a gas can from the shed, and fills up, seeing Cody emerge from the sugarhouse to watch. She stores extra fuel in the caddy, shifts into neutral, and hits the start button, slowly opening the choke until the idle

120

sounds healthy, actually glad for the five minutes or so where she can't hear anything but the engine. Cody doesn't question her, instead looking down at the machine as if she'd walked a two-humped camel out of the shed.

She puts her helmet on, then holds up Seth's, from the passenger seat. He doesn't take it. She huffs, calls out, "I won't tell anybody you rode bitch."

She pushes the helmet into his chest until he grabs it, then she climbs onto the driver's seat, feet on the rails, gripping the handles. Cody glances around—no one watching—curses soundlessly and, with a rough scrub of his hair through his cap, jerks the helmet on and slides into the space behind her.


THEY DRIVE THROUGH the clearing and into the woods until they hit Yellow Trail, so called for the yellow markers painted on occasional tree trunks years ago, pointing the way down the five-mile route to Tillman's Lament, which lies on the outer edges of the town of Dermott, about three-quarters of the way around the base of Waits Mountain.

It's intimate, more than she anticipated, being pressed between his legs like this, and it's a relief not to have to talk over the sound of the Ski-Doo. She's ridden with Seth or Holly many times, but Cody is bigger, taking up way more space in the back than any of them do, and he obviously doesn't trust her navigating skills. He won't put his arms around her, but a couple times, when she has to throw her weight into the curves, his knees squeeze her hips with a viselike intensity that makes her suck in her breath.

After parking the snowmobile and hiking a steep seven-minute trail that gives the impression of leading nowhere, they arrive below Lament. Owl rests on her heels, giving Cody time to take it in.

The thick, bluish-toned ice floe burgeoning from the eight-hundred-foot-high rock face is massive, with tiers of icicles dangling from the overhangs, some well over six feet long, creating the look of a sculpture both honed and hacked, nature's dual identity captured at once: beauty, brutality.

Cody manages silence, five full seconds of it, as he paces toward the rock, staring up.

Owl took a calculated risk—it's a favorite weekend destination for climbers, and there's almost always been other parties here when she's come with Seth and Holly. Today's no exception, two ice climbers working their way up a column on the left, balancing some thirty feet above the talus below, their helmets and parkas incandescent against the floe.

"How are they not falling?" Cody doesn't pull his gaze from the climbers.

"Ice axes and crampons, those metal spikes they strap on over their boots. They kick the toe spikes into the ice to make footholds. Watch." Owl points to the highest climber, now in the process of working her axe free. She pauses, then swings it into the ice above her head, ducking slightly to let a spray of ice deflect off her helmet. "That's tripod position. See? Her body's a triangle. Legs wide, arms narrow above her. Most stable shape in nature."

"Okay. You just pull that out of your ass?"

Owl shrugs. "Seth taught me." As if it weren't the turning point of her life, somebody filling the empty vessel inside her that needed this, something tactile, cold air expanding her lungs, and muscles burning, and an unshakable solid sense of presence and place.

"You do this?"

"No. I go bouldering. But Seth does ice climbing, rock climbing. Did. Before his knee really got bad." Hesitates, venturing a bit more: "It always ached after we went, but he said it was worth it. Pay for a day of getting out there."

"Wow. Special ops and extreme sports." Cody snorts laughter and dabs his cold nose with the back of his hand. "And he looks like just a regular old shitkicker."

"I never said special ops." She has no idea who Seth was over there, feeling an innate dread of the sun-and-sand-bleached memories locked inside him, what it's like to have a homemade bomb go off under the Jeep you're in, feel your knee blown half off your body. Truth of what war really does to you. "And he didn't have to hire you."

Cody turns on her instantly. "Hey, he was looking, so was I. That's how it works. Don't act like he did me some charity and I owe him. *Fuck* that."

Owl presses her lips together until they're bloodless, imagining the pure satisfaction of kicking him directly in the ass, but instead she forces herself to brush past him like he's done to her, not breaking his gaze until she's made it clear that he didn't win; she just isn't going to waste any more words on him.

She walks to the base and watches the climbers on her own for a while—a breathless moment when the lower climber seems too tired to continue, hugging the floe for so long her climbing partner calls down to check on her—but then the woman nods and tugs her lead crampon free, using mostly the strength of her left quad to support herself as she drives her spikes into the ice and boosts herself upward.

Cody studies Owl longer than she knows, then paces away, turns a few pointless circles—mutt that can't lie down; entertains himself by stepping up onto a couple of the larger boulders to survey the view. Things get lonely fast. He false-starts calling to Owl—a jab, anything to spur conversation—but knows she won't hear. He pegs a rock into the snow by her feet hard enough to raise a puff of white.

She spins, staring darkly—a scowling little kid with pigtails sticking out from under her hat. Christ. "Let's see some bouldering." He calls it from the top of a slab of rock, putting on a grin. "You got skills, show me."

Owl lowers her chin. "This is a five-eleven." When he obviously doesn't get it: "Rating system for climbing? This is one of the hardest on the mountain."

"What you got in your bag, then? Jerky?" Kicks off the snowcap and plunks down to sit on the rock, legs hanging down, hand mining his chest pocket for smokes, the pack a touchstone, not bringing them out. "I'm staying right here till you prove you ain't all talk, Bird Girl."

Her helmet's in the pack. Her climbing shoes, roll of tape, left there from the last time she went out. She also brought a couple bottles of water and some granola bars, out of habit—just in case, all of it, she'd told herself. But now faced with Lament, she admits her eagerness to get up there, grab a piece of the rock for herself. "I can't do ice," she says slowly. "I don't have the tools." And her chalk bag and the crash pad are at home. She's never climbed without them. Or Seth. And she knows he wouldn't want her to. "You have to spot me."

HER FINGERS PROTECTED with white tape, boots swapped for her Scarpas, she fastens her helmet and sizes up the only section of rock low enough for bouldering that isn't covered by the floe or too close to the other climbers. Immediately sees a crack she can slot her foot into, an edge within fingertips' reach above it.

She gets herself stabilized, then checks to make sure Cody's still beneath her. Wonders if she has a death wish, trusting him to break her fall if she loses her grip. No ropes in bouldering, no harnesses, just your own strength and judgment, which is why Seth always says never go any higher than twenty feet. And always with the crash pad below to catch her if she fell.

She won't go far. Just a quick climb to show Cody who's all talk—across the angled slab to the overhang above. Top out there, then back. Twenty-foot traverse, no more. Do it.

Owl slides the rubber soles of her climbing shoes along the cut in the wall, working her fingertips along a dime edge, following it as far as she can before she starts looking for the next handhold. There's a good jug—a deep, wide hold—about three and a half feet above her head to the right, the direction she needs to pull herself in. She wishes she'd done more stretching before she started. Rushing things. Stupid.

She reaches one hand up for the jug, clings on, adds the other, then pulls perpendicularly, hauling her body over while bracing her toes against the slab. Already breathing hard—she's forgotten what a workout bouldering is, every part of your body thrown into just staying on the rock, searching for the next edge to hold your weight.

Cody calls something—she thinks—and she hazards a glance toward the ground. When did he get so far away? He says it again; she reads, *You got this?*

Turns away, teeth gritted, determined to top out, stand straight up on the roof to look out over everything, make him small.

Grunt of exertion as she swings herself slowly, gaining momentum, her right foot out to touch the edge of a broad flake; over time, a slice of rock has broken away, leaving a gap a few inches wide that she can use to make the final stretch.

Tries to slot her foot, but there's nothing—no gap—and she gasps as her toes slip, her right leg dropping, jerking her hard enough that she pulls a barn door, her right side swinging out into space. Dangling, body twisting out, left side doing all the work, no chalk, hands grimy and sweat-greased—*shit*.

It's not in Owl to cry out, all chaos trapped inside, eyes wild as she grimaces, trying to swing herself back to nab her handhold before her left arm gives out.

She gets it, but barely. Breathless, she cranes her neck to see how she missed. Ice, frozen down inside the flake, filling most of the gap, shadowed and preserved during the last thaw. No room

126

for her foot, barely an edge for her to balance on that won't be slippery, treacherous. It's that or surrender, inch back down and drop to earth, where Cody's laughter is waiting for her.

She *wants* that overhang. Face screwed up, extends her right leg all the way out, toe feeling for the edge of the flake. Bends her knee, flings her right arm out, bringing her hand down with a smack onto the overhang. Digs her fingers into the craggy, uneven surface, and pulls herself across the divide, lingering only a second, right hand and foot braced, before throwing her entire upper body into dragging herself onto the overhang.

Muscles throbbing, Owl manages to slowly unfold herself into a standing position on the corner of the roof.

Below, Cody applauds.

# 12

In the musty quiet of the cloakroom, Owl brings out her list, written carefully on notebook paper, in case she's accused of not taking enough time with the assignment.

Ms. Z sits with her forearms resting on the desk between them, fingers entwined as if physically grounding them from signing, watching Owl center the notebook in front of herself. "You seem ready. Go first. We'll take turns."

Owl clears her throat, shifts in her seat, looking down at the paper. "Number one: I want to move our desk." Takes a quick check of her teacher's expression, goes on: "I can't see your face with all the light behind you. It makes things harder."

For a moment, Owl wonders if Ms. Z will confess to blocking her lip-reading, but instead she unclasps her hands, pushes her chair back. "All right. Where would you like it?"

Shrugs uncomfortably. "Doesn't matter. Just . . . not in front of a window."

Ms. Z stands, takes one end of the desk, waiting for Owl to grasp the other, and together they walk the desk toward the opposite end of the entryway, Ms. Z positioning her chair beneath the list of rules hanging on the wall. "Better?"

Owl nods.

"All right. My turn." And Ms. Z's hands snap into action: *I need us to sign everything together.* Emphasis on *together*, fists meeting to make small circles. Watches Owl stiffen, straightening in her seat. "I understand how you feel about speaking vocally. It's important to you. But I'm a teacher of the Deaf. It's my goal to help you see ASL as a skill, not something that sets you apart. So we'll both speak aloud as we sign. Fair enough?"

"I'm not fast like you. I lose what you're saying."

"Then give me one of these." Signs, *Slow down,* drawing her right hand gradually up her left arm to her elbow. "Let's try to make this practice for you, not torture. I don't expect you to be perfect." Holds Owl's gaze. "Truly. If you're having trouble, tell me."

Owl exhales slowly, nods.

"Okay." Ms. Z rests back against her chair, signs, *Next.*

Owl's gaze returns to her list, hesitating before reading the biggest risk she took on this page. "Two: What do you want me to talk about other than school?" Forgets to sign, labors through it, needing to redo *school* because she left out the two "claps." "You said that I'm giving you nothing. Not like your other students."

Ms. Z. hesitates, searching for diplomacy. "You're more closed off than they are, yes."

"How?" It's a question that's bothered her over the weekend, how these other nameless, faceless Deaf kids know how to naturally provide something Owl doesn't. "What should I say?"

"That's up to you. It's nothing I guide them in. I suppose the signing helps them feel more comfortable with me, so they talk a bit about themselves, their lives, as we go over their work. Say what you feel."

"I feel like I don't know you." Owl pauses, flipping through mental flash cards, images of the signs she needs next, some of which come up blank, and she has to fumble. "Mr. Duquette lives down the street. Mrs. Montrose-Perlman lives in St. Beatrice. They've been here ever since I came to this school." Hesitates. "Can I ask things about you? You always ask the questions."

"Within reason."

"Where do you live?"

"North Conway, at the moment."

"Do you have—?" Tangled, Owl drops the verbal word *children*, focuses on the sign, which she thinks is something like patting an invisible kid on the head, one in front, then one off to her right.

"No."

"Then why do you want to teach Deaf kids?"

Ms. Z looks back steadily. "My older sister was born profoundly Deaf. I learned sign before I spoke my first English word." Smooths her hair back in a swift movement, pearl earring reminding Owl of an insect's tiny egg, found beneath a green spring leaf. "Her Deafness defined who we were as a family."

"How?"

"A million ways. Some big, some small. We relocated from Rhode Island"—checks herself as Owl signs for her to slow down—"to Connecticut so that she could attend the American School for the Deaf. When she went on to Gallaudet, we moved again, to be close." Hint of something—amusement, exasperation—crosses her face, disappears. "Ironic, with how hard my mother worked to make sure Mari would always be self-sufficient, she was the one who had difficulty letting go." She visibly pushes aside the memory. "You must at least have someone in your family who speaks a second language?"

Owl falls still. Then: "My aunt is Passamaquoddy." Doesn't know the sign for the tribe, so fingerspells each letter instead.

"Does she ever use that traditional language around the house?" Watches the way Owl's gaze strays uncertainly. "Just another example of communication." Reaches into her bag for something to write with. "Nobody should ever have to stop speaking because they're afraid they won't be understood."


"IS HE COMING over today?" Aida's question is like a steel bolt hurtling through Owl as classroom background noise goes up, up, everyone gathered in their project groups, Griffin having dragged his chair over to join them.

"Every day. Until sugaring's done."

With a sound of outrage, Aida throws herself back against her chair, staring at the ceiling. "You are so lucky. I want some hottie to hang out at *my* house, getting all sweaty and taking his shirt off and stuff."

"It's March. He's not going to take his shirt off." Owl's aware of Griffin's gaze flicking between them as he *tap-taps* a pencil against the tabletop; she has no intention of explaining Cody. As if she'd even know where to start.

"Whatever. Like I can trust you. You didn't even want me to know about him."

Heat creeps up Owl's neck; for someone so oblivious to other people, Aida still has the uncanny ability of a childhood friend to see right through to Owl's backbone—when she chooses. "It wasn't that. He's nothing special." Her right side is still sore, even two days later, from badly pulled muscles she earned Sunday trying to show Cody what she's worth. "Not even nice."

"Who wants nice?" Aida says. Griffin laughs at that, and Aida cuts a narrow-eyed look at him. "And you should be taking notes, Mr. Kiss-Ass." Darts a look for Duquette. Across the room, helping another group pick out some of the local history books he's borrowed from the St. Beatrice Library for project research. "Girls want excitement, okay? Not . . . perfect attendance awards."

"Girls want mean, not-special, exciting bastards." Griffin nods. "Okay, good notes."

Owl laughs; after a second's irritation, Aida decides to go with it, grin surfacing. "After Saturday, my mom was all over me about who Cody was, what he's doing at Owl's place, blah, blah. And I know she was whispering with my dad about him after I went upstairs—I could hear them."

"Why?" Owl looks at her. "Cody didn't do anything wrong."

"Doesn't have to." Aida speaks lightly. "Just has to be there with the right equipment. Instant threat to my mom. You know, she asked if Holly was at all worried about having him around. With you being there and everything."

Owl straightens, affronted; as if she and Cody were nothing but combustible chemicals, never to be placed on the same shelf—or, worse, a couple of animals in rut, Cody chasing her down like the bull moose who dented in the automatic garage door of a house on Mill Road last year, ramming it with his antlers in pursuit of a cow who'd escaped his advances through the side yard and was long gone. The story made one of the biggest papers in the state.

Griffin glances over his shoulder. "In about two seconds, Duquette's going to come over here and ask how it's going. I don't think he wants to hear about your sexy syrup man." Sets his pencil down. "Come on. We have to pick something from Coös County history that we can make a project around."

Aida blows out a sigh. "I don't know. What do you guys want to do? How can there even be a history of this place? Nine billion years of bears shitting in the woods? And who cares anyway? Unless they're doing fireworks and cotton candy for this Founding Day, I'm out."

Griffin holds up the project information sheet, wafting it back and forth at her. "We have a topic list to choose from. Open your eyes. Read. Go-o-o-d."

"Well, excuse me, Baby Genius." Another furtive look for Duquette.

"I say we go with the copper mine." Griffin stabs his pencil through the binder holes in his notebook. "I've been up there before. My dad took me a couple times." Aida pulls her mouth to the side, says nothing; it was impossible for the whole school not to bear witness to the Baptistes' loss when Greg passed away, how Griffin had pulled into himself for months. "It's cool. Maybe we could make a model or something. Anybody remember how to papier-mâché?"

"I never knew how to do that." Aida's attention reconnects with Owl's, the unspoken almost-argument that never stopped. "*I* didn't say anything to Holly about it, okay? It was my mom. I was just telling you."

"Well, it's stupid. The whole thing." Though peripherally aware of Aida's chin lifting defensively, Owl's too deep in a buzzing, agitated place to process that she's crossed a line.

"Then why didn't you come to Van's on Sunday? For real."

"I already said. They needed me at home." Owl's voice is coarse, making the next table look over.

Aida flushes, looks away. So begins the silent treatment.

IT'S COLD, BUT Owl wears her mittens with the removable fingers for dexterity, bringing her drawing supplies to the blind to seize the last hour or so of full daylight, before the rays begin to wane over the treetops. She wants to recapture the moment the male fox stared out at her from the depths of the den, framing the hole in the embankment with some initial sweeping lines, evoking a bird's nest at first, disorder soon to be tamed with shaping, shading of the charcoal.

She hears two footsteps, hard *pocks* of boot soles punching through the fresh crust behind her. Panic ignites when Cody crashes onto the branches beside her. He's already laughing as she clamps her art pad to her chest, squeezing her eyes shut.

"Pee a little bit?" Grinning.

Owl releases a shuddery breath. "Maybe." Grabs up her pencil and eraser before he rolls on them, her annoyance mostly for show; really, she's watching him sprawl there in the snow beside her as if it's completely natural—this close-ness—propped on his elbows, leaning his head to look around the blind. Ever since she smelled him the other night on the deck, she can't help trying again, breathing in through her nose, but she's not close enough to catch anything but maple smoke trapped in the wool of his coat. "Who's watching the evaporator?"

"Seth. I'm on a fifteen. You okay with that?" Pauses, squinting at the embankment. "What're you *doing*?"

"Quiet." Points her pencil. "Red fox den. Don't bother them."

"Ohh. Saw you staring at a hole in the ground. Figured it was something you'd do for fun around here." They exchange a look, and she fights a smile.

The change between them is tangible, a few degrees tilt, but there—Owl's only evidence that maybe Sunday wasn't a complete act of idiocy on her part. After she got home, she'd put her climbing gear away, refusing herself ibuprofen to soothe the throbbing of her pulled muscles or the two ripped fingernails on her left hand. Punishment for becoming someone she barely recognized in her need to prove herself to Cody. What were the chances he could've broken her fall if she'd lost her grip on that rock, like a real spotter? What would've happened if she'd needed him to take her to the clinic in St. Beatrice with a broken arm or leg? Seth and Holly were counting on her to help with the sugaring, and she'd brushed so close to complete disaster that she could almost taste the last, swift gasp of frigid breath before she tipped outward, arms spread in open air, nothing waiting below to catch her but a pile of jagged scree.

"What's this?" Cody reaches out for the art pad. "You draw?" Watches her flap the cover shut. "Let me see."

"No."

"What, they suck or something?" When she ignores him, busying herself by tucking her pencil into the spiral binding, he rests back on one elbow, stripping blunt green needles from a branch with his fingers, the smell fresh and aggressive. "Bet they're all pictures of me."

Laughter bursts out of her—he's ridiculous—but she hadn't realized the tension she was holding on to until it breaks, the result of an afternoon spent in Aida's doghouse. Without Aida's grip on her arm, voice in her ear, all that seems to be left is the fuzzy background clamor of the classroom and the Suburban ride home, where Owl hears essentially nothing at all. Maybe that's the idea, Aida's real punishment: forcing Owl to see how much she needs her. Owl imagines—tentatively—having a friend, just one, who knows sign. She imagines constructing a wall of silence together around Aida whenever she acts like this, show her how it feels to be bricked in with a whole world happening on the other side.

He tosses needles one at a time, aiming them through the gaps in the blind. "There are foxes in there right now?"

"Might be. They're mostly nocturnal, so they could be sleeping."

"Or you could be watching an empty hole."

"Want to go check?" Smirks at his hesitation, shakes her head. "You're scared of animals."

"Now, I told you about that scared shit." Watches the needles scatter on the snowpack. "Should've known you'd be some kind of rat whisperer, the way you were screaming at me about hunting that first day."

She looks at him hard for a second. "Somebody was leaving coil spring traps on our land. Know how they work?" Sets her pad down. "Spring-loaded. Fox smells the bait, steps on the pan"—she slaps his hand between both of hers, grips tightly, feels his forearm muscles stiffen, resisting—"jaws slam down her paw."

Cody holds her gaze. "Yeah? Cuts it off?"

Shakes her head. "Plain jaws. They just squeeze. She can't get away. Can't reach food or water. Nothing to do but wait for the hunter to come back for her." She clutches until she sees what she knows must be in there, some spark of recognition behind the veined blue-gray granite of his eyes, until his attention is focused full on her. "Some hunters . . . they don't check their traps much. After a couple days, she'll get desperate. Start trying to chew off her own paw." Her fingertips trail from him, rest in loose fists on her thighs. "She'll kill herself to escape."

They're quiet together, Cody pulling himself into a sitting position, watching the den, then the woods. Finally, Owl says,

"The vixen's pregnant. I haven't seen her in a while. And the male's been bringing food."

"Think she had them?"

Her shrug can't conceal her excitement, sitting up on her knees now for a more direct view of the den.

"How can you know?"

"I'll just keep coming back. Might see them playing outside here sometime when they're old enough. Fox families stay together a long time. Until the kits are almost grown."

He gets to his feet with a sigh. "If you do, take a picture. I've never seen a baby rat."

"They're not like rats. They're like dogs." But he's already walking away, hand digging into his chest pocket for smokes.

When he's gone, she finds herself scanning the tree line, as Cody had, slowly, the mosaic of shadow and light. Art pad tucked under her arm, she inches back from the blind on her hands and knees, as always, standing and making her way toward the woods along the edge of the clearing so as not to interfere with the den.

Owl places her steps carefully as she enters the trees. It's too late to look for a man's footprints that may have been left last week, any trail erased by the snowstorm.

Owl walks without a clear sense of how far to go, reaching out to touch low-hanging branches, looking for any recently snapped. It was dusk when she and Seth were in the blind together that evening . . . Someone would've had to stand close to the edge of the clearing to know they were there. This was the rough direction Seth turned in that night, toward whatever sound she'd been unable to hear.

When she sees it, it's part luck, part observance, scanning the ground for the one thing she knows might be visible in more shallow snowfall, using the toe of her boot to flick apart any small mound at the base of any tree, most of them clumps fallen from overloaded branches above. On the fifth try, she finds what she was looking for.

Two crushed, sodden cigarette butts. Newports.

# 13

"You two going to be okay on your own today?" Seth studies Owl over breakfast the next morning.

Holly watches closely, fingers tight around her coffee mug.

Owl knows her job, in silent agreement with Holly: nod immediately, make sure she doesn't give him any reason to think about canceling his two-thirty appointment with the orthopedic surgeon at Androscoggin Valley Hospital, even if being alone with Cody right now made Owl's body feel strung with high-tension wire, a marionette jerked across the face of Lament, unable to trust herself because she didn't know when, or where, the next foreign impulse might come.

Holly's taking time off to drive Seth—driving himself a long way is near-impossible for him now, between working the accelerator and the roughness of the road—but Owl thinks it's mostly to see with her own eyes that he goes. "You need us, call," Seth says. "Whatever it is. Don't care if it seems like a small problem. Something goes wrong with the evaporator, just kill the fire, stop the process. And you know you got Gunnar and Wallace right down the road."

"God forbid it come to that," Holly says into her coffee.


MUTED SUN SCALES the sky to midday, begins its slow sinking toward late afternoon. Shadows play across the sugarbush, the dry-bone clack of branches in the breeze.

Owl stands in the farm's empty driveway, Mrs. Baptiste's Suburban disappearing over the rise behind her, looking toward the sugarhouse. As Owl watches, Cody appears in the doorway, leans there, shoulder to the frame, gazing back.


THE COLD SNAP has held; slower sap day, the work in the trees going quickly with lighter buckets. They talk little; whenever they happen to meet up at the tank, Cody sticks his hand out for her collection bucket, dumping it in for her, saving her the climb up onto the trailer. Owl doesn't thank him, instead stealing the seconds to study him, the shape of the cigarette pack in his coat pocket, trying to solidify her many questions into something that might get her the answers she needs.

When they've emptied the day's haul into the storage tanks, Owl's voice stops him on his way to the evaporator: "I'm heading inside." Swallows, takes a breath. "Do you want coffee—something?"

She doesn't know what he'll say—or even what she wants. He turns, his face somehow new in its unguarded study of her own, taking a moment before he gives a shrug. "Yeah."

They go into the cabin, Owl holding the door, letting him in behind her, watching his back as he looks around the stillness of the kitchen and living room. Breakfast dishes in the rack, a pair of Seth's gloves forgotten on the table.

"Seth leaves the pot on." Owl sounds curt to her own ears, trying too hard to make clear that this isn't any special effort. Pulls a mug from the cupboard, relieved when there's enough coffee left that hasn't burned onto the bottom of the pot by this time of day. Cody doesn't pick up the mug when she sets it near him, and as she gets herself a drink from the fridge, she notices his gaze traveling the ceiling, as if listening. "They're not here."

He nods a little, taking his mug, and she slides the baking tin his way. By the time she's looked up from taking a brownie out, he already has one half-eaten, pushing the second half into his mouth in a move so rough yet seamless she doesn't even see crumbs.

"Hungry?"

Wipes his hand on his coat. "Always."

"You should've had more on Saturday when everybody brought food. We're still eating leftovers." Hesitation. "You could've sat down with us."

"Not my scene." Downs some coffee. "Moms. Kids."

"You did okay with Lulu." She points toward the bathroom door to show who she meant.

"Oh. Well. Most of the places I got stuck in growing up had

142

little kids running around. You get used to them bouncing off you and getting in the way and stuff."

"Wasn't just the little girls bouncing off you."

He looks over, has another sip, a smirk working across his lips. "You mean Streaks."

"Aida." Watches as he shakes his head. "She's a friend." Owl's word choice is deliberate, the *a* giving some distance, still feeling too resentful to say *my*; definitely not *best*. Aida spoke to her only a couple times at school today, the usual slow thaw once she decides to acknowledge Owl's existence again. They've been going through this since they were little—Aida running things, doling out punishments when Owl doesn't remember her place—but Owl's tolerance has worn thin, and now Aida's every move seems calculated to hurt her: snarky expressions whenever Owl contributes anything in their project group with Griffin, a deliberate pause before answering Owl's few questions, leaving her in suspense as to whether or not she'll respond.

"I was thinking you didn't have friends." Cody doesn't take his gaze off the old wooden barometer hung on the far wall as Owl gives him a flat look. "When I was seventeen? Couldn't keep me home. Out with my boys all the time. Hop a bus or whatever, hang out in Red Oak, or one of the parks. Getting fucked up. Chasing"—stops, changes his words—"looking for girls."

"Two years changed that?"

He shakes his head slowly. "YDSU did. Juvie lockup." Sets his empty mug down. "Two nights. I can't be shut in. Guys I hung with did six months here, a year there, no big. Pissing their lives away in a cage with a bunch of losers even more messed up than they were. I'm not doing that. Not getting trapped in that."

Conversation stalls. Cody leans forward, gaze following the line of stairs to the loft. "That's my room," Owl says.

"Yeah?"

Pauses, forcing her body to stillness, determined not to let a jiggling knee or fidgeting fingers give away how much this offer is costing her. "If you really want to see my drawings, they're up there."

He takes a few steps toward the stairs, assessing her in a way she returns with a frank look, then glances over toward the back hallway one more time, as if Seth or Holly might suddenly come rushing out and catch them.

She hangs back a little, watching how he slows near the top as he reaches the curtains, just as Seth does, then moves one panel aside to check out the room before he enters. Aida's been in her room, of course, and the Boulier sisters, briefly. No one else but family.

By the time she's in the loft, he's made his way over to the wall near her bureau, looking at the sketches of the mother deer and fawn she did last year, a much rougher, unfinished picture of a scattering of broken robin's-egg shells she found in the grass beneath a nest.

Silence goes on too long. "Not bad." He doesn't turn, keeps going from drawing to drawing, a quick study before moving on.

She shrugs, a small defensive stab in her middle, wounded pride even after she had convinced herself it didn't matter, nothing he could say.

He lingers over the drawing of the splintered antler she found on a hike, maybe evidence of where two bucks had battled, the ground well trampled. "Where's this?" Taps the corner of another sketch, the waterfall into the basin.

"We call it the Notch." She goes toward the stairs, ready to head down, all this seeming like a mistake now, an embarrassing overstep on her part, none of this anything that he would ever want to see. "About an hour's hike away."

"You gonna take me there sometime?"

She throws a look over her shoulder and sees he's really waiting for her answer. "If you're lucky." Starts toward the stairs.

"Hold up." His hand lands on her shoulder, firm pressure, and she jerks around partway.

His gaze is on the top of her head, his height giving him the perfect angle to see the place she covers with a side part raked into her scalp with a pintail comb after every shower. He touches without permission, too focused on the line of pinkish-white scar tissue that stands out against her pale hair, pressing his fingertip to it. "What's this?"

With a firmness of her own, she pushes his hand away.

Then—a moment's fearlessness—she pulls the covered elastic from the end of her right braid and untwists the three segments, raking her fingers through until her hair hangs loosely, letting him look.

She doesn't expect his touch again—quite the opposite; maybe she wanted his shock, revulsion. But his fingers trace the full four inches of the scar with a sort of patient, thoughtless fascination, not seeming to flinch from the worst place, the spot she hates, the last inch where the flesh puckers and twists, a florid peony pink, despite the surgeon's best efforts, where no hair will grow again. She lifts her head, steps back when she isn't sure if he's going to take his hand away.

"What the hell happened to you?" he says.

Again, his face so different when genuine emotion is right on the surface. Can imagine what he might've looked like as a kid, before everything.

"Skull fracture. That's why I can't hear much. Auditory nerve damage." Barely a beat before adding the obligatory: "I was lucky."

Snorts softly. "Bet you felt real lucky." He takes her in, standing with one-half of her hair hanging to her shoulder, tightly waved from being plaited while wet. "Took a header, huh?" A quiet, casual summing-up that gets a smile out of her.

"Yup."

"And then you had to come here."

She nods, waiting for him to ask the question no one has posed to her since Seth and Holly stopped making her see that child therapist in Stokely, when it was obvious that, after a year and a half, Owl had nothing left to say to the woman, who'd never been more to her than a stranger making listening faces, the two of them riding on the same carousel of questions about Daddy, the scenery a never-changing blur. Worse, the questions about her mother—what can you say about someone you barely remember? *She left us. Left me with him. Knowing.*

Cody doesn't ask. He takes a few steps away and pops a drawing down from the wall, not bothering to remove the tack. "Can I have this?"

It's the sketch of the Notch. Owl's nonplussed—no one's ever asked before. "I guess . . ." But he's already walking past her with it, folding the sheet into quarters. "Were you in our woods the other night?"

He stops at the curtain, looking back.

"If it was you . . . please just say." Waits, her fists pressed to the sides of her thighs. "I need to know." Whatever reason he had for coming back doesn't matter, not in comparison to this. "I found your cigarette butts." Like maybe he'd stood there, watching her and Seth from the convenience of darkness, smoking, listening to them talk.

"Okay. I probably took a break there sometime. I know how freaked you are about smoke around the sap."

"Near the den?"

"I dunno. Maybe." Lifts his brows. "That it?" He doesn't wait for her to nod before he ducks through the curtain. Calls back, "We boiling or what?" She hears the first few bumps of his feet on the steps. Then he's out of range.

# 14

"I need to go to Griffin's house after school." Owl doesn't say it until she's gathering her backpack before going out to meet the Suburban the next morning, glancing over at Holly, dressed for work in her forest-green Van's polo shirt, dark-wash jeans, and boots. Holly hesitates in packing her lunch. "We're working on a project. It might take an hour and a half?" Can't stand another second of waiting, says, "I'll ask Trini for a ride home." Irritating—asking Aida for a favor—but she also knows the spot she's putting Holly in and hates the awkwardness.

"No. It's okay. That's pretty much when I'll be coming home from work anyway. I'll finish up a little early."

"Are you sure?" When Holly nods without looking at her, Owl leaves it alone.

Seth is outside, opening the sugarhouse for the day, getting ready for Cody's arrival, and they raise a hand to each other from across the yard. The appointment with the surgeon went well—Seth's been deemed a good candidate for knee replacement, with a follow-up appointment scheduled for next week and a phone call coming eventually to set a date for surgery.

Owl still feels like she got away with something yesterday while they were at the doctor, even though she and Cody hadn't broken any established rules. But she'd still taken a minute to wipe clean any trace that Cody had been inside the cabin, washing and putting away his coffee mug, even taking the tack down from her wall on the off chance anyone should notice a drawing missing. No one's ever set any guidelines about who she's allowed to ask up to her loft. Yet she hides Cody. She hides that she let him touch her scar.

OWL, AIDA, AND Griffin spread their stuff—backpacks and papers and phones—all over the big table in the Baptistes' dining room. They're watched over by a row of baskets on the mantel, all different shapes and sizes, woven into fluted-looking geometric patterns. Aida scrolls madly, not taking much part in the brainstorming until Mrs. Baptiste comes in, setting down a bowl of chips and an armload of soda cans in the middle of everything, wiping condensation from the cans on her jeans. "Yeah, I wouldn't open those right away if I were you guys." She's wearing one of her slogan T-shirts—NO ONE IS ILLEGAL ON STOLEN LAND—beneath an unzipped red hoodie, her long hair loose around her shoulders. "Everybody good? Need anything?" Watches wryly as Aida fumbles her phone facedown onto the tablecloth. "You guys know what you're doing yet?"

"Copper mining. I guess?" Griffin glances at Owl, who shrugs agreement; now that she's in their house, she feels reluctant to meet Mrs. Baptiste's eye, wondering what the woman thinks about the fact that Holly never called—if maybe she assumes Owl didn't pass the message on at all. "We got some books from Mr. Duquette. No internet sources allowed."

"Well, good for Mr. Duquette. You kids think truth is spelled W-i-k-i—any fool can write those things."

"You kids today," Griffin quavers, groping blindly around on the table. "Hand me my teeth."

His mother holds her fist up. "You're the one's going to be eating his Doritos through a straw, motehsan." Turns, hands held up as she goes into the living room. "All right. Butting out."

Once she's gone, Aida grabs a handful of chips. "Your mom is so awesome."

"Pretty much."

Owl's book is marked through with Post-it notes—*A Descriptive History of Coös County,* a maroon library binding holding together some of the driest old-fashioned writing on the planet—but at least she found the kind of statistics and facts that teachers seem to salivate over. Aida's back on her phone, hasn't moved. Tickle of annoyance. "Did you find anything about the North Plover dig?" Owl asks her.

Shoulder goes up. "I didn't have time last night."

"You didn't read?" Glances at Griffin. "You knew we were meeting."

"I just said I didn't have time." Stares at Owl over her phone, puts it down roughly. "It's not like we can't still work on it."

Owl bites her lip, then flips open to her first Post-it-marked section harder than she really intended, the cover smacking the tabletop—a statement.

"Yeah . . . so I found out the North Plover mine closed in 1973." Griffin looks between them, clears his throat, as he flips through the thick, musty tome he'd chosen. "Open pit mining for smelter ore—"

"Are you seriously mad about this?" Aida, intense, across the table at Owl.

Owl lifts her gaze slowly, emotional boiling point achieved. "You knew *we* would do the reading, so you thought you didn't have to."

A tight, indignant sound from Aida's throat. "We had math, and those questions for English, too. I'm so sorry I didn't get to every tiny little thing."

"I had to work after school, and I still got to it."

Griffin keeps his eyes on the table. Aida buckles, without a comeback—then: "Like flirting is work."

Owl stares, gripping the table, stripped off all memories of ever being this person's friend—swimming together in the little aboveground pool in Aida's backyard while deerflies dive-bombed their heads, going to each other's houses to exchange gifts on Christmas Eve every year, birthday parties where they were each other's only guest who wasn't family. "Who'd want to flirt with me, right?" Each word bitten off, staccato.

Aida's expression tightens. The specter of last year and the other older boy, Riley, with his short-buzzed haircut, Realtree camo sweatshirts—backwoods cool in every way—now here in the room with them even though his family moved last June. The things Owl read from his smiling lips, spoken to Aida, in the community hall during gym—*Hear how she talks?*—and Aida, her best friend, who did nothing but glance over from across the room anxiously, to see if Owl had picked up on it.

Now, in the Baptistes' dining room, Aida turns from his memory, looks off to the far corner, arms crossed.

"Guys . . . this is due in less than two weeks." Griffin speaks carefully, neither girl giving him her attention. "Can we just—"

"Forget it." Aida grabs her phone, shoving her chair back. "I'm going home."

She leaves the dining room, and a minute later, they see her through the far window, dropping down onto the wheelchair ramp put in place for Mr. Baptiste's use, coat on, hood up, hunched over her phone.

Mrs. Baptiste comes in. "Uh, Hurricane Aida's outside calling her mom. I couldn't even talk her into waiting in the kitchen. What's going on?" Neither Griffin nor Owl want to be the first to speak. "You know Trini's going to be on the phone to me later if Aida's off her feed in the slightest. Fess up."

"She's just mad. Nothing new." Griffin tosses his pen down onto the table, shoving his hands through his hair. "Whatever. Let her go home if she wants. Owl and I will figure it out."


AND THEY DO, at least partially, Griffin coming up with the idea of making a cross-section model of a copper mine they find in a book, sort of like an ant farm: "We could put it behind a piece of plexiglass or something—like different types of sand or dirt to represent the ore and veins and stuff, with a little hole dug down through to be the vertical shaft. Labels stuck on everything." Both avoid turning to the window when Trini's Jeep pulls in and Aida walks to meet her.

"Seth might have something. He's built displays and things for festivals before. Could be plexiglass." Owl works the tip of her pen on a corner of notebook paper, bearing down hard, a mass of concentric swirls. "How will we get the sand layers to stay put, not get mixed together? It has to go all the way to the Stokely school."

"Yeah. Haven't gotten that far yet." Griffin releases a burst of laughter, and Owl joins him. "Also, if you have any ideas on how to build a teeny-tiny mining cart system that really works, let me know."

"You're the one going to MIT." Checks the time on her phone; Holly's due any minute, and Owl's determined to make it seamless. "My ride's coming." As she stuffs her things into her backpack, Owl's attention is drawn by the baskets, and she walks over to look at them more closely, particularly the one in the center, with the careful, needle-etched tree silhouette. "Are these made of wood?"

"Birchbark. From our trees right out back."

"Your mom made these?"

"Nope. I did." Sees her surprise. "Well, she made that one. And that one. But the rest are mine. Making baskets in the traditional style is basically an endangered art, so Ma really wanted to get me into it. A lot of it is about showing respect to the tree, taking the bark in a way that won't hurt it."

153

"They're beautiful." There's a framed photo collage on the wall nearby. As Owl shrugs on her backpack straps, she leans in to study the pictures: Griffin and his parents standing together toward the back of a big family reunion group shot; Griffin growing throughout the years: a laughing little kid with his hair shagging in his eyes, another picture of him in full traditional dress, leggings, fringe, feathered headband, frozen in dance in a line of other tribal members.

Griffin follows her gaze, nods. "Sacred circle at Recognition Day in Houlton when I was like eight."

"Cool." She leans closer, studying the details, the obvious crowd in the background. "Wish I could see that."

He leans against the wall beside the frame. "Does your aunt really not have any contact with her tribe at all?"

Owl doesn't want to betray Holly's privacy, unsure where the line is. "I don't think so." Glances toward the window for signs of Holly pulling in. "I've never met her family. She doesn't talk about them much."

Griffin nods slowly. "Must be hard. Wolastoqiyik is part of who I am, you know? Even living so far away from the river and tribal lands and everything now. I always know I've got a place there. Ma made sure of that." He looks hard at the picture of his child self. "I think she'll move back there after I graduate. Dad moved us down here to take the choke-setter job—got to go where the work is, right? Then he got sick. All kind of felt like it was for nothing." He pauses, and Owl looks down, not wanting him to feel stared at, knowing how much she hates it. "This powwow coming up in July will be the first one we've gone to since Dad. Feels like Ma getting back to herself, her people."

Owl nods, casting about for recognition within herself, something to relate all this to, the thought of a large and varied family forever anchored to a broad and churning river. Of history, ancestry, blood. Her hook cuts through water, snagging nothing.

OWL MAKES SURE to be out the door before Holly shuts off the engine, tossing her backpack onto the floor space as she slides in next to her aunt. Holly's looking at the face of the Baptistes' small house: dark brown clapboards, stone chimney, whisper of smoke.

Holly glances over, smiling distractedly. "How'd it go?"

"Good." Except that Aida might never speak to her again after this. Owl envisions the permanent silent treatment, carrying straight through summer vacation and into their senior year, plodding along behind Aida in a yoke of shame, for what she said today. Owl tries to just feel the relief of purging that infected, stinging place left by Riley, letting the brand sear into Aida's skin for a while.

Holly backs the Land Rover down the twisting driveway, Owl gazing out the window at the trees blurring darkly, holding her question in her mouth, tasting the risky flavor of it. "Do you know how to speak Passamaquoddy?"

Holly's quiet a moment. "Why are you asking me that?"

"I . . . No reason." Realizes she's made it seem like this is the Baptistes' doing, like they've coached her, when in fact, she's been wondering since her meeting with Ms. Z. "I just never hear you use it." Owl fidgets—in too deep, no way to reverse—picking at one of her torn fingernails. "Is it . . . because Seth and I aren't . . . ?"

When she answers, her words are slow, deliberate. "Doesn't seem like there'd be a lot of point, would there?" Gaze unwavering on the road ahead.

Confirmation: The flaw is in who Holly spends her days with, in Owl, in Seth. Owl waits, counting seconds. Finally pulls from inside, "You shouldn't stop speaking just because we wouldn't understand." Then she turns back to the windshield, heartbeat fluttering rapid, afraid of having ventured too much, not enough.

# 15

"Cody. You up for a drive?"

Owl and Cody watch Seth work his way down from the cabin along the snowy path on Friday afternoon with a stick in his hand. He reaches them as Owl is looping the storage tank hose back onto its hook, and she sees Seth's holding a wooden cane she's never seen before. It's hand-carved, narrow, and varnished to a shine.

He leans on it, the most self-conscious she's ever seen him look, mouth lopsided, obviously determined to keep the conversation on work and his gaze on Cody. "New evaporator's in. Thought maybe you'd be willing to take the truck down to West's Farm Supply and pick it up. Whole hell of a lot cheaper than having it shipped." Cody reaches out, taking the keys to the F-350 from Seth's hand. "I'll come with you, give you a hand. It's a haul down to Errol, and even with GPS, it's not easy to find West's."

Cody's expression stays immobile, but Owl doesn't miss the way his gaze goes to her before he nods once and starts over toward the pickup.

Owl touches Seth's arm as he turns, keeping her voice low. "Stay here. The drive's too long."

"He can't load that thing by himself."

"And you can't help him." She looks down at the cane, and he shifts, closing his mouth on whatever he'd planned to say next. "I'll make sure he gets there. I've been enough times."

He stares at her doubtfully. "You want to go?"

Keeps her face neutral, nods. "I can."

Cody watches as she settles herself in the passenger seat beside him, snapping her belt, shaking her braids back from her shoulders. "Just you?" he says, keeping an eye on Seth through the windshield, still standing in the yard, leaning heavily on the cane as he looks at them.

"Just me." Takes her phone from her pocket to pull up the GPS. "You want to end up on Route 26. Drive through North Plover to St. Beatrice, and you'll start seeing signs for the off-ramp."

As they pull around the circle of the drive, passing close by Seth, Owl meets eyes with her uncle; the distance between them instantly magnifies, the safety glass a convex lens. On impulse, she puts her palm to the glass.

He raises his free hand, fingers outstretched, and then his

158

form is reduced to the side view, another piece of shrinking scenery, farm left behind.

IT ISN'T UNTIL they're approaching Houlihan's that Cody speaks up. "Want to stop?"

She appraises him. "I'm a little young."

"A lot young." He presses his shoulders against the seat, flexing his back. "Bet you fifty I could get you in."

Nothing about the dim shop front with its goblin-light shamrock entices her. "Don't you need Wallace for that?"

Cody looks over, bouncing his hand against the wheel a few times, probably wondering who told. "They know me. You don't think I can talk my way into a place like that?"

Lifts her shoulders, turning to her window. "It's behind us now anyway."

Doesn't occur to her until a couple minutes later that maybe he'd been trying to impress, that she'd stymied him; maybe the girls he knows in Manchester never pass up a drink—or a guy who can lie his way anywhere. "Your exit's coming up." The black-and-white sign passes by—leaning, rooted in snow. "There's a place I could take you on our way back through St. Beatrice. If we make good time." Wonders if he can tell that she's had this in mind since she offered to ride with him, that now she's the one holding her breath for an answer.

"Yeah? Better than a dive bar?" When she glances at him, he's smiling, and, in her relief, she joins him.

"Much."

• • •

THEY DRIVE PAST the Dixville Notch State Wayside, wooded peaks powder-blasted, then get themselves turned around on the back roads of Errol, a bit of light snowfall speckling the windshield. They finally make it to West's Farm Supply, run out of a renovated three-story barn on the owner's property, a row of snowblowers and walk-behind salt spreaders lining the gravel parking lot.

The evaporator is waiting in the loading dock, gleaming stainless steel wrapped in clear plastic and zip ties, and it takes Cody and the owner muscling and maneuvering it up the ramp with dollies to get it into the pickup bed, where Owl stands, throwing her whole weight into inching the evaporator flush with the rear window on a beat-up wool blanket Seth had tossed down to make it easier to slide.

Covering the whole thing with a blue tarp, Owl works tie-downs through the bed anchors and tosses the excess straps over the top of the evaporator to Cody, who catches them and does the same on his side. More than once, she sees him watching her hands, mirroring how she threads the straps through, then jerks them tight.

"BETTER STOP HERE." They're nearly ready to turn off 26 when Owl points to a little convenience store on their right. "Last chance for gas."

"We can make it back."

"Redlining it, maybe. Pull in. And it takes diesel." Studies him critically as he releases a pent-up breath and parks alongside one of the green pumps. "You don't show up on E."

160

"He's your uncle. Like he's going to care."

"You borrow someone's truck, you fill it up." Said slowly, like all it might take is a memory jog, amazed that this simple truism needs to be spoken aloud. "Don't you know that?"

Cody glances over reluctantly—and beneath that, maybe, uncertainly. "Well, *you* paying? 'Cause I got dick for cash on me."

Owl tugs her nylon wallet out of her back pocket; she feels ridiculous carrying a purse, like she should be wearing lace gloves or something. Hands him the twenty inside. Won't come close to filling the F-350's huge tank, but better than nothing. Watches him pump, hunched away from the wind, glancing over his shoulder at the store as customers come and go, as if he might be spotted by someone he knows out here in population two hundred.

HER ANTICIPATION BUILDS as they pass the state park sign for Lake Plummet, then, minutes later, the St. Beatrice exit. They turn off onto the usual tired Main Street, Holly's vehicle gone from the curb near Van's at this time of day. They've made good time, and then some—with how Cody drives, it's the fastest round trip to Errol that Owl's ever been on. "We're going to the lake," Owl says. "Don't follow the signs."

She gives directions down a side road, passing dilapidated frame houses from the 1920s or '40s, before the mine closed, or modulars with open garage doors, giving views of junk shadows, basketball hoops trailing rotted nets abandoned by children long gone, trailers with topspinner clotheslines coated in ice. It's a drive, where they're going—perhaps a bit

161

longer than she remembered, watching the scenery peter off to almost nothing but woods, only the occasional homestead peering out from overgrown lots: Airstream campers or plywood shacks with generators outside to power lights and heat.

"Right here," she says, sitting forward just as she's begun to doubt herself; the turn-in she remembers appears from the overgrowth on her side of the road, barely big enough for three vehicles to pull off. "We have to hike in."

"'Course we do."

They've got decent daylight now, but Owl still pockets the flashlight from the glove compartment, just in case. Her phone light would be little defense against the kind of blackness that falls out here.

Snowmobilers and hikers have been here since the last snowfall, making the way generally easy to follow, except when boulders or fallen trees obscure it, forcing her to pause, search for the next sign of an opening.

Cody walks behind, cursing as snow sifts down inside his boots. He alternates between the same two pairs of socks, all that were clean when he bailed: no-show athletic, leaving his ankles exposed. Coughs, occasionally, into his fist, hoping maybe she can't hear it. Hard to tell what she catches sometimes, what slips by her.

Eventually, they come out onto the old logging road Owl remembers from summers past when she'd come here with Seth, grass growing in a broad strip down the center, insects buzzing a droning fortress of sound even she found inescapable. Now, snow; for her, silence.

They walk side by side, Owl glancing over at him. "Giving those black lungs a workout."

He grudgingly takes the hit, angling to watch her. "Ready to tell me where we're going now?"

She pauses, pointing off ahead. "I think it's about twenty more minutes on this road before we reach the tramway."

"Uh-uh, nope. I don't want to hear 'I think.' You're supposed to be the guide." He bites his already-chewed thumbnail. "What the hell's a tramway?"

"Ghost trains." Can't hide a glimmer of pleasure at his immediate head jerk. "That's what they call them."

Stops, letting her gain a bit, then swings back into step. "Wha-a-at?" Gives her shoulder a bump—playful, but the sensation of his hard muscle and bone lingers against her, like a trace detectable only under black light. "You're not wasting my time with some snipe-hunt-scare-the-city-boy shit, are you?"

Her look is dour.

"Right. Owl don't play."


THEY VEER FROM the path only once, Owl walking into the trees without a word, reminding him of the day with the deer; he stays on the road, watching her kneel in front of a tree crisscrossed with scratch marks.

She runs her fingers over it, glancing at him. "Black bear marking tree. Ran his claws all over this. Might be a den near here." Snaps a pic with her phone, grinning as she sees him quickly check the woods behind him. "I thought you were all set to piss on a grizzly?"

The first sign of change is rusty heavy-gauge wire looped through the tree branches along the road, hanging down into the bushes in places. "Back in the 1920s, a logging company built a tramway between here and Iroquois Lake. Made it easier to move the logs out." Owl picks up her step, eager to get farther into the site. "When the company went under, it cost too much to transport the trains out of the woods, so they left them." Points to the bushes, where massive iron wheels protrude from the snowbanks. "That's all that's left of most of the cars." Sees him slowing and breaks into a trot. "Come on."

The road widens gradually, and signs of the tracks appear, crumbled, the ties completely rotted away to leave only corroded iron runners heading off into the woods in both directions and heaps of scrap jutting from the snow. Glimpses of openness beyond the trees—iced-over Lake Plummet—and the first touches of sundown darkening the horizon. Not much time before they'll have to head back.

Owl leads him to the ghost trains. Two steam engines and a caboose, still whole, backed up near some collapsed timbers, all that remains of an engine house that once enclosed them. They're capped with snow, long drips of ice frozen down the length of their muscular twenty-five-ton bodies.

She lets Cody go to them first—he should have the full experience, the surreal sense of discovery, the only comparison she can think of is that of running, as a kid, toward a new playground, the immediate pull to climb on everything, touch everything, claim it. And he doesn't disappoint, going straight to the first engine, swinging up onto the narrow steps to the engineer's cabin, so full of snow he has to kick it free from the doorway just to get a look inside.

She wanders toward the caboose, what she remembers being her favorite car, giving Cody time to walk around the other cars, give in to the irresistible impulse to climb up on the rear steps and try to turn the big iron wheel that controlled the couplings, long since rusted in place.

There are reasonably fresh footprints on the caboose steps, and she hesitates before peering through the open doorway, the wooden door gone from its hinges—mentally touching base with the knife in her pocket. Most anyone you meet in these woods is generally harmless—probably all she'd find is some hiker with his feet kicked up, smoking a joint—and Cody's here. That changes the odds.

But whoever it was has come and gone, the long shotgun shaft of the car empty, snow only blown in a couple feet at either end. The small, high windows let enough daylight in to see, and she turns as she hears Cody coming up the steps behind her, swinging around the doorway with a breathless sort of speed that suggests he hit a patch of ice on the way. She's rewarded with the expression in his eyes; some sign of whatever enthusiasm drives us toward that new playground to explore and conquer hasn't been fully extinguished in him, either.

"The engineers used to sleep back here on long rides. You can see where there was a woodstove and sink before people stole them." There's a space for two cots, one at either end of the car, nothing left but the bolted metal framework for a box spring to rest on. Owl goes to the step system built into the wall, boosting herself to the face-to-face benches beneath the windows, meant to give engineers a view of the full length of the train.

She didn't expect Cody to join her, but he's up there almost as quickly as she is, sitting across from her. The space is tight, their legs mingling again, hers between his. The contrast in their bone structures, the length of his femurs, the utilitarian construction of his knees drawing her focus for a beat longer than she intended, and when they lock eyes, she can't remember what her defenses feel like, how not to show her naked fascination with him.

Raises her phone, unthinking, has him framed before he changes expression, and the shutter closes on his slightly dilated stare, lips parted, hands resting on the bench on either side of him, young and old at once, lustful and wounded.

His hand moves the phone aside, down to her hip, leaning toward her, a rustle of outerwear, and they're nose to nose, eyes open, blue gray to dark brown, close enough to make Owl's vision double; loss of sight overwhelmed by touch, his lips and chin trailing down her cheek first, the faintest friction of stubble, testing closeness.

Part of Owl falls, slowly turning into some shared abyss; another part's astounded, hyperaware of this first, *a first*, and her movements toward him are gradual, hesitant, sliding her face against his until their lips meet, not knowing what to do, how to do it right, just doing.

Fragile bridge of trust, every passing second that neither of them pulls back securing another cobblestone, then another, until Owl moves out onto it, eyes closed, gripping two handfuls of his coat, because there's open air between them and to her right, no armrests or railing. He automatically steadies her with a bracing of his left arm—a blunt, unconscious shelving back on the bench—without taking his lips from hers, and it's proof she needs: he has strength, but won't use it against her.

It becomes a question of oxygen, Cody first to stop, settling back just enough so that they can both breathe, his gaze on her face like it's this new discovery, this thing he'd never expected to have and can't decide where to begin with it.

The daylight has dimmed low outside, a hurricane lamp starved of wick; she finds her voice, husky, full of this thing shared between them: "We need to get back."


SETH IS IN the chair at the head of the kitchen table, edged out to keep his bad leg as straight as possible, watching the driveway as the F-350 pulls in upon the final act of sunset, circling around to the sugarhouse with the evaporator tarped and well rigged to the bed—Owl's work. Familiar flash of pride, amazement at how much she's learned, absorbing through osmosis, example, few words. He's no great teacher.

Relief hits next, sending him out of his seat to the window, thoughtless, as if the knee weren't there, awakening the band saw, grinding, reverberating off the joint, his fist clenched around the head of the hated cane as he watches Cody swing out of the driver's seat, followed by Owl out the other side, going back to drop the tailgate. "They're late," he says, making Holly look up from the counter.

"Yes, they are." Unperturbed, pastry blender scraping against the bowl as she cuts Crisco into flour. "A little." He leans closer to the glass, the drive to get out there and help almost irresistible, and she stops mixing the dough, coming up behind him, slipping her arm around his waist.

The teens are talking, voices indistinguishable from this distance, Cody in the bed behind the evaporator, Owl saying something as she walks toward the shed—going for the dolly. Didn't need Seth there to tell her. Cody says something back, and she laughs, a rare clipped sound, like something released from a box before the lid is slapped back down, always hard-earned. Seth shakes his head. "Thought she couldn't stand him."

Holly's smile is small, ironic; with a shake of her head, she gives his shoulder a bracing pat, kisses his temple, then returns to the making of the meal.

# 16

A warm spell casts during the night, a shifting, melting sway. The woods, free of human occupation, sigh and crack, drop loads of melt from treetops, with weighty punctuating thumps.

In the den lies the vixen, side gently rising and falling, eyes slits as her four wriggling kits suckle at her belly. They still wear their newborn coats of charcoal gray, but their eyes and ears have begun to open, teeth begun to cut, making their mother jolt occasionally as she's nipped in the musky, soil-dark keep.

THE CABIN PANES are liquid with snowmelt Saturday morning as Owl picks around her breakfast, agitated, her insides appropriated by a hummingbird in a patch of red lobelia, buzzing, alighting, then on to the next bloom without settling. It's so unlike her—no resemblance—not the saw-whet girl who keeps watch from on high, biding time, tensed for every sound.

She's sick with nerves to see him, would die a private death if she didn't, not knowing what to expect or how to act with a night between them and what happened in the ghost train. The ride home hadn't been bad, neither of them speaking much, Owl unable to decide if this was natural, both of them testing to see if they could still fit in the spaces they occupied together before, if they even wanted to. Cody's gaze found her in the rearview a few times, Owl looking directly back, and the space beyond—that pull—held so much more potential than anything that had come before.

Holly's taking her time with breakfast, pouring herself more coffee. Saturday is her one day off this week, and Owl flees the cabin, afraid her aunt will ask about that extra forty-five minutes it took them to get back from West's yesterday, unaware of how Holly leans forward in her seat, watching Owl's ski cap bob out of sight down the front steps, her slight figure breaking into a near run across the front yard to the sugarhouse, faster, faster, taking the doorstep at a leap.

MINUTES LATER, WALLACE pulls up with Cody in tow, followed by Gunnar on his snowmobile, the excuse of helping Seth install and brick the new evaporator a convenient reason to hang around the sugarhouse and swap stories for the morning. Wallace's presence is enough to drive Cody down into himself, jaw tight as he's exploited for his youth and brawn—lugging cinder blocks for the evaporator to rest on and bricks to mortar along the inside of the combustion chamber—Seth the only one he takes direction from without obvious resentment. Owl watches from the periphery, trying not to show her anticipation for this morning's tap check, not even sure if Cody sees her standing by the storage tanks as he blows by on his way outside after Wallace's most recent advice on how to lift with his knees so he doesn't end up the walking wounded like the rest of them by the time he's forty.

"Been hearing about you two down at the market," Gunnar says to Wallace as Seth mixes mortar in a bucket. There is only one market, the Korner Store, in St. Beatrice, where you can get a few basic groceries—bread, milk, TP, beer—without having to drive all the way to Market Basket or Walmart in Stokely. "Saying you and the boy been raising some hell at Houlihan's."

Wallace gives a coarse laugh. "Yup. Most nights."

*Think that's smart*, Seth says—Owl lip-reads—while he's directing his words down toward the mixture of cement, sand, and lime, *fueling him up on booze all the time?*

"Well, Christ, he'll just get it someplace else." Mottled flush in Wallace's unshaven cheeks—Owl can't tell if it's emotion or the blossom of high blood pressure—and his gaze glosses right over her, as if she has no more comprehension than a post. "At least if he's with me, I can keep an eye on him. Better than him sneaking off with a bottle of Jack somewhere, getting busted for DWI, isn't it?"

Seth nods, saying nothing more, but Gunnar's gaze is skeptical. "Heard some stuff got smashed up Thursday night. Boy shot his mouth off at the wrong guy."

"Oh. Yuh. Aw, hell, it was just some empty bottles. I smoothed it over."

Owl's gaze finds Cody through the window. He's paced away from the sugarhouse for breathing room and is leaning against the side-by-side, hands braced on the frame. He looks over then, meeting her gaze, and she knows—it's their time.

AT THE SUGARBUSH, a game of pursuit, short-lived: Owl climbs out of the passenger side as soon as they stop, grabbing her pail and heading into the trees on the right-hand side of the road, looking back once to see him following, at a distance, that stance of his, head down, hands in pockets.

She darts through the bush, abandoning her usual orderly tree check, testing if this is really happening, that this sense of thrill, power, isn't some game she's playing alone; she's never known it, never dreamed it for herself, can hardly believe she might be holding it in her hand. Drops the pail to the snow, a bread crumb, then finds an old, thick maple to press her back to, waiting, counting silently, eyes closed, seeing if he'll close the rest of the distance.

Picks up on the final scuffs of his footsteps as he nears, and she steps out, grabs him, his hands covering hers, and pulls him around the tree with her, the two of them ending up against the trunk, smiling into each other's faces, and this time the kissing doesn't require anything of her, training wheels off, returning to what they began yesterday with an energy that melts any doubt she had.

So when he pauses, breathless, saying, "This is okay, then," close to her ear, she cuts him off with, "Yes," then, "Yes," reaching up to hold his face, direct it back to her, as a breeze winnows through the bare branches, a rattle and a hush.

AT VAN'S ON Sunday, Owl keeps a watch on the door, anticipating the usual clamor of Aida's entrance.

In the sugarhouse, Seth and Cody will be boiling all day into the night after yesterday's haul, and with today's temps, more of the same; Owl will be back in time to help with the second tap check and bottling. She feels outside herself, a sense of having stretched beyond her own form, looking down at the top of Owl Dotrice's head as she straightens the boots—the razor-straight part in her hair, the braids—a girl she no longer quite seems to be. Yesterday in the trees began her metamorphosis, a slow discovery of wings folded to her back, not yet fully open—and with her every step, she knows she might take flight, drawn by something in the distance that hasn't taken form.

The glass doors push open, and Owl glances quickly, finding Holly doing the same from behind the counter: a guy who tends bar down the street at Houlihan's, Declan, early thirties, no jacket, two gold chains showing around his collar, a look of harried panic Owl recognizes.

Holly's already reaching into a box under the counter, holding up a roll of receipt tape. *Here.*

He catches it. *You guessed, huh?*

173

*Whoever's ordering down there needs to get their head on straight.*

*I'm the one who—* Sees her smile, relaxes. *Right. I owe you, Holl. Better get back—boss would kick my ass for leaving the till.*

Once Declan's on his way, Holly walks down to the end of the counter, leaning on her elbows, getting Owl's attention before she speaks. "Where's Aida today?"

Owl shrugs, a sharp motion, hating the sullen feel of it. Too much like guilt, which she doesn't feel—honestly—only regret at things having gone so irretrievably south with Aida that they can't talk at lunch, finally giving Owl her turn at gushing, going over every lush detail of what's happening with Cody. Or maybe it's more regret that Aida is the only one she has to tell, now that Owl has a picture of a boy on her phone, too—a real one, his gaze full of Owl at the instant the shutter closed—which she brings out to look at whenever she can, trying different filters over it. She likes black-and-white the best.

Holly looks at her, drums her fingers lightly. "She seemed pretty surprised not to find you here last week."

"She knew. I texted her."

Holly nods slowly, takes quick stock of the two customers over by the camping gadgets, obviously engrossed, then says, "Can I talk to you out back?"

Everything around Owl stills as she follows her aunt into the stockroom, the familiar crowded surroundings taking on a heightened sense of vividness, in this second, where it seems her wings will be clipped—so soon, before she's even gotten a feel for weightlessness.

174

Holly leans against a desk overloaded with packing slips and wire baskets with billing information. "I wanted to say something. The question you asked me after I picked you up the other afternoon—about why I don't speak Passamaquoddy . . . I didn't really answer you. You took me by surprise, I guess."

Oxygen returns; Owl buoys, nods.

"First of all, I'm not fluent. Not many people in my generation are. And speaking those words . . ." Shuts her eyes. "Being Passamaquoddy is different things to different people. Being Indian is. For me, it's personal, and it brings up some hard memories. I don't share a lot." Releases a breath, firms her fist on the desktop. "But I want you to know that not wearing it on my sleeve isn't even close to the same thing as being ashamed. Okay?"

Owl flinches, blood rushing into her cheeks, remembering her artless use of Ms. Z's words. "Sorry. No. I didn't think that." Again, words fail her; she hates the thought of putting her foot in it again. "The Baptistes didn't ask me to say anything. It wasn't their fault. Just so you know."

Holly nods once, stiffly, and Owl turns to go to the main room but is immediately stopped by her aunt's voice: "The stories we used to tell, at night?" Owl looks back, breath held; they've never spoken of it during the day, as if some spell might be broken and their power stolen. "I shared those with you because I wanted you to have them. Inside you. Like I do." Holly's expression is composed now, distant. "They're the most precious things I have to give."

• • •

MONDAY AFTERNOON, STEAM churns from the sugarhouse cupola, a stark gray flag against the coming dusk.

Cody keeps the fire going—he has all day—the sap boiling down to the proper thickness, while Owl, Seth, and Holly work in the sugar kitchen, bottling and stickering and boxing, rows of glass maple leaves now resting on their sides, gleaming golden in the lamplight.

After eating their supper in the sugarhouse, Owl carries the dirty dishes inside, careful not to be caught watching Holly pull sheets and spare blankets from the hall closet, tucking an extra pillow beneath her arm.

"THINK YOU'VE GOT everything you need."

Well past eight o'clock, sugar kitchen shut down for the night, Owl waits in the sugarhouse doorway as Seth looks over the stack of bedding Holly left on the cot mattress. "You know where the bathroom is inside if you need it. Help yourself to the fridge. You run into any problems, don't worry about waking me up." Seth sniffs, steps back, using the cane to rest on. "Don't sleep worth a damn anymore anyway."

Cody looks up from where he stands over the evaporator, pulling the skimmer through the foam in the back pan, straining impurities, nods once.

"Make sure that the damper's closed most of the way before you bunk in. Enough heat in here right now to keep you warm through the night fine without adding any more wood." Seth glances away from the firebox, giving a rueful half smile. "Sorry. Didn't mean to go all Wallace on you." Gets a cough of laughter from Cody, who shakes his head, looking down to his work. "You got this. 'Night, kid."

Owl holds the door for her uncle, gaze drawn to Cody as she knew it would be in this moment's privacy, no one's eyes on them for the first time in dragging hours, and she meets his stare fully, risking dangerous seconds before shutting the door gently behind her.

Before she reaches the house, Owl looks back at the sugarhouse window, finding Cody's outline in the dim light inside, still tracking her as if by body heat through the dark.

THE FOX SKETCH is done, at least for now; Owl isn't totally satisfied with the shape of his ears, but any more shading or erasing will surely ruin it. Around ten thirty, she tacks it above her bed, begins a new one, this time of the vixen stealing out of the den in the darkness, more from imagination, since the pics were too dark to tell much but basic shape. Owl's creating, but also stalling, heart rate higher than it should be as she sits cross-legged. Sleep an impossibility, knowing he's out there.

Ten to midnight, she goes to her window, pulls the curtains aside. Sees the faint glow in the sugarhouse, as if he's turned off all the lamps save one.

Brushes out her hair, puts on lip balm, for what it's worth—beeswax stuff without tint—unfamiliar with primping. Wears her chukkas again, uses the softest steps she can manage, pausing at the bottom of the stairs a full thirty seconds, eyes closed, trying for a depth of hearing she simply doesn't have

177

before crossing the dark living room to the rack, where she carefully puts her coat on. Front door is best, farthest from their bedroom.

Then she crosses the span between cabin and sugarhouse, simultaneously the longest and shortest distance she's ever bridged, pulse high and thudding in her throat, drawn by that flickering, inconstant light.

# Part III

## MAPLE SYRUP GRADE: Dark

*Nearing season's end;*
*deeper color, robust flavor.*

# 17

When the door swings inward, Owl sees that Cody has made up the cot, the hunter-plaid blanket tossed over the comforter, pillow propped against the wall, as if he'd been sitting there, facing the door.

Now, he's kneeling in front of the open firebox, using the poker to turn over logs consumed to a molten orange, casting his face in a harvest glow as he looks at her, taking her in as she leans her weight against the door to press it shut. He doesn't register surprise, but neither does his gaze leave her as he closes the box door and the damper most of the way, getting to his feet.

She takes a couple steps into the room, simultaneously strung up with nerves and again feeling so weightless that her feet could lift off, toeing air, until she and Cody are eye to eye. "I wanted to come out sooner," she says.

He pulls off the leather firing gloves, tosses them onto the nearest counter. "I figured."

Cody walks to her, cupping the side of her face with his hand, big and calloused, sliding it back to run his thumb over the curve of her ear, into her loose hair. She leans into it, supported, then moves in to kiss him, shutting her eyes, unsurprised as she really does feel her feet leave the floor by a couple inches.

He carries her with him easily, walking her toward the bed, and she fits beneath him with a rightness that both soothes and alarms. She's grateful her body can find its own way, but a spill of images falls through her mind's eye—stripping off clothes, things moving too fast, control lost or stolen, and she nearly sits up—but he isn't pushing or tearing, doesn't seem any more intent upon *taking* than she is. By inches, she settles her head on the pillow, tendons in her neck relaxing, and allows her hands to travel where they want to. Beneath his flannel and T-shirt to his bare back, into the depression of his spine, then the nape of his neck, fingers slow-dragging through his hair.

Time recedes beneath a warm tide, better part of an hour dissolving between them, hands above clothes and under, Owl guiding his touch away when it strays beneath the elastic support of her bra, her instincts saying not there, not yet. They reach a natural pause, Cody rolling onto his side, the two of them lying face-to-face in the quiet, only the occasional skitter and pop of the fire accompanying them.

He touches her hair for a time, smoothing over it, fingers finding the scar again, tracing it; she tries to tell what he's feeling, what compels him to touch the thing her own hands steer clear of—something like fascination, maybe morbid curiosity—and she says, "I can tell you what happened." More a test of his response, trying not to feel the dull shock of her offer, more than she's ever made even to Aida. Even with Seth and Holly, it isn't spoken of, none of them needing a reminder of that time, always trailing them from a distance like some skeletal, distempered stray.

His gaze doesn't waver from the scar. "If you want." Tone noncommittal.

She looks at his face for a long time, not sure of the starting place, or how much Cody or anybody would even want to hear. "I used to live with my dad. My mom . . . left us when I was really little. I don't remember her." Lie. Sensory memory—a body, a scent and a warmth, held in the lap cradle of a hard, thin woman's frame. Seth met her once and said she was just a girl, barely eighteen when she had Owl—but these aren't details Owl knows how to pass on to another person, give credence to. "Life wasn't good there. He wasn't right."

"He beat on you?"

Flashes held in place by mental fire doors, details crashing against the barrier, until it's all pressure, all pain, the past she won't allow to break through to engulf the present. One incident from when she was tiny still burns through into her dreams sometimes: the red sauce, cheap stink of processed tomatoes, mixed with the salt of tears and mucus, stickiness all over, shuddering, gasping in her seat at the table, blue plastic dish overturned, and the sense of him coming at her again, a huge moving mass filling her vision.

"I'm not sure what I did. That last time." Narrowing her eyes unconsciously, briefly striving to see back. "When you get a head injury, you can lose memories of when it happened. Sometimes it gets erased. Started with something about my shoes. Wasn't putting them on when he said . . . wasn't going fast enough, something. We were going somewhere. Nowhere special." Tension of the argument, her own voice whining, peevish little girl with a perfect skull and perfect hearing, Daddy high above, hands trying to steer her shoulders. "We lived on the second floor, and we were taking the back stairway. I'm not sure—I wouldn't go, I guess. Stopped walking. Got stubborn." The wrench of her shoulder; the slap; screaming at him.

Cody waits, still unreadable.

"He"—*I fell*—"threw me." She feels so sick in that dreaded pause.

"Down the stairs?" Tone sharp.

"I didn't hit any of the stairs." Shrugs. "I was little. He used all his strength. I landed on the concrete floor at the bottom. I guess there was a rubber mat down there. It broke part of my fall. That's why I ended up with this"—gestures to her ear—"instead of having to relearn how to walk, talk, do everything. That's what everybody meant when they said I was lucky."

Cody makes a harsh sound. "Anybody who said that to you is a fucking idiot." Rolls onto his back. Owl stares, uncertain how to respond; that includes pretty much every nurse and doctor she dealt with in the hospital. "Like you're supposed to thank your dad for not killing you. You got a right to live."

No one's ever said it quite that way before. She props herself up on one elbow, facing him, counting breaths, because

184

the confession isn't done—if that's what this is—and now she needs for him to understand all of it. "When the doctors asked what happened, I told them the truth. My dad . . . they arrested him at the hospital, took him away. He didn't fight it. I don't think he ever really thought I'd tell. It had always been just us. You know?" Draws a slow breath, fighting the tightness in her chest. "They let me give video testimony for his trial." Imagines her child face stretched across a flat-screen, still swollen and purpled from impact, hair buzzed short from surgery, head bandaged on one side, speaking to a courtroom full of strangers—*My daddy hit me, and*—"He got twelve years."

"Should've gotten life. No, somebody should've thrown his ass down a couple flights of stairs, see how he likes it. See how he likes having his head bashed in." Cody sits up abruptly, brushing into her, one arm around his knee as he stares forward. "They did that, eye for an eye? Be a hell of a lot less kids getting the crap kicked out of them every day."

"What I said got him put away." Not even sure what she's looking for—judgment, sympathy, even praise.

Cody jerks around to face her. "Being a sick bastard got him put away. Don't take it on you—I don't want to hear that." Turns to face the dim room again, bitten fingertips digging at the fabric of his jeans. "That's how they play it, over and over, all these guys—don't you get that? Their game is so friggin' old, but it keeps on working, because little kids don't know any better." Points a finger at the air. "I'm going to keep my boot on your neck, right here, and you're gonna thank me for it, every day. Thank me for letting you have that much air. 'Cause

185

one of these days, I might just decide to step down.'" Puts his leg out straight, knocking the blankets onto the floor in a heap. Climbs over her to get off the cot, jouncing her around as she watches, speechless.

He goes to the workbench, where his coat is draped, pulls his pack of Newports roughly from the pocket, setting it beside the lighter on the bench as he shrugs the coat on. "I've done it, you know. Testified. I mean, I've gone to court for my own shit, but this was like what you did. Only I was in the room. With one of these pricks I'm talking about."

She sits up slowly, trying not to look self-conscious as she plucks down her shirt hem to cover the waistband of her jeans again. "Who was he?"

"Foster dad. My second-to-last placement. His wife was just as bad. Three of us kids reported them to our caseworkers, but one girl got scared, backed out."

"You must've been scared, too."

Shakes his head, pulling his hat down low.

She swallows, gaze trailing down to the sheets. "What did they do to you?"

Cody palms his lighter, then pulls a cigarette out, turning it over in his fingers. "Two pervs get married, decide to take in some kids. Fill in the blanks." Puts the cigarette in the corner of a smile curved to a hook's point. "Bonus points for creativity." Before Owl can react, he says, "Be back," and heads out the door into the night.

The sugarhouse is a flickering cave, the equipment unfamiliar shadows as she curls down onto the cot mattress, processing what Cody just said. Her mouth's dry, body hot with outrage, sympathy she knows damn well he doesn't want, wondering if words exist to prove to him that he wasn't wrong to tell her.

When he returns, he doesn't look at her—she'd dreaded this, hoped he wouldn't do it after such closeness—tosses his stuff back on the workbench, sniffs, then comes over and drops heavily onto the cot, clothes exuding fresh smoke, forearm across his eyes.

It's a push; she knows it. Heel of the palm to the diaphragm—trying to knock her back to her loft. Last chance.

Owl leans over, kisses his brow at the hairline, then presses her body to fit against his, open palm on his chest. He lowers his arm, looking at her with unguarded eyes. Confirmation of what she knows to be true—the absolute worst thing is carrying a deep and private belief that you're unworthy of anyone's touch.

THEY SLEEP FOR a time—Cody never wakes, turned to the wall, one arm crushing the pillow beneath his head—but Owl rouses to the first glow of dawn outside the windows, giving the treetops definition against the still-dark sky.

She gazes at him—needs to get back inside, be asleep in her loft long before Seth and Holly wake—but the effortless wonder of last night, their entrance into something wholly their own, keeps her spellbound, reluctant to leave.

The fire is out, the air in the sugarhouse chilled, and she puts her slippers on before stepping down on the bare floor and going for her coat.

A buzz from the workbench startles her. A notification—a vibrating phone, ringer off. Somebody managed to sneak through the holes in reception. It's in Cody's coat, plain black rubber case scuffed at the corner, slid mostly free of his inner pocket. She realizes she's never even seen him hold it, let alone check messages.

Glances at him, still unmoving. Slides the phone out just enough to wake it up. It's old-looking, maybe one of those pay-as-you-go models. More than just one notification waits: There's a line of them, a couple different DM threads, previews showing just the first snippets visible without his access code.

Miguel, thirty seconds ago: *Dude wtf get back*

Jonas, seven hours: *You've got till Tues to get your stuff—then I'm . . .*

Miguel, nine hours: *U mad*

AngelKayla, two days: *Ballard is still looking for you, PISSED—WRU???*

Evie_2682, four days: *Please answer baby. Love you.*

Owl's gaze remains fixed on the last message, cold pinpoints raising on her flesh before she recognizes the name. Cody's mother—Wallace called her Evie.

She looks over to where Cody sleeps, knees bent, drawn down into himself, then replaces the phone carefully before slipping outside, that last image of him covered in blankets narrowing to a seam, then nothing as she shuts the door and crosses the yard, the only sound she hears the soft, rapid crunch of her own footsteps.

• • •

OWL VEERS TO the fox den, really running now. Knows she's pushing it with every extra minute she stays out here, but it's a rare chance for an early morning visit, and this is the foxes' time, woods layered under dimness, quiet.

A stir in the bushes some fifteen feet over from the den— maybe as far as the vixen wants to go at this point—and Owl sees one of the kits, toddling on what might be its first venture outside. Hard to make out much but grayish fur, a round belly.

The others stay hidden, no doubt closer to their mother, but this one walks along the edge of cover, navigating the strange sensation of the crusty snow as Owl snaps pics, zoomed in as far as her phone can go without totally losing focus.

In an instant—the vixen thrusts through the brush, closes its jaws on the kit's scruff, pulls it back into the fold.


OWL HUDDLES IN her bed, sleepless, watching almost an hour pass on her digital clock face before the first jet of lamplight shoots up against her loft curtains—Seth, awake— followed moments later by the scent of percolating coffee, and she knows she's done it, pulled it off, a combination of relief and guilt overwhelmed by the sudden weight of her own exhaustion.

One question follows her down into brief sleep before her bed shaker goes off: A phone left untouched, locked for days on end. *Please answer baby.*

# 18

"Tell me about the project." Ms. Z spreads orange segments on Owl's paper towel as she bites into a slice of her own.

"I will," Owl says, signing it, moving her open left hand past the side of her head, looking down at the row of flawless crescents. "If I can ask you something."

"Sorry. I didn't understand that."

Owl hesitates, reshaping her sign, crooking her index finger at her teacher.

"Trading a question for a question?" At Owl's shrug, Ms. Z smiles a little, nods, brings both hands out from her chest, fingers planked together, thumbs up. "Go on."

"Why do you bring this?" Owl uses what she thinks is the sign for orange—squeezing a C shape next to her mouth. Is rewarded when Ms. Z doesn't correct her, instead finishing her slice, dabbing her fingers on the paper towel.

"Well . . . because I have to leave the Stokely school around eleven thirty to get here in time for your study hall. I usually eat lunch on the drive, and fruit can be challenging while at the wheel."

"An orange every time?"

Ms. Z clears her throat, taking another slice. "You tell me why you think I bring it. I can see you have an opinion."

"I think it's about being perfect. Or . . . correct." Owl doesn't have the exact sign for the second word and shakes her head, substituting with *I don't know.* Ms. Z supplies, forefingers out, two taps of her right hand on her left, and Owl repeats it.

"You think that's what I expect of you?"

"I don't know. I used to."

"Shamed by an orange. Questionable." Ms. Z's gaze travels over the framed sign of old rules and punishments for mis-behaving students, and Owl's follows, reading BOYS AND GIRLS PLAYING TOGETHER—I LASH, TELLING LIES—7 LASHES. "How about this. Tell me what it is about an orange that means per-fection to you."

Owl searches her memory, mouth screwed to the side, then ventures a circle, drawn in the air. Exhales sharply. "No, the math word—'sphere.' I don't know it." She waits as the teacher supplies a rotation of her cupped hands, then repeats it. Eyes go to the ceiling as her hands search the air and her memory, again dropping the verbal side of her words in her effort to find the sign. *Perfect skin.* Unbidden, she thinks of Cody, her hands on his back, smooth, seamless. The impossibility of last night, of knowing that he was still asleep just feet away in the sugar-house as she walked down the driveway to meet Mrs. Baptiste this morning, this boy she now feels bonded to in a way she's never been to anyone. *All grow the same.* Only knows how to sign the end, rocking her left hand back and forth, thumb and pinkie raised.

"Sameness means perfection?"

"People think so."

"But do you?" Ms. Z's hands hover, waiting, as Owl looks at her, at an impasse, unsure how to phrase how often the word *perfect* enters her mind—memories of how her senses worked before the fall, how effortless it seemed, existing in sound. "The thought that we should all be striving toward sameness is a little too depressing for a Tuesday afternoon, don't you think?" Gets a rueful smile out of Owl and nods. "How's the project going?"

"Good." Explains how she found some partial pieces of plexiglass in Seth's workshop, the idea behind the copper mine model. "Griffin's got them at his house now. I'm going over again this week so we can finish it."

"I thought there were three of you?"

"There are." Owl's hands pause. "I don't know what Aida's doing."

"She's not helping?"

Another hesitation, debating how far she can trust this common ground she seems to be finding with Ms. Z. "Not really." Make that not at all; today's their next in-class work session, and Owl's dreading it: Aida sitting primly, facing away from her, barely acknowledging anything even Griffin says. This time, Owl's hands get away from her, signing out, *She's mad at me,* before she can second-guess.

192

"Ah." Ms. Z bites into another slice, pausing until she can sign again. "That must be hard. Having all your classes together in a space like this." Gestures dismissively toward the old walls, coated thick with layers of white paint, reapplied each fall for a new school year. "Could you tell Mr. Duquette about it?" At Owl's near-frantic headshake: "Do you want to tell me?"

Owl's gaze comes up, surprised, searching her teacher's face, her own temperature upping, a fine dampness rising at her temples and beneath her arms. Checks the closed door to the classroom. Finally, in sign only, *A boy.*

In this case, Ms. Z's impassivity is a relief, no disapproval or encouragement showing in her manner as she nods, dropping her verbal end of the conversation as well. *Griffin?*

*No. Griffin's a friend.* Owl's hands rest curled on the table, remembering the sign but slow in pulling it out, twisting the X hand shape into the corner of her mouth: *Jealous.*

*Jealous because she wants the boy, or because she misses you?*

Owl frowns, unprepared for the question. "All I know is . . . she thinks it should be her, not me." Forgets to sign everything but *not me.*

It's a while before Ms. Z speaks. "I have a challenge for you. Feel free to say no, but consider it seriously before you do. The day you bring your projects to the Stokely school, I'll be there. Meeting with my students in the resource room, from about ten to eleven thirty. You'll have a chance to stop by, get introduced." Watches Owl's expression go still. "This could be a good thing, Rochelle."

Owl's hands go to her lap, below the level of the table and

Ms. Z's view. Rise hesitantly, as if on an updraft, one finger to her temple: *I'll think about it.*

"That's all I ask." Ms. Z nods, picks up one of her two remaining segments. "Do you want to know why I really bring an orange every time?" Deposits the slice on Owl's empty paper towel. "Most shareable of fruits."

AT LUNCH, OWL goes outside, Aida stays in with the other kids, the broken state of their two/one-ness impossible to miss. Owl knows the others are watching, talking, but walking the circuit alone is a combination of punishment and willfulness without Aida's arm connected to hers, her words deposited directly into her ear, down, down into her brain—some liquid polymer of hot boys, hovering mothers, and general frustration with the mountain walls holding her in. Owl circles the flagpole, facing doggedly forward, all the time wondering if Aida ever looks out the window at her or if she's focused just as determinedly on forced conversation with Savannah, the Fifteen who Aida has always called a Tragic Case: corduroy jumpers and print turtlenecks, church on both Wednesdays and Sundays, sprout pita sandwiches in her lunch box (actually uses a lunch box).

Motion catches her eye by the older students' door; Owl makes herself face forward, holding her breath, mind racing to figure out what she'll say if it's Aida, how determined she really is not to be the first to apologize.

But it's Griffin, his usual slope-shouldered mosey, not over to Owl but toward the swings again, earbuds hooked in, not paying her any obvious mind.

Owl does a few more turns, stops by the dirty, icy ridge of plowed snow to watch him, then walks over, sliding into the swing beside him. He nods without meeting her eyes.

Their boots don't stay still long, that childhood inclination to push off stirring their soles against the crust, toes giving lift, soon their legs pumping, bodies twice as heavy as they were when this act of leaving the ground was daily, ages seven, eight, nine, making the swing set screech and thud, and Owl shuts her eyes, leaning into the wind, into the exact moment when her body rises high enough to leave the seat.

IT'S LIKE NOTHING has changed when they come together again, Owl and Cody. With Seth nearby in the sugar kitchen catching up on bottling, Cody's who he always is, jingling the side-by-side keys, appropriated early, in his coat pocket, jaw muscle jumping a little; she darts her gaze down and away, hoping he didn't notice her attempt to connect, relieved she hadn't put anything more out there.

On the drive, she faces away, last night's burnished intimacy on repeat in her memory, wondering where she'd misstepped, if it were ever possible not to with him. But she can be this hard, pretend she expects nothing, wants nothing. If she has to.

As soon as they turn onto the access road, she feels the vehicle slow, glances over to see him shut off the ignition, then place his hand on her thigh. Owl lifts her face to his, his expression clouded, searching, with already a touch of defiance, another opening for her rejection.

She covers his hand with hers, squeezing hard, and leans in to kiss him, feeling his immediate response, fingers lacing together over her knee, pressing down as their bodies reconnect.

SUPPERTIME, TALK OF tomorrow's follow-up appointment with the knee surgeon. "I wish they would just set a date for the surgery and be done with it," Holly says, sliding a bowl of green beans over to Owl.

"Hell no, not when they can drag it out over as many appointments as possible. Suck people dry with co-pays." Seth chews hard, drinks ice water, a tightness to his expression, pain singing a relentless aria.

"Well. We'll get through it."

"Mm."

"Or we can curl up and die. There's always that option."

Owl sees a grudging twitch at the corner of his mouth. "Yeah, all right. Quit my bitching, huh?"

"Something like that." Holly drops a wink at Owl, who smiles down at her plate.

The meal finished, Seth takes his turn with the dishes, Owl drying and putting away, while Holly goes to deal with the laundry in the stackable in the bathroom. The landline rings, a rarity, generally telemarketers or recorded voices plugging one politician or another. Seth goes to the living room to answer it, his limp more pronounced in the evening. Owl

196

glances over as she runs the dish towel over a plate, catching Seth's words popping up in text on the CapTel screen: *Hello?*

The pause afterward extends longer than normal. Then, *Seth?* Another pause. *It's me.*

Owl watches, hands still moving at her task, seeing her uncle's gaze riveted on the far wall, his hand curled tightly around the head of his cane.

Two, three more seconds—then Seth stabs the OFF button with his thumb, bringing the handset down hard enough that Owl can hear it even from where she stands.

His foot connects with the end table, sending it against the wall, heaving coasters and magazines to the floor; Owl stares, plate gripped to her chest as he grabs the phone cord and yanks it free of the wall socket in one motion.

Holly appears at the end of the hallway, stopping at the sight of the mess. "What? What happened?"

Breathless, Seth throws the cord down, then slings the cane against the wall, where it clatters onto the end table, like a gleaming, mottled root; then he hobbles down the hallway, light from the bedroom snuffed out as the door slams.

Owl's and Holly's gazes meet across the room. "Was it him?" Owl's own voice a shrill call, repeating. *"Was it him?"*


STUNNED, VIOLATED SILENCE fills the cabin, heavy banks of it in open spaces, misty tendrils creeping around doorways, settling over the separate bedrooms and the sleepers, who shift and frown, waking before the sun to watch shadows move with the changing light before they surrender to the day, dress, switch on lamps.

Owl hesitates halfway down the stairs at the sight of Seth already sitting in his recliner, legs propped up, a book resting open on his thigh, untouched, facing the front windows. He turns as she crosses the rug toward him, and she can see he slept as badly as she did, his eyes reddened, glassy. "Hiya."

She nods, putting bread in the toaster, then makes her way back to sit on the ottoman in front of him, a familiar posture from growing up: mentor, pupil. More like devotee—she sees it now, a bolt of clarity—starving little girl being fed attention, approval, each passing year bringing more faith that his hand isn't going to come down against her, that her life with Daddy wasn't normal, that this could be better. Seeing Seth like this, exhausted, standing guard when his own leg can barely support him, brings a rush of affection, gratitude—and, unexpectedly, the truth about Cody is on her lips. Such an important change shouldn't be kept from the people she's trusted with every moment since age seven. Shouldn't be navigated with sneaking out and silence, paramount to lies.

But the thought of Cody's face if he found out she'd told Seth—any of the adults—is enough to stop her: darkening, betrayed, turning away so soon after becoming fully human with her, risking her judgment, rejection. And the truth was half his, wasn't it, to keep or give away; how could she take it on herself to hand it out? Instead: "Holly asleep?"

He nods. "She was up pretty late last night."

"Sorry."

Squeezes his eyes shut. "Don't apologize for him."

"I'm not. But . . . I don't want anyone to worry."

"Not on you, kid. I'm calling the sheriff's department in Lancaster soon as they open. See what we can do about all this." Seth looks over at the end table—still shoved to the wall, the magazines and coasters tossed back onto the surface—then down at the cane leaning against his recliner. "This used to be your grandpa's, know that? He carved it. It's been in the back of our closet ever since he died." Humorless smile as he hefts it. "The doctor said, 'Get a cane,' and I didn't want to be walking around with one of those aluminum things from a medical supply place. Seemed stupid not to use the one we had."

Owl examines the smooth, knot-darkened wood, then Seth's expression: no softening there. "Nice work."

"Yeah, real nice. He could make anything with his hands. Skills I'll never have." Seth lays it across his lap, gripping the curved head. "He used this for about a year before he died, when the cancer got into his bones." Pause. "I also saw him bring it down across the back of his best hunting dog's neck. *Whack*, just like that. Macey didn't stop barking when he said to."

Owl doesn't speak, watching the gleam of the cane under the lamplight.

"That's who he was, your grandpa. Not a bad man, mostly, but sometimes . . ." Jerks his chin. "I couldn't wait to get out of here when I was your age. You believe that? Enlisted as soon as I turned eighteen. Thought I'd see the world, bust some heads, come back to this mountain when

I could look the old man square in the eye and say, 'See? Did something you could never do.'" Thin smile. "Didn't play out quite that way. By the time my knee got blown out, he was sick, had been for a while. Didn't tell me, of course. Waited until he came to see me in the VA hospital when I was back stateside. I couldn't miss how much weight he'd lost, and he was walking with this thing. Said there was no point in saying anything while I was deployed. Nothing I could do about it. And, god knows, Joel"—takes a quick glance at Owl when he says her dad's name—"he was no help. Your grandpa ended up leaving this place to me, and I came to see there was no place I'd rather be. With both of them gone"—his dad, his brother—"it was different. More about me and Holly than all that stuff gone by."

She watches him, holding her breath, reading everything, nothing, into his silence, not quite sure what she's hungry for. "I remember . . . with Daddy . . . you never knew what he'd do."

"He was always like that. Even growing up." Flat light in Seth's eyes as he watches the window, the gradual spreading of daylight behind the dark treetops. "Your grandpa being who he was—that's no excuse. I don't know. I'm sure the prison shrinks had a crack at your dad, came up with some reason why a man would do what he did." Pauses. "I didn't want to believe it. When I first got that call from social services about what happened, that you were in the ICU, they'd arrested your dad, and me and Holly were all you had left for family, Joel and I hadn't talked in over four years then. I didn't even know that your mother had left. But when we got there, to your room, and I saw you in that bed, asleep . . ." Shuts his eyes a moment, barely more than a slow blink. "So little. Head bandaged. And all the shit—the desert, everything I was running from—was right there, wrapped up in one little kid. In my family, all that ugliness. Just goes to show, you never really get away. But still . . . that's when I knew I was done running. Because all I wanted was to be there for you." He's silent. "I stopped having a brother that day."

Owl wishes she could second that, say that Daddy wasn't the double exposure around every early memory, the blurred presence reaching from far corners of her subconscious, shadow hands that stretch and undulate.

"What'd you do with your letter?"

"Got rid of it." She presses her chin hard into her bent knee. "He has a new address. An apartment in Dover." The question forms, escaping her thoughts like a drop of rainwater, falling before she can catch it: "What was my mother like?"

She doesn't meet his eyes right away but can feel him staring, caught off guard. "Well . . . I only met her the one time, and she didn't say much. Sat there on the couch beside your dad and held you. Small . . . real light-blond hair like yours. Let Joel do all the talking." When Owl finally looks at him, his expression is apologetic. "The social worker on your case thought she might've been a runaway, said they didn't have her real name, and that's why they couldn't track her down after you ended up in the hospital. I guess her job cleaning houses was under the table, paid in cash." He pauses. "All I can say for sure is that she had sad eyes. And while I was there, she held on to you some tight."

# 19

Afternoon, just Owl and Cody on the farm again.

Back from the tap check, Cody turns from disconnecting the storage tank hose from the bulkhead to find Owl standing behind him, having retrieved her hiking pack and two pairs of snowshoes. The larger pair she tosses down onto the ground in front of him.

"Ever walked in these?"

"DAMN IT." CODY sinks into a drift up to midcalf again, jerks his boot free, covered in white from snowshoe to jeans.

Owl watches, not making much effort to hide her smile. "Stick to the path."

"What path?" Swats at a branch heavy with white. "How can you even tell where we're going?"

"Because I've been this way a hundred times. Just follow me." She stamps her right foot on the trail. "It's packed under here. You don't sink. Top's powder."

He grunts, makes his way over, coming up alongside to give her backpack strap a tug. "Gonna do some more climbing?"

She doesn't look away from the opening in the trees ahead, scattered with abstract shards of afternoon sunlight fallen through the canopy overhead. "No."

"Yeah, that's what you said last time." Waits. "Whatever. I thought it was hot."

"Even the helmet?"

"Especially the helmet. What'd you think I meant?"

They laugh, and Owl has a quick impulse to reach for his hand—conjures an image of them walking together that way—before glancing away fast, afraid he'll see the desire play across her face. Can't imagine he's ever held hands with anyone, not like that—tender—pictures him twisting free, laughing at her, and she speeds up her step, doubling the distance between them.


THEY CHECK THE marshes for moose, finding a line of the big heart-shaped hoofprints in some mud near the partially thawed water, another smaller trail with a dragline belonging to a muskrat, but the animals themselves are well hidden, returned to the deeper labyrinth of the woods.

By the time the elevation grows steeper, boulders crop-ping up as the Notch rises above them, Cody is coughing, occasionally spitting off into the trees. This time, Owl doesn't make a remark about black lungs, watching with unease, wondering how much damage chain-smoking can really do to a nineteen-year-old, how many years it takes before you get cancer in the bones, like her grandpa—who maybe smoked, maybe didn't; she doesn't know. Wonders how long Cody's been doing any number of things to break down his body before its time.

The waterfall is moving again, outcroppings of ice still hanging in bearded stalactites the length of the cliff to the basin, which is water again, the depths reflecting the murky slurry gray of the sky, with brown undertones, flashing an impression of fatal cold up at them like some remorseless eye.

Cody stops at the sight of the fall, transfixed. Owl gives him the time everybody deserves on their first trip here, pac-ing around on her own, checking out the path through the fissure in the rock, gauging if they can make it all the way up to the plateau, given the shifts in snow and ice since she was last here. She doesn't go to him until she sees he's drawn near the edge of the cliffside, staring down.

He doesn't look over when she walks up beside him. "It's like . . . hypnotizing. Kind of makes you want to jump. You know? Follow the water."

She takes a handful of his coat. "Yeah. Don't."

They wend their way upward, through the rocky passage-way, Cody behind Owl, using the same handholds she does, mimicking her steps, until his higher clearance of vision fills with the massive, flat plain of the ledge. "Holy shit."

Owl nods, some pride going through her, knowing she can't take credit but still feeling some ownership, pleasure in sharing a secret he would never have otherwise known.

THEY END UP as close to the edge as she'll let him go, lying together on the rock, which rapidly cools beneath their small patch of body heat as the lowering sun drains the warmth from the day. Owl doesn't notice—her coat is unzipped, the privacy sumptuous, more so than in the sugarhouse, and again, sense of time loses integrity, becomes something they stroke through without flow or direction, their touch the only tangible thing.

After the glimpse of sky she steals over his shoulder is noticeably tinged with pink, she remembers—Seth's appointment—and sits up partway, mind racing to gain some sense of how long they've been here.

Cody rests back slightly, his hand still under her hoodie and thermal Henley, tracing shapes on her bare stomach. "They're gonna be home soon, huh?" Watches the motion against her clothes. "They'd lose their shit if they knew."

"No." Defensive. "It's not that."

"But I am the first guy you've been with." Gaze fixes on hers momentarily until he finds whatever he's looking for and drifts back to the endless view; she frowns slightly at his certainty, that her inexperience is so obvious. "If that's not it, what is it?"

She straightens, focusing on drawing up the zipper on her coat. "They're worried." Hesitates. "I told you about my dad." A beat passes. "He got out of prison a few weeks ago."

"He's *out*? That's bullshit. How'd he get parole?"

"Good behavior, I guess. He's been writing letters. Seth and Holly got one. I did, too."

Cody's eyes are wide, incredulous. "Yeah? Fuck'd he have to say for himself?"

"I didn't read it."

"Why not?" Sits roughly forward, jerking his coat around him. "You didn't trash it or burn it or anything, did you?" Cuts a look her way as she shakes her head, drawing away from his unexpected intensity. "Good. Don't let the sonofabitch off that easy—I guarantee that's exactly what he figured you'd do. Probably wrote it because his lawyer or sponsor told him to go 'make amends.' Thinks to himself, 'Hell, they'll never read it anyway, so I'll just say whatever jerkoff thing comes into my head and get to feel all warm and fuzzy inside, like I made things better.'" Face tense, drawn, he stares hard at the acres of woods spread out before them, then snaps into motion again, pushing to his feet. "Nah. You don't let him." Walks a circle, staring down at the thin scrim of ice hardened into a shadowy crack in the rock. "You read every word, and then you ream his ass. Cuts both ways, right? He had his say. Now you get yours."

"Maybe I don't want a say when it comes to him. Don't need one."

"Yeah, you do. Everybody does. 'Hey, Dad, you gonna take back smashing my skull?'" Scuffs the toe of his boot hard against the edge of the ice, sending hairline cracks throughout. "'Know what it's like not being able to hear for shit? You gonna fix all that by saying sorry?'" Pauses, gives a disgusted laugh, shaking his head. "Try to murder your kid, and they give you early release. What a friggin' world."

Murder: he's cast the die out there, no retrieving it. Her stomach tips, seems to bob sideways, capsized, and she covers her mouth, pressing back queasiness; the distant Rochelle voice cries out insubstantial protests, small fists beating Owl's insides. "Assault."

"What?" Residual sharpness in his voice.

"Aggravated assault. That's what he was convicted of." Watches him shake his head, finds herself rushing to explain. "He didn't plan it. That's all it means. He didn't bring me on the landing to . . . He was always exploding, over everything, any little thing—you never knew when. That time, it went too far." Frustrated by Cody's expulsion of air. A bitter laugh. "I'm not making excuses for him. I don't."

"People like that live on excuses. It's how they fucking survive." Shakes his head, a sudden black sarcasm blossoming. "Seth gonna be able to deal with your dad trying to get at you again?"

Something in his tone makes her pause, studying him hard. "What's that mean?"

"You know." Rattles an invisible bottle between thumb and forefinger. "His problem."

It takes her a second. Connection's made—and her frown deepens. "He has to take those. They're for his knee." No sign he's heard. "The pain's really bad. He's getting an operation."

"Yeah? Better hope they don't prescribe him more Percocet, or he'll never get off it."

Sits straight, gone stiff with indignance, fear. "Yes, he will."

Cody doesn't face her directly, but what she can see of his expression is scathing boredom. "Owl, Percocet's oxy. My mom's a pillhead—anything she can swallow, stick up her nose. I know what I'm talking about."

"I thought she quit."

"She never quits. Who said that?" Shifts his head and shoulder. "Rehab doesn't take. Fakes it until she makes it, then right back hooking up with her old dealers, spending everything we got on more shit. Or maybe she stops the pills for a while but doesn't dry up, so nothing really changes. All the time telling everybody how hard she's trying." Curses, a string of them. Disjointed, unmatched beads left dangling. "I'm going down."

Owl watches as he disappears, leaving her sitting on the massive plane of rock, where all at once the wind seems vindictive, hurling her braids like coarse yarn, the last human holdout on a planet returned solely to the wild.

WHEN SHE GOES back down the path, she finds Cody standing along the cliffside again, turned partially away, looking off into the basin. A motion of his hands, a reflective flash that drops from sight, and he turns, cigarette raised to his lips, cupping his fingers to block the flame from the wind. She waits, watching, until he pinches the Newport, exhales.

"You have to take it back." She stands, tense as a bow as they face each other. "About Seth. I can't pretend I didn't hear." Swallows. "You've got to say you didn't mean it." Is quietly aghast to feel her arms shaking inside her coat.

He gazes at her, not answering for a long beat, his expression remote. Then: "I didn't mean it."

She holds her spot uncertainly, then turns to continue down the path, gingerly, tilting her good ear toward where he stands, trying to tell if he's following, how far back he might be walking, distancing himself from her.

No sound, no sound—then touch, his fingers around her hand, snatching it up like some smooth stone found by chance, clutching it to his side.

They walk home like that.


THEY'RE LATE GETTING back to the farm, and there's little time for goodbyes; Cody continues down the road toward Wallace's house, no particular hurry, Owl racewalking along the fringe of the property, eyes on the F-350 parked in the drive, already halfway up the steps before she remembers she should hide her hiking pack, come back for it later.

She's bent over, stuffing the bag far beneath one of the Adirondack chairs, when the sense of being watched makes her stop, look up.

Holly's standing there, halfway between opening the storm door and shutting the inner door, which she swiftly does, never taking her gaze from Owl—caught, all of her hastily concocted explanations blurring to uselessness in the face of her aunt's surprise.

"We thought you were upstairs." Holly looks to the chair, a telltale strap poking out from underneath. "Where are you coming back from?"

Owl rests on her heels, taking a slow breath. "The Notch."

Holly folds her arms, studying her. "Not sure how I feel about you going there by yourself." Pauses, looking toward the sugarhouse. "Unless you didn't?"

Owl shakes her head.

Holly lowers herself into the chair on the opposite side of the door, leaning forward, hair draping over her shoulder, hands clasped loosely between her knees. The silence is delicate, a spider-silk construction preserved on morning dew. "Seth told me that you took Cody to Lament the other day." Watches as Owl sits in the other chair, running her nails over the texture of the wood grain. "You like him?"

Owl hesitates, nods.

"More than a friend?" Another nod. Holly sits back, seeming to consider—this new territory is shadowed, hard going. "Well. If you ever want to talk . . ." Questioning glance. "You know I'm here. Right?"

Relief, gratitude, in her final nod.

Holly stands. "Come in and make the salad, okay? And . . . you should know, the reason Seth's not in a great mood tonight . . . Part of it's the long ride and his knee, but he also got into it over the phone with one of the sheriff's deputies earlier today. They said at this point there's nothing they can do about your dad calling here. We don't have a restraining order, and we can't file for one unless he calls back after being told not to. Basically, we have to wait and see if it happens again." Holly gives a lopsided smile. "You can imagine what your uncle said to that."

BUT ALL SETH says about it at the supper table, after sitting mostly silent, head resting on fist as he spears his food with his fork, is, "I'm getting the landline number changed. Not waiting around for some judge to push our paperwork through."

Owl hesitates in her chewing, then looks back to her meal. The prescription bottle in the cabinet has new magnetic properties, pulling her attention now that she'd do anything to avoid looking at it and forget what Cody said.

*Pillhead.* Cane rests against Seth's leg. *He'll never get off it.*

IT ISN'T UNTIL later, when she's in the bathroom getting ready for bed, gazing through her reflection in the mirror as she brushes her teeth, that she allows herself to relive her time with Cody at the Notch. The afternoon's compelling mix of bittersweetness—the crisp, cold sound of footsteps through snow, fingertips hot points sliding over chilled skin, the harshness of his voice. And the flash of motion and light as she came up behind him at the ledge—the sun reflecting off his lighter— where he'd talked earlier about following the water down.

Following. Falling.

Owl lowers her hands to the sides of the sink, seeing it again. Not daylight bouncing off a stainless-steel lighter. The flash was too low, winking below his hands, not in it, one quick flip before it disappeared below her range of vision, blocked by his turning body. Not like steel. Glass.

Like the screen of a phone.

# 20

Math. Owl's work, shown on notebook paper, spread out between them, Ms. Z bent close over the desktop as she tries to decipher Owl's tangled calculations, see where she went wrong.

"You're making this harder than it has to be." Her signs flow, and Owl watches, appreciating it in a way she hasn't before; perhaps it's because Owl's getting better—she can feel it—quicker, able to snatch up simultaneous meaning, vocal and gesture at once. "Math is about memorization. That's it. 'Why' is for English class. If you remember that, I guarantee, this number phobia of yours will cease to be." Stops, pointing at the page. "You made a mistake in your basic addition here. It threw off the whole problem. Try again." Owl takes the notebook back, starts erasing. "Have you given any more thought to stopping by my classroom on Founding Day?"

Owl nods. "I will." Adds, *Probably*, sign only, moving each hand as if testing a weight.

"I hope so. I'd like to see you there. The other kids would, too." She doesn't seem to notice Owl's doubtful glance at the thought of kids she doesn't know, particularly kids who can hear even less than she can.

Owl corrects the addition, shaping her numbers slowly, attention straying back to the list of rules and punishments: 5 LASHES, 10 LASHES, 20, boys and girls venturing into each other's territories. "I have another question."

"Go ahead."

"How do . . ." Catches herself, hunts for the signs, all the while nearly taking the question back, swallowing it down. "How does someone know if they're in love?"

Ms. Z's gaze lifts, holds gravely. "With math?"

"All I mean is . . . love. Not just . . ." Owl shakes her head, fumbling now. "I mean something real." Wishes she could rewind herself, jitter backward through the door into the classroom, sit with her head turned resolutely away from Aida, redo this into a session where she never, ever opened her mouth about something so silly.

But the flash of the object falling into the basin, brushed from Cody's hands so casually that she almost missed it, won't stop winking from her mind's eye. Because who throws their phone away? Who doesn't unlock it to answer DMs for days at a time—urgent ones, asking if you're okay, if you're even still alive? And despite it all, why is she ruled by the dread of crushing this feeling, this inner weightlessness, of the inevitable long spiral back to earth?

214

"Well . . . what's real to one person isn't necessarily the same for somebody else. I suppose it's all in how you feel, inside yourself." Moves her bent middle finger up her chest. "Not necessarily in what someone gives you in return. Reciprocation isn't validation. Does that make sense?"

Owl pinches her bottom lip, pensive. "Have you ever been?" Like a question of travel.

It hovers there. "I don't know how appropriate . . ." Goes still half a second, deciding. "I don't think this is something I should discuss with a student."

Mortified silence, both of spoken word and sign, all four hands still, as if slapped. Owl's gaze freezes, then skitters to a random corner, heat filling her face, pricking at her eyes until they water, the rest of the session focused around blinking furiously and never connecting her gaze with her teacher's until at last the bell rings.

LATE AFTERNOON. SUNSET peach-orange, burning through the random gaps in the treetops surrounding the Baptistes' house.

Inside, Owl and Griffin are sitting at the dining room table. They've screwed together a plexiglass case, with smaller pieces glued in place to make the main shaft and the different levels of the mine, as well as a cage for transporting miniature miners, twisted from Mrs. Baptiste's jewelry-making wire. Owl pours leftover all-purpose sand—salvaged, like the plexiglass, from Seth's shed—into the top, then Griffin adds layers of clear craft glue and a stripe of yellow craft sand to represent the copper

215

ore. The entire time, though, Owl grapples with the humiliation that made her bolt from Ms. Z. And she's determined not to ask Griffin about Aida's absence here—until she can't bear it anymore, the question emerging explosively, a demand: "She's just going to take a zero?"

Griffin looks up at her as he gently shakes the case, testing to see if their method of keeping the sands separate actually works. "She said she'll do the written part."

Infuriating being avoided, talked around instead of to; Owl smolders, mulling. "She doesn't have any reason to still be so mad." But . . . it's hard now to remember exactly what was said and how Owl said it, if it had maybe sounded like she was calling Trini stupid. Never meant that. She'd just felt desperate to get everyone's eyes off her, speculation away from her and Cody. Now, look what they've become. Trini and Aida saw it even before Owl did. Owl folds her arms on the tabletop, lowers her chin, first taste of humbling doubt having a grounding effect. Questions if this whole thing didn't grow as much from what she was beginning to feel for Cody as from being sick of Aida: combination of embarrassment, denial, fear of exposure.

"It's Aida. Not like her reasons need to make sense to the rest of the world." Griffin finishes off the top layer, gives the box a shake, watching the sand settle. "But I don't think that's it anyway. Not anymore." Sinks into his chair without taking his eyes off the strata. "I think she's feeling guilty. Doesn't know what to say." Owl watches him, brow furrowed. "About Riley."

"He *told* you?"

"No. She did. After it happened." Griffin glances at Owl. "She wasn't making drama or whatever. She didn't know what to do. She told me that she was just standing with him when he said it, and you read his lips from across the room, and it was too late—it's not like they were talking crap about you together." Hesitates. "She wasn't agreeing with him. You know. She felt really bad."

Owl grapples a moment, wound scraped fresh—Griffin, sitting there knowing what was said, the memory of Riley's words from the smiling sardonic mouth. Owl wants to hide, feels dragged around to see herself from the outside and is sickened by what lies there. "She should've said something then. Should've made him—" Her throat seals off, and she looks down, lips pressed in a line.

"Yeah. She should've." Folds his arms on the table. "But . . . I mean, you guys are Aida and Owl. You go together. Since forever." Griffin gazes at her. "What he said? Your voice. You just don't waste a lot of words, that's all."

She'd read exactly what Riley thought of her voice, right from his own lips, and the wound was still open, the crawling pain of infection. She and Riley weren't close—obviously, not really friends, but not enemies, either. She'd never guessed, never knew he could hate her. All her studied care to keep her voice low, level, dreading the thought of being the only one in a room who didn't know she was speaking too loud, making a fool of herself, was crushing.

"Everybody knew he was a jackass, Owl."

"Everybody thought he was cool. You used to hang out with him."

"We hung at school because we were together every day, doing the same work. Doesn't mean he was my best friend.

217

And maybe sometimes he could be cool, but most people just didn't want to get on his bad side. Because then he'd make fun of them." Shrugs. "I wasn't sorry when I found out he was moving. I don't think anybody was. And for sure nobody cared what he thought. About anything."

They lapse into unsettled silence, broken only by Mrs. Baptiste leaning into the room with a subtle *rap-rap* on the wall with her fist.

Griffin looks over. "Knocking before coming into your own dining room. Interesting."

"You, I'm ignoring." She faces Owl: "Making popcorn. Want some?"

They join her in the kitchen, sitting on stools at the counter while the microwave turns.

"So," Griffin says, with an exaggerated stretch, clearing his throat, "how's the syrup business?"

Owl can't help but laugh. "Pretty good. Same."

"You know, Indians invented maple sugaring. Showed the whites how it was done." Cracks open the soda his mom slides to him, grins at Owl. "That's another one you owe us."

As they talk, the minutes get away from Owl; Griffin's the first one to notice Holly's arrival, turning toward the window when he hears her car door shutting.

Holly's already on her way up the path to the door, and Owl freezes, then slides to her feet, doing a racing mental inventory of how spread out her stuff is, how long Holly will need to stand here before she rounds it up—

But Mrs. Baptiste has the door open; whatever she says, her back to the room, is lost to Owl, but Owl sees Holly's reaction past Mrs. Baptiste's shoulder. Hesitating on the steps, gaze going to Owl, food and drinks in front of her and Griffin. She pauses, then nods once. "Tea would be nice. Thanks."


"WAS THAT . . . OKAY?" Owl glances over at her aunt as they drive home. Fifteen minutes spent in the Baptistes' kitchen, Holly bobbing a tea bag in her mug as she and Mrs. Baptiste chatted, Owl and Griffin eating and talking about school while Owl kept one eye on Holly, afraid she might miss a subtle signal to leave.

"Yeah. Fine." Holly takes a breath, adjusting her grip on the steering wheel. "Lovely, actually. Winnie's a good person. I do know that." Gives Owl a look as she nods carefully. "I'm not making much sense, am I?" Slows as they take a sharp curve, the cliffside sheer rock, blasted out of the mountain over a century ago to build the road. "I guess . . . when I feel pressured, I push back twice as hard. No matter how well meaning that person might be. Stubborn ass, huh?"

"I get it," Owl says slowly. "I'm not saying I know what it's like for you. I don't. But feeling cornered makes me want to dig my heels in, too." Closes her mouth deliberately, letting Holly know that she's not going to pressure her for more answers, won't make that mistake twice.

Holly's eyes go to her in the rearview mirror, appraising. "Sometimes I wonder if your uncle and I have gotten out of the habit of changing. Letting new people in. Even changing our minds." Her gaze travels the unraveling roadside forest. "Hazards of isolation, I guess."

# 21

Morning Suburban ride. As Owl clambers in, Griffin, in the passenger seat, eyes closed, raises a fist to her, throwback *Breakfast Club*–style. Owl grins as she settles into her seat, allowing her gaze to stray toward Aida for the first time in days.

On the other side of the purple backpack barrier, Aida is bent over her phone, hood of her coat rucked up around her collar, obviously no idea how tangled her hair is inside it. Owl's seized by a painful rush of affection, blood to a sleeping limb, and puts her hand into her coat pocket, bringing her phone out far enough to read the text she'd composed and left open while she waited for Mrs. Baptiste to arrive, unsure if she really wanted to send it. *Meet me @ lunch?*

Looks down at Aida's dirty road-salt-and-snow-battered high-tops, hot-pink laces. Touches SEND.

OWL'S HALFWAY THROUGH her third lap around the flagpole when she sees Aida framed in the schoolhouse doorway, watching her.

Aida never answered the text—admittedly not much chance between the car ride and school starting, if the message made it through the spotty reception at all. Aida never gave a sign all morning, focus completely turned away from Owl, as it has been for over a week.

Now, Owl watches as Aida comes down the steps, hands in her coat pockets, hunched against the wind as if it's as cold out as it was a month ago, not pushing fifty-five, brazen sunlight gleaming through fast-moving clouds.

Aida looks at her from beneath her hood, the two of them making wary, reluctant eye contact. "Got your text," Aida says, touch of sullenness in her tone.

Owl shifts her weight, looking to the pavement as she gathers what she'd planned to say. "Sorry if you thought I was talking crap about your mom."

"If I *thought?*"

"I didn't mean to. It came out wrong." Watches Aida nod a little, brows drawn together, mouth screwed to the side, not jumping in with an apology of her own. Owl exhales, struggling to remember pushing won't get them anywhere but into another fight. "But you weren't being nice to me, either." Hesitates. "And I brought up the thing with Riley— what he said—because we never talked about it. And it made me feel . . ." Surprised by the tightening of her throat as much as she is her hands, lifting, wanting to sign; she lets them, letting Aida watch, uncomprehending, riding out the emotion by moving outstretched fingers down her face, a sign like falling tears, until the constriction subsides. "You didn't tell him he was wrong."

Aida's quiet, staring at Owl's hands, a brief paralysis, before she looks straight at her face. Aida's eyes are brilliant ice blue with tears. "I didn't know what to do. When he said that. I mean, he knew we were friends. I just . . . wasn't expecting it. And then . . ."

"I think you wanted him to like you more than you wanted to stand up for me."

"No." Aida shakes her head. "It was just a thing that happened. I didn't plan it." Her hip juts, folded arms tighten as Owl says nothing. "What about you? You freaked so bad about Cody I figured it had to be true." Waits. "Well? Was I wrong?"

Owl gives a barely perceptible shake of her head.

"Knew it." Glances away, savoring a grim gratification before fixing her scrutiny back on Owl. "So . . . what's that mean? Does he know?" Stare intensifies as Owl nods. "You guys are, like, together now?"

Owl takes a quick assessment of Aida's expression, pained as she realizes only now how badly she wants Aida to be happy for her—to gush, ask a million questions. The way it should have been at the start.

"Oh my god." Still a certain hardness beneath the surface, keeping Owl from showing too much herself. "Like, out in the open? And Seth and Holly are okay with it?"

"Kind of. I don't need everybody in the world knowing, but . . ." Owl shrugs, reaches for her phone, an itching compulsion making her open her camera roll, holding up proof, the pic she'd taken of Cody on the train, the look on his face undeniable as a written confession, still covered in the black-and-white filter.

Aida looks for a long moment. "Wow." Watches as Owl puts her phone away and takes a few steps on their usual route, then falls in with her, close enough to ensure Owl hears, but no arms linked. "What have you guys done?" Her meaning obvious. "So far."

Owl looks over sharply, then stares at the asphalt, focusing on walking, on forcing things back to normal, even if they don't feel it. Not yet.

FIRST THING OWL notices in the sugarhouse that afternoon is the cot, stacked with fresh sheets and folded wool blankets again. Ready for him.

The sight has a soft impact on her whole body, like a tingling collision with a bank of fresh powder, and she turns to Cody before she can think. Seth's right there, talking to him by the evaporator—something about temp, Seth gesturing in the flow direction of the pans. Doesn't seem like Holly could've told Seth about their conversation on the deck after Owl got back from the Notch; Owl would sense something, a shift in him, some discomfort, if he knew, unlike Cody's flawless poker face, as if she hasn't come into the sugarhouse at all.

She goes outside, beating him to the driver's seat of the side-by-side, taking off as soon as he's seated beside her, two near strangers waiting for the farm to be out of sight.

THEY VISIT THE fox den later, Cody coming during his smoke break while Seth watches the evaporator, dusk falling around them as Cody fits himself into the blind beside her.

"How's my picture coming?" Tips down the spiral binding of her notepad maybe a millimeter before she snaps it back up, and he smiles, shaking his head. "That good, huh?"

"You really think it's page after page of you?"

"'Course. Rats aren't coming out. Nothing else worth drawing."

"Well, I just saw one. And the vixen." Holds up her phone, can't keep the smile out of her voice. "One kit keeps sneaking out on her own, and the mom comes after her, drags her back in."

"How do you know it's a girl?"

"I don't, for sure. I just think it might be." Looks over as his hand finds hers, tip of his thumb following the shape of her bones, exposed in her fingerless gloves. She pulls free to cover his mouth with her hand as some dirt trickling down from the opening of the den catches her eye.

The kit tumbles out, losing traction halfway and sliding sideways to the snow, a scrabble of paws as she rights herself and heads up the slope toward the bushes, unsteady on new legs. As they watch, the vixen follows—Owl feels Cody start slightly at the speed and size of her, emerging from a hole in the ground with a mother's panic, catching the kit in a second, again by its

224

scruff, and trotting back. The kit dangles without resistance, blue eyes preternaturally bright, passing over the blind. Then back inside, another trickle of dirt marks their passage.

When they've waited long enough that it seems like the foxes won't be coming back out anytime soon, Owl lowers her hand from Cody's mouth. "Still think they're rats?"

He keeps looking. "I want one."

She ducks her head, silent laughter. "I don't think they make great pets."

"They'd get used to me after a while. One of those babies could live in my pocket."

"Babies grow up."

"Whatever. I'd be an awesome fox dad. I'd give them treats and stuff, and they'd love me."

"You're going to keep bugs and dead mice in your pockets? Because that's what they eat."

"What the hell—why do you have to piss on my dreams? I just want to walk around in a coat full of fox puppies, okay?" Owl laughs harder, and he pretends to tackle her. The two of them ending up rocking back in an embrace, nearly nose to nose, Owl kissing his smile before she can worry what might happen if Seth chose this time to come up the path. As Cody starts to get to his feet, he says, "I'm staying tonight."

"I'll be out." Doesn't want to let go of his hand as he steps away. "Late."


GLASS MAPLE-LEAF BOTTLES rest on their sides along the sugar-kitchen countertops, amber liquid drained of its glow in the dark room, firelight flickering through the partially ajar doorway.

It's approaching one a.m. Together, they're a dark mound in the cot, some clothing discarded onto the floor.

It's colder tonight, but the blankets form a cave roof above them, pulled high to trap their mingled body heat, Cody on top, still in his T-shirt, though he coaxed hers over her head a few seconds ago, Owl helping, glad to be rid of another barrier between them, their solar plexuses taut against each other, rising in tandem. She's aware of his fingers sliding beneath the straps of her gray sports bra as he kisses her throat, her collarbone, as she works his shirt up, just knowing she wants to be skin to skin, wants to follow wherever he's leading.

No plan on her part, no calculated dividing of territories, how much she'll surrender. The stopping place comes to her as naturally as the start: a tightening in her gut, a sense of the ground falling away when she realizes her jeans are open, his kisses are on her stomach, and, in a rush, she needs to feel solidness beneath her, some control.

She rolls to the side, fist beneath her chin. Straddling her, he watches a second, then drops onto his back beside her, one arm behind his head, looking at the shadowed eaves, the ductwork of the exhaust system leading upward to the cupola.

She feels the need to speak first. "I'm not . . . on anything." When he doesn't answer: "I've never been to a doctor to get on the pill, I mean."

"Didn't think you had." His voice is hoarse, unreadable, and she turns her head to look at him, wondering if he'll expand upon that at all. "It's good, probably." Gaze still following that pipeline to the stars. "You know when to slow down."

Doesn't feel like much of a feather in her cap, over here cooling and half-clothed, compared to the hot surge of moments ago: all too easy not to think, to let her animal self cleave to the current.

He rolls onto his side to face her, resting his hand on the dip of her waist, firm pressure. "Season's almost over. Seth said."

She nods, wondering if this is the opening of a discussion she isn't ready to have. Thinks again of the message previews on his phone. "Your mom will be glad you're back." Testing.

Silence. "I don't live with my mom." Tone near disgust, he jackknifes into a sitting position so quickly it startles her, makes her prop herself up on her elbow, watchful now. "I moved out as soon as I turned eighteen. Nothing the state could say then."

Shrugs, touch of defensiveness. "I wasn't sure. Where do you live, then?"

"Got a place. Had a place. With a couple buddies of mine." Shakes his head. "I told you. After this, I'm gone." After this—as in the farm, the season, and them, together in this bed. Glances over, eyes heavy-lidded, trace of insolence on his lips, taking her in: bare shoulders, pale hair a snarl against the pillowcase, blanket falling almost exactly where he last kissed. "Does that bother you?"

Emotions a tight coil, making her frown, consider, prop her head on her hand. "I don't know. This is where I should be. My home."

"How do you know?" No sarcasm now. "You haven't been anywhere. Just your dad's and here. How can you know this is the right place? Maybe it's the only time you haven't been treated like crap, gotten your ass kicked."

"No. It's more. I can't explain it. I just feel it." A fleeting nakedness in his eyes before he faces away, firelight casting his flank in a warm gleam, muscle molded beneath flesh, flesh stretched over ribs. She sits up straighter. "Give me your number. Then it won't matter where you go. We can always text." Waits without breathing.

He gets off the cot, circles to where their clothes lie together. "Can't. Broke my phone."

"Let me see. Maybe we can fix it."

"Yeah, no. Screen's smashed." Pops his head through the collar of his T-shirt, shrugging into his flannel. "I trashed it. Like, a while ago."

And now she's certain of what she saw, the flash of the phone dropping down into the basin, no way to call him on his lie without admitting that she searched his pockets. Looks at him levelly as she rests back, gaze straying to the row of empty glass syrup bottles lined up on the windowsill, various sizes and shapes they've offered over the years. "Have you ever even had any?" Thinks out loud, sees him glance over. "Our syrup."

"No."

She pushes the covers back, climbing out. "You're making it. You have to at least try some."

She goes into the sugar kitchen, switching on the bulb over the stove range, pulling a stainless-steel pot from a cabinet, a candy thermometer from the drawer. At the shelves, where last season's leftover stock is stored, she chooses one of the souvenir-sized maple-leaf bottles. Empties it into the pot and puts it on the heat, waiting until small bubbles become boiling white foam. Checks the thermometer, waiting until the temperature hits 235 degrees.

Turning the heat off, she grabs a shallow pan and goes through the main room. "Give me your shirt."

He pulls his flannel off and tosses it to her—she could've grabbed her own hoodie, but she's coveted this—and she wraps herself in it, the fabric smelling strongly of smoke, both maple and cigarette, boy deodorant, that one-note soap. She opens the door a short way, making sure the cabin is still dark before stepping outside and kicking at the snow alongside the foundation until the crust breaks open and she can get at the looser powder beneath, packing a few inches into the bottom of the pan before slipping inside.

Cody follows her into the kitchen, leaning against the plywood center table to watch as she uses a spoon to drizzle lines of hot syrup over the snow, where it solidifies instantly, becoming shiny and smooth. Owl wraps a strip around the spoon, hands it to him. "Tire sur la neige. Sugar on snow?"

"Okay." He looks at it.

"You eat it. Like taffy." Holds it out farther until he takes it; he gives it another hard look, then takes a quick bite, and she lets him consider while she scoops up a strip of her own and eats it with her fingers. Checks back, and sees he's devoured the rest of it. "Doesn't taste like the fake maple they sell. Part of it's boiling with wood fire, instead of gas. The smoke adds to the flavor."

He takes another strip—eats it whole—then another, leaving the snow clean, and tosses the spoon into the pan, resting his elbows on the tabletop. "We make good syrup."

First time she's ever heard him take ownership of any of it, including himself in the process from tree to table, and she smiles a little. "Now you know."

# 22

Owl sleeps for three hours, hard and dreamless, after their hands had fallen away from each other and their bodies spooned together, her forehead pressed against his bare back, drifting off to the rise and fall of his breathing. Her internal clock wakes her roughly an hour before she'd get up for school on a weekday, so she doesn't hurry, pulling on her jeans, stepping out into the dusky light of the yard, noticing a bare patch of dead grass for the first time, at the center of the drive, where the sun falls hard at midday.

Walks up the cabin steps, pressing the door gently shut behind her, depositing her boots on the rack before heading for the stairs, mind registering the smell in the kitchen a half second too late to warn her: brewing coffee.

"Owl."

She stops. Judging by the force in Seth's voice, he's already said it at least twice, from too far down the hallway for her to hear, a mistake he never makes.

She watches as he comes into the living room, cane in hand, dressed in jeans and zip-front sweatshirt, sleeplessness written in the lines of his face, sockets of his eyes, unshaven jaw. Takes her in with a sort of stunned consternation as she stands there, caught in her stocking feet, Cody's flannel bagging down to midthigh.

"What's going on?" Crosses the rug, stopping at his chair. "What were you doing outside?"

Again, obvious time to lie, to say *Visiting the foxes* or *Snowshoeing*. But Cody's shirt, right here in front of him, impossible to miss; and her hair, loose, unbrushed, like she never wears it—all of which he's staring at with increasing understanding, emotion traveling the range of his face. Her mouth tries to form any word, any way out, but excuses leave her and she simply stares back.

"What is this?" Tosses his hand out, as if to jerk the flannel between thumb and forefinger. "This his?"

Holly comes out of the bedroom, tugging her robe on, expression watchful as she walks up behind Seth.

"I couldn't sleep," Seth says without turning. "Heard her coming inside." His gaze doesn't leave Owl. "She was out in the sugarhouse."

Holly shakes her head. "You spent the night out there?"

Owl looks between them. No safe haven. "Yes."

She watches the news crest, break over them, Holly's eyes wide, turning to Seth, who's gone still, tense, knuckles white around the cane head. Someone needs to speak—pressure builds as the pause drags on—but Owl's answered, doesn't know what could come next but apologies, and something in her pushes back against that, full-force.

Seth starts for the front door, Holly saying, "Wait—"

"You don't need to." Owl's tone is barely controlled, heart rate picking up, as she follows him outside, down the steps.

Seth doesn't look back, stopping only when the sugarhouse door opens. Cody watches them, zipping his coat to the top as he gazes at Seth expressionlessly, unsurprised, eyes slightly swollen from sleep.

Owl stops where she stands, raising her voice to Seth: "Don't talk to him about it. Talk to *me*."

Seth jerks around to Owl, their gaze locking in an interminable moment. Then he says to Cody, "Get back to Wallace's," his voice low, flat.

A pause, then Cody straightens from the doorframe, eyes traveling over the two of them impassively before he steps inside, never speaking.

Owl watches as Seth walks past her, and she follows him into the cabin, where Holly leans against the counter, arms tightly folded.

Owl stops at the table, throwing her hands down, part disgusted, part despairing, as she watches him. "Are you going to talk?"

Seth stops, head low, close to the shoulder, jaw working; looks at her. "Can't believe you'd do this."

"Do what?" She signs as well, dashing her right forefinger down her left palm, exasperation, hands sinking at Seth's withering expression, one he's never pinned on her. "Which part?"

"Jesus, Owl! Come on! You're not stupid. Though you got me wondering, pulling this crap."

Holly's trapped midpoint between them, choosing to talk to Owl first, deliberately pitching her voice down when she says, "You never said it was like this." She casts a sidelong, entreating look at Seth, who's angled himself unsteadily to stare at her. "Owl, go up to the loft."

"You knew about this?" His voice unbelieving.

"I knew something, yeah. Not this." Sees her niece not moving, says sharply, "Go to your room. I need to think." Turns her back on them as she bangs the kettle down on the burner.

Owl wavers, speechless—has only been sent to her room here maybe twice, ever—but goes up the stairs—will not run—stiff and powerless. Once she's in this soundless space, whatever they say next will be lost to her, and they damn well know it, too.

She jerks the curtains shut behind her—deprived of even a door to slam—then sits on the bed, one leg bent beneath her, squeezing her pillow before punching it down, wondering how far Cody is along the frozen roadside now, if he's feeling at all like this—snared, dragged to the ground.

Shoves the pillow aside, grabs her drawing supplies and tosses them onto the bed, flips to a blank page. Opens her camera roll and starts sketching hard, none of the usual care taken in shading and detail, forming something entirely from broad strokes and remorseless lines.

• • •

IT'S NEARLY NOON when Holly finds Owl lying on her bed, doing homework. Holly nods toward downstairs, and they go together, Owl catching a flash of motion as the front door shuts the moment that her vision clears the slant of the eaves. Seth, going out.

Holly pats the table, where she's made Owl a sandwich; she stands at the sink for a minute, washing the few lunch dishes left behind by herself and Seth, giving Owl a chance to tuck into her food after going all morning without breakfast.

Holly folds a careful line in the dishcloth, drapes it over the neck of the faucet; then she turns, gazing at Owl, who hasn't looked away from her aunt's back the whole time, toying with her empty glass.

"I didn't realize. When I asked if you liked him and you said yes, it just didn't occur to me . . . I had no idea this was a mutual thing. That you two were . . ." Shakes her head, still seeming dazed. "It was the first crush you've ever told me about. I guess I didn't think things would move this fast."

"Why is everyone so surprised?" At Holly's questioning look: "That he likes me back."

"Who else have you told?"

"Just Aida."

Holly sighs, rubs her forehead. "It's not that I don't want you to have crushes or . . . date, but I wish you'd done this differently. Sneaking out? That's not you."

Owl shakes her head slowly, sifting through thoughts, motivations. "I wanted to be with him. You wouldn't have said yes."

Holly stares, lets out a short laugh. "Well, you're being honest, I'll give you that." Joins her at the table, gathering her cardigan over her front, a pained crease across her forehead. "Did you use protection?"

"We didn't do it."

"Owl."

"It's true. We slept together. It was sleep." Gazes straight back at Holly's doubtful look. "We kissed and stuff, but we didn't . . ." Uses a shake of her head to brush off the rest, trying not to think of the early hours of morning, after she'd dumped the snow into the sink to melt and they'd returned to the bed, how the sports-bra barrier had seemed to cease mattering, how it had eventually joined her shirt in the pile on the floor. Another first. "We weren't trying to hurt anybody. It wasn't about anybody else. It was about us." Looks toward the door, where she last saw Seth vanish.

Holly doesn't speak, gazing at Owl as if seeing someone else sitting there, vaguely familiar, half forgotten; then she leans back, legs stretched to brace her bare feet against the bottom rung of the opposite chair, looking out the window at the pale-gray sky for so long that Owl wonders if she's free to go. "I do get it, you know." Expression mild. "My parents never wanted me to be with Seth. They always made it about them, not us."

Owl sits slowly forward, hopeful relief at being pulled closer, ready for another scrap of Holly's life that came before. "Why didn't they like him?"

"Lots of reasons. White. Army. Not an Indian's best friend, historically speaking, you know?" Wry smile, gone in an instant. "They wanted me to marry within the tribe, like my sisters did. Even had a guy they kept pushing me toward, son of a friend." Glances at Owl. "No interest, of course." Owl smiles hesitantly, waiting. "When I started college, I was still living with them on the res, waitressing double shifts, doing classes part-time. That's when I met Seth. I put off bringing him home, and when I finally did . . . it went as badly as I was scared it would. Mom just won't—" Seals the words with a shake of her head. "She never gave her blessing. Wouldn't witness our vows, none of it. We had a fight. And that was the end of Mom and me." Silence. "I was so sick of them not respecting my choices. But my sisters can do no wrong, you know? Because they keep Mom happy, popped out those grandbabies. They all still live a couple streets away from each other, you know. My kid sister, Lottie, messages me sometimes. Says it's nice. Always sends me online invites to family things. My grandmother's ninety-fifth birthday party, last year. As if Mom's going to just welcome us through the door." Holly shrugs. "My parents said I was going to lose myself, get whitewashed. Forget who I am, where I came from. I gave up my friends on the res, left school to move out here. So maybe they were right."

Owl looks at her hands, damning white, like the rest of her. Her and Seth. Thinks of everything Holly put aside to be here for them. "Do they know about . . . ?"

"About you?" Nods slowly. "They know. I told them, years back. It was the only time I ever tried . . ." Shuts her eyes, weathering the memory, until the smile returns, tinged with irony. "Lost cause."

They sit with the finality, then Owl stands. "I should go check the trees."

"No." Holly stops, tries to soften her tone. "Let Seth do it today."

"But he can't—"

"I know. But he needs some time. Okay?"

Owl looks down, tugging at a fray in the cuff of her hoodie sleeve. "What's he going to do about Cody?"

"Not sure. But like you said, for us, this is much more about you than Cody. You went around us, hon." Holds up one finger when Owl starts to protest. "Seth's taking it hard. You don't need me to spell out what you two have. You broke his trust." Holly's eyes dark, solemn in a way they seldom are. "It's not going to be an easy fix."

# 23

Houlihan's signs are off, one a.m. last call made. Declan says the usual—*Don't have to go home, but you can't stay here*—regulars not sparing him much of a laugh. Dec's just the weekend guy and they don't owe him no favors; not like Les Houlihan, who's been wiping down this bar since Dec was in diapers and probably saved half the guys in the place from putting their head through a windshield driving home wasted one time or another. Saint Les of Assisi. Light a fucking candle.

Dec fumbles his keys out of his pocket, in the usual hurry to shut out the sight of cloudy shot glasses and even foggier faces looking at him from the leatherette stools, glancing over his shoulder at the scrape of a shoe over pavement.

There's only a solitary gooseneck light over the rear entrance, to cast a glow in the tiny employee parking lot, but it's not unheard of for some of the customers to hang around outside in the cold, have a smoke the wife won't put up with back at the house.

One silhouette is outlined in the dank, mold-smelling space between the bar and the storage shed, where they keep stock. Head oddly smooth and cocked in examination, black hole for a face.

"Who's that?" Dec straightens beside his Impala, voice deepening, roughening, to cover for the shot of ice sent through him at the sight of the guy.

He sidles out, the fucking ginger from earlier, hood up over his head; lambskin leather jacket must've set him back a good five grand. Should've traded skin with the lamb—something wrong with the guy, sick or something, stripped down to nothing but bone and sinew and a sandblasting of faded freckles, which look to continue below his collar, cover him, animal's markings. "Sure you can't help me out?" Tortured, rusty-thin nicotine voice; gonna be talking out of one of those boxes in the windpipe before much longer.

Dec goes back to digging for his keys, fighting hard not to look like he's hurrying. "Told you, man. I never seen a guy like that."

"Yeah?" The ginger comes around the tailgate, hands in his pockets, takes a few wide steps to stop beside Dec. "'Cause I got to talking to some of the hicks in there, an-n-nd a couple of them claim they've seen you serving him before. Like recent." Cocks his head to the other side, mouth in a line, brows raised, then leans forward on the balls of his feet. "We're talking just over the past few weeks he would've been around. Make it worth your while if you can tell me where to find him."

240

"Can't help you." Not grassing anybody up to this guy, and sure as hell don't need it getting around that Houlihan's has been lobbing beers to a kid with no ID. He doesn't care if Wall's grandson is underage; probably is, even with all his swearing up and down that he's twenty-one. Been nice having anybody younger-looking than Dec in the place, gave the customers somebody else to rag on.

"See, I think it's more that you don't want to." Leaning, in Dec's space, a sour, thirsty smell lurking beneath cologne, his eyes bloodshot, and this isn't right, the whole thing, Dec's instincts saying, *Get out.* "What's the matter? You don't like me or something?"

"Too cold for this—'night." Dec double-clicks his electronic key fob, jerks the driver's-side door open, already seeing himself peeling out of here, taking off down the sleeping street.

"Hey, wait. Buddy?"

Dec glances as he turns, and something explodes between them, a flash of light, a muffled pop, like the Black Cat firecrackers Dec and his buddies used to drop off overpasses in high school, then run like hell. And that's his last thought—*Black Cat*—as the side of his ass grazes the seat and he falls to the ground hard, a hole torn through his side into his heart.

The ginger lets him lie there and bleed for a moment, studying him. Rests his boot on Dec's outstretched hand, pressing down, waiting for a response. Stands on his fingers. "Didn't like you, either."

# Part IV

## MAPLE SYRUP GRADE:
## Very Dark

*Darkest shades from end-of-season runs;*
*most intense flavor.*
*Not to be brought to the table.*

# 24

Composite toe. Waterproof coating. Foam-cushioned insole.

Sunday, Owl sorts boots, a pile of empty shoeboxes and crumpled tissue on the bench behind her. A relief to be at Van's after being shunned from sugaring yesterday; Seth stayed away until late, maybe working, mostly avoiding her. He'd eaten breakfast and was out in the sugarhouse again this morning before Owl came downstairs, stretching the silence, the dread, the waiting. She wonders if Cody will even show up for work today, what will happen if he does, wishing she could just text him and ask how he is.

Holly tags a pile of camo hip waders and jackets behind the counter, glancing over with a greeting as customers come in, all of them shaking off a spitting, offended sort of rain. The bear bench stands empty, seat worn to a shiny concave. No Aida.

Owl pulls out her phone, bites her lip, types: *Are you coming?*

Doesn't press SEND for another couple moments, holding out, even though they're supposed to have made up. It sits uneasily, the whole conversation around the flagpole, that sense of a lingering barrier between them: showing Aida the pic of Cody, which should've stayed private, answering her question in some detail—*What have you guys done? So far*—maybe not because it felt right but because she felt like she had something to prove. Especially to Aida, queen of online hookups, scandalous chains of ones and zeros, all amounting to nothing Owl can see, not even the electricity of one single physical touch.

Hesitates. Hits SEND anyway. Pockets the phone.

Minutes pass. Knows that with Aida's signal booster at home, there's no chance her friend isn't using her phone right this second.

Approaching a full five minutes later—a response: *Mom said no. Sorry.*

Line appears between Owl's brows. Texts: ?

*Who knows—pissy again.*

Owl rests on her heels, double-taps Aida's response to leave a thumbs-up, then puts the phone away, uncertain if she's disappointed or not. Never known Trini not to do her big shop on Sunday, but Owl isn't sure she wants Aida to know everything that's happened—getting caught sneaking in, Seth so angry he doesn't even want to look at her; it all feels too raw, newly humiliating out here in public, like she's wearing a sandwich board printed in bold: CAUGHT WITH A BOY. NOBODY THOUGHT I HAD IT IN ME. Then she remembers Holly's words—*broke his trust*—and resentfulness dies in its tracks.

Trash next, hefting huge bags of packing materials—Styrofoam peanuts amounting to almost no weight at all—stacked by the loading dock doors. Owl slings one bag over each shoulder and carries them outside without bothering to grab her coat.

Raindrops patter on her face as she crosses the lot toward the dumpsters, in full view of the street, as a few vehicles pass by, mostly people on their way to the weekly ritual of an early lunch at the diner after church.

A PLATINUM-COLORED SUV, moving a bit below the speed limit, brakes when the driver notices her from the corner of his eye—nothing but a little stock girl in a green company shirt, made gnomelike by the bags she's lugging. The red-haired man continues scanning the dead street, seeking—bass pounding the trapped air of the cab, brain ticking away like a beetle under glass—barely sparing a glance to the bar where, in the rear parking lot, a bloodstain has all but washed away.

HOLLY'S LAND ROVER crawls to a stop by the cabin. Owl's out of the car first, bundled in her Carhartt, feet rapidly scaling the steps to the deck.

Cody watches, framed in the dimness of the rain-dotted sugarhouse window, pans seething steam behind him, the sweetness and moisture leaving its usual dewy condensation on his skin.

Seth's at his shoulder; didn't notice him crossing the room from the kitchen, where the older man has spent their morning of work—mutual silence, neither of them acknowledging the other—taking in Cody's view of Owl piling firewood in her arms, crouching low to pull stove lengths from a depleted stack, braids trailing down from beneath her cap.

"You hurt her, she'll be the last person you ever hurt." Seth's tone is measured, his attention never wavering from Owl, who now goes into the cabin door, held open by Holly. "Guessing you probably know that." Nods to himself. "Maybe that's even why you did it."

Cody won't react, squinting against nearsightedness and gray daylight, at a deck where there's no one left to look at.

"Long as we understand each other." Seth returns to the kitchen, accompanied by the hollow placement of the cane, a steady metronome.


THE NEXT MORNING, Monday, they're waiting for her in the kitchen, Seth and Holly, marking the first time Seth has shared the table with Owl since Saturday. A ghost of her uncle, taking his suppers in the sugarhouse, barely glimpsed disappearing around the corners of outbuildings, returning to the trees.

She stops at the sight of him, staring, debating how much hurt she'll allow to seep through into her words. "You're going to sit with me?"

He nods once. "Grab yourself something to eat while we talk. Mrs. Baptiste's going to be here in a couple minutes."

Instant oatmeal she doesn't want, cinnamon-apple scent wafting up as she sets the bowl in front of her, a prop—anything to get this started, whatever words he hasn't been able to bring himself to say to her for nearly three days.

But Holly begins. "You can go back to helping with the sugaring." Watches Owl straighten in her seat. "But we need to know we can trust you."

Owl rushes to answer, a hurried glance between them, but Seth cuts her off with an air of getting this off his chest: "I never worried." Shakes his head. "Never once, about letting you two work together. Didn't even occur to me that you'd . . . Then, finding out like that?"

He looks straight at her, and Owl wonders if maybe she didn't have it easier when he was avoiding her; that look, somehow holding in it everything they are to each other—every undeniable truth of the three of them, how they've chosen each other in spite of the odds—finally crushes her little ramrod ego, whose best defense has never gone any deeper than *But I wanted to.*

"We need the help with the end of harvest, so he stays. Wouldn't make sense trying to train somebody new at this point. And something tells me I wouldn't have a lot of luck trying to keep you two away from each other anyway, huh?"

Holly cuts in: "We want to believe that your word is still good, where Cody is concerned." Looks at Seth, so much of this obviously discussed behind their closed bedroom door at night.

Owl's look darkens. "It is."

"Then promise me that we don't have to worry about you sneaking around or keeping things from us ever again. We're not going to try to stop you from seeing each other. Just . . . have it be out in the open."

"Okay." Waits, realizes they're waiting for her to say the word. "Promise."

OWL ISN'T SURE what to expect at tap check that afternoon—if Seth might ride along with them to the sugarbush, chaperoning, a humiliation so unbearable that she doesn't allow herself to consider it in detail. Limbs loosen with relief when he stays a short distance away, pottering in the shed, making his presence known but saying nothing as she and Cody leave in the side-by-side.

Cody's laughing as he shuts off the engine, not noticing her distraction. "When's he gonna cap my ass?" When she doesn't respond, he's quiet a second. "Figured he'd be waiting for me with a shotgun yesterday."

"Then why come back?" Looks over at him, brows raised, not sure who her tartness is aimed at; him, for being unreachable while she dealt with the aftermath of their night together, or herself, for going about everything so wrong, tarnishing her word with people who, more than anyone, deserved better.

"Wanted to see you." Pauses. "Is that stupid?"

"No." Can't help a faint, disbelieving laugh. "I want that."

"Was it bad? Did they give you a lot of shit?"

Owl shakes her head. "I think I hurt them. Scared them. I said I wouldn't do it again."

No more talk as they walk together into the trees, Owl stopping as Cody's hands find her hips, turn her toward him, bodies pressing together.

"We shouldn't." Lays her hand flat against his chest, wanting to feel the beat there, if only briefly. "He knows how long it takes to check the taps."

"Never worried about it before."

"Now he knows about us. It's different." A second of self-loathing, talking about Seth like that, an adversary, pitted against the survival of "us." "They didn't say I couldn't see you."

He moves back a little. "Just not in a way that's worth anything, right?" He gazes at her bare, questioning look, steps away as if to head into the trees. Then: "I can show you something."

She shakes her head. "What?"

"It's a walk."

Tries to tell if he's teasing her. "We have to check the trees."

Flash of a smile as he heads toward the side-by-side. "So work fast."

THIS TIME, HE leads the way through the trees, heading east of the farm at a steady rate, like he really has a destination in mind; without snowshoes, certain places are hard going, Owl grabbing low branches or bracing herself against tree trunks to keep from losing her footing and spilling forward.

Can't think what they'd be going to see. How could he know something about her woods that she doesn't? When would he have had time to learn it? Maybe something to do with the foxes—like another den, some sign they've dug a second home. She glances back, thinking of the full horizontal tank of sap waiting on the trailer, and Seth at home, counting the minutes they've been gone, probably assuming they're hooking up somewhere, all over each other the moment they were out of sight.

About ten minutes later, he stops, slightly breathless, looking around at the treetops, circling around them, as if searching for something he recognizes. Owl waits, watches, ready to call him out at the first sign he's messing with her.

"Ha." Slaps his hand against a broad tree trunk, drags his palm down it as he starts forward, watching his feet—counting paces.

Owl goes to the tree, leaning close. An *X* is notched into the bark, showing the fresh green wood beneath, small enough that no one would notice it who wasn't looking. Sets her jaw, goes after him.

Cody finally stops, fifteen paces away, grabbing a low, thick branch, hefting his weight and bracing the toe of his right boot into the trunk long enough to reach higher, into gnarled branches, feeling for something. Owl's gaze travels up, sees a length of nylon cord, nearly invisible against the clotted snow, leading up, out of sight of the ground. Glances over, sees the light of a clearing coming through the trees. Knows this place; the fox den is just through there. Not far from where she found the cigarette butts in the snow.

He fumbles, curses. "Hand me your knife." Takes it from her, hacking through the line just above where it's tied, then lets go.

An object drops from the treetop; he'd anchored it over a high branch, using the cord like a pulley to raise it some twenty feet off the ground. It gets stuck just above them, and he grabs branches he can reach and shakes them, until the object falls into the snow at their feet.

It's covered in a couple of white trash bags, sealing out the wet. She watches as he unties them and peels them down, revealing a black backpack inside. It's the one he wore the first day she encountered him, on the access road—realizes she hasn't seen him with it since.

He unzips the front compartment, slides it down closer to her so she can look inside.

A gallon Ziploc bag full of money. Cash, twenties and fifties, bound with elastic bands, five wads in all. More than she's ever seen in one place at one time.

He opens the seal, angles it toward her. "You can touch it." Nods when she hesitates. "Go for it."

Owl picks up one stack, peeling the top layers back, not sure what to do with it. People talk about the scent of money; she puts her nose close. A musty, handled smell, passed around, belonging to everyone and no one. Wrinkles her nose and drops it back in the bag. "Why do you have it?"

"Because it's mine." Takes a couple stacks out, watching the bills cascade as he flips through. "A guy owed me, and now it's mine." Holds it out. "Have some. I don't care."

She's startled—instant discomfort; shakes her head.

"Whatevs. Do what you want." Puts it away. "Gotta have money, though. You want to run your own life, take care of yourself, got to have it. And more than you can make ringing up fucking groceries or cleaning toilets, like they want you to. Fuck being broke. I'm sick of it."

"How much is there?"

"Twelve K." At her stare. "Was more to start with, but . . . had some things to take care of. This is what's left."

"If it's yours . . . why are you hiding it out here?"

"Like I'm going to leave it in that RV with Wallace hanging around? That's where he's got me—sleeping in a camper. Don't need him up in my grille. Probably start charging me rent. Two K a week to live in his yard." Snorts laughter, zips up the backpack. "Safer out here. Know where it is, get to it easy." Sees her watching him. "I hid it here that first day, when nobody else was out here." She thinks of the Newports in the snow, the night Seth heard someone in the woods. Cody must've come back to check on the money.

He looks at her intently. "You can't tell anybody about this, okay?"

"But . . . if it's yours—"

"I earned it. That's all you gotta know. This is start-up money once I get where I'm going. Like, savings. I'm gonna be set. Not touching it until then."

"I thought you didn't know where you're headed."

"I don't. I'm talking about finding the place. Like you said." Rubs the back of his neck. "Where I should be, where it feels right." Compressed silence: "You could come."

Stares, thinking she misheard. Ventures, "Go with you?"

He stands immediately, crooked half smile. "Don't sound so excited." Pulls the trash bags over the backpack again, dragging the drawstrings tight.

Blindsided, she gets to her feet, buying time by brushing snow off her jeans before she speaks. "I just didn't expect it."

He slows a little. "We work pretty good together, right?" Gazes at his hands as he knots. "Feel like we get each other more than other people do. Figured . . . this much cash, I could take care of both of us. At least for a while." Grabs the cord and heaves it up at the branches, two tries before it snags up high enough to satisfy. "I know you like it here and all." Shrugs. "But there are other good places. Has to be. Then we won't have to say bye. Ever."

Owl folds her arms, waiting as he boosts himself up to tie the cord around a lower branch again, securing the bag out of sight. Drops to the ground again at a brisk walk, brushing close by, leaning down into her face with a grin: "Just fucking with you."

She watches him go, stymied, knowing better.

# 25

The morning is pure wind, Owl and Aida using the Suburban as a block, waiting as Griffin and Mrs. Baptiste help the little kids pack their project—a trifold poster pasted with images of the logging industry—into the back beside the model copper mine, a folded blanket keeping them from rattling together on the drive to Stokely.

Owl and Aida stand close but don't talk, Owl's view of the world limited to the gap between her hood hem and collar, which is pulled over her nose. A bit of the faded teal floss of Aida's hair flutters in her peripheral vision. Owl hopes a week or so will bind their broken bones together again, heal the last of this silence, Aida's small-smiling distracted aloofness that Owl can't quite put a name to. Knows what a relief it would be to tell Aida, someone, about yesterday, unburden herself, though Owl promised to keep quiet about the money. To tell Aida that he'd asked Owl to leave with him, words that woke a distracted, agitated spring fever in her, lying on her side staring at the darkness last night. Leaving the mountain. Leaving Seth and Holly. Leaving the trees. Unimaginable; yet he wants her, and the possibility is there, always has been, an open door waiting.

Micah has his hat pulled over his eyes, grinning, the Boulier sisters spinning him in circles, pushing him back and forth between them, laughing as he staggers away across the asphalt, faking drunken dizziness, until Mrs. Baptiste, driving and chaperoning today, calls him back, ushering all of them into the warmth of the cab. The other two Suburbans owned by the school are parked nearby, the rest of the kids getting in, voices raised in the excitement about any change of routine, the sound carrying across the desolated town to the border of woods beyond.

THE AUDITORIUM OF Stokely Area High School is cavernous, folding tables set up from end to end, kids grouped by grade setting up dioramas and poster-board displays, a stage along the back wall with purple velvet curtains with a banner strung across reading COÖS COUNTY FOUNDING DAY. There are events happening in the town center this afternoon—snow sculpting and sledding and food vendors—that the kids have been promised after teachers and parents have had a chance to tour the auditorium, and the projects have been graded.

The schoolhouse kids walk together, trailing Mr. Duquette and Mrs. Baptiste, staring around at all the unfamiliar faces, the entire building seeming labyrinthian, two stories with some portable classroom units outside, athletic fields surrounded by chain link spreading out beyond.

"Oh my god, two o'clock, two o'clock." Aida's back in form, surrounded by a feast of unknown boys, arm locked through Owl's, leaning in close to Owl's ear. Owl's relief is complete, grateful now to slide into her usual role, the part she thought she was sick of: Aida's appendage and sounding board. "Holy friggin' hotness."

"Where?"

"Right *there*."

A boy in a hoodie with a logo Owl doesn't recognize and expensive sneakers, looking like he spent an hour combing and pomading his hair into a molded sideswept style. "That's four o'clock."

"So I can't tell time, okay? *Ohmygod*." The boy is looking now; Aida covers her face, collapses into giggles against Owl's shoulder. Owl gazes back at the boy a moment, letting Aida hide against her, keeping her supported until her paroxysms pass. First time ever, experiencing a detachment, without embarrassment, judgment, even much interest. A sense of being older.


OWL'S THIN, DISTORTED reflection flickers across the hallway floor tiles beneath diffused lighting, locker sentries lining both walls, a hall-of-mirrors look, both infinite and depthless.

Ms. Z told her the classroom number—Special Education Resource Room 202, a hand-painted banner over the door made by students, couldn't miss it—so Owl takes the broad staircase up, glad for the hush, classrooms mostly empty, almost everyone down in the auditorium.

She sees the banner first: Some talented artist had formed calligraphy letters above the double doors. Advances slowly in the mode of a dreamer, all sensory input, no perception or identity. Doors with high panes of reinforced glass grant a view inside a large room flooded with light, walls covered in posters and charts and student artwork, round tables with chairs in the foreground, cluttered teacher desks arranged here and there.

It's no effort to spot them: Ms. Z sits with two students, a boy and a girl, at the far left table. Ms. Z is in the chair facing the doors, wearing a familiar dark floral blouse with a cranberry-colored cardigan over it. The kids are angled toward each other, the girl tall and lanky, hair close-cropped, wide-spaced eyes intensified by smoky makeup, the boy shorter and stocky, vivid grin adding expression to his signing.

They're all signing—one picking up right after the other, some game of intellectual toss, emotion glimmering from face to face, hand to hand, their comprehension that swift.

Owl moves closer to the glass, seeing Ms. Z laugh—a real laugh, transformative—at something the boy has said, the words lobbing past Owl so quickly she catches only a notion here or there—*maybe they won't, do you think, no way*—so disorienting that she shuts down the flow of information. Stops processing, jerks back the hand raised to the brass push plate.

Ms. Z catches movement from behind the glass—in time to see Owl's face pull back, expression remote, eyes already distanced in the second she turns away.

Ms. Z leans against the open door, watching Owl hurriedly descend the staircase; gestures, *Be right back*—forefinger to herself, away, then back—to the other kids.

MS. Z'S FOLLOWING, Owl knows it—could feel the vibration of her footsteps on the stairs far above—but Owl won't stop, her doomed flight reaching the first floor, a secretary jerking around in her seat behind the office window, maybe yelling at Owl to slow down, who knows. Can't go back to the auditorium—doesn't want Aida or Griffin seeing any obvious sign that she's melting down, near tears.

An exit looms; Owl hits the crash bar, swinging out into the shock of cold fresh air, which she sucks in, going stiff-kneed down a couple concrete steps to drop onto her butt on the bottommost, huddling against the short railing, knuckling away tears. A flickering thought of Cody: *What's he doing now?* Pictures his blurred outline backlit by the dim sweetness of the sugarhouse—wishing for his presence, somehow managing to ensure that she never feels alone on the fringes of things.

The door opens behind her, Ms. Z's oxfords stepping down into Owl's field of vision as she sits beside her. Owl keeps her gaze down, watching her teacher grip her knees, focusing on the soft woolen finish of Ms. Z's brown houndstooth slacks as the quiet stretches on.

"Why'd you run off?" Ms. Z speaks up, knowing Owl isn't watching her lips.

Owl doesn't say anything until she works down the tightness in her throat. "I don't belong in there. I'm not like them."

"In what way?"

"*Real Deaf.* I told you. I can't sign like that. You *know* I'm slow. Why'd you—" Bites off the rest of the sentence, needs another deep breath. "They'll think I'm an idiot."

"Ah. The root of the problem. Fear of looking stupid." Waits, stiff against the cold, until Owl raises a baleful look. "Can I ask why you have such a low opinion of the real Deaf kids? Jamique has partial hearing, too, by the way. Before you judge." Adjusts her grip on her knees. "I'll let that sink in."

Hesitates. "He's still better than me."

"Your words, not his. And Nia is one of the nicer human beings I've met. Not generally one to crush a person's soul upon introduction." Corner of her mouth moves as a slight smile passes over Owl's lips, fades. "What makes you assume they're going to hate you for not being like them?"

Plenty of feelings to support it, few words. "I don't know. I'm afraid they will."

Ms. Z stares at her, then looks off abruptly, a few rapid blinks. "Give them a chance. Let someone surprise you by being kinder than you expect. It happens. From time to time." Glances back at her. "Are you and your friend still fighting?"

"Not really."

"Good." Takes a breath. "I'm sorry I didn't answer your question the other day. I opened the lines of communication, then shut them down without an explanation. Not fair to you."

261

"It's okay—"

"No, you weren't wrong to ask. I meant it when I said I want us to talk to each other." Hugs herself, running her hands up her arms to warm them. "I have been in love. Just the once."

Owl looks over curiously. "What happened?"

"She married someone else." Ms. Z keeps her gaze on the distant street across the dead and windswept soccer fields, cars small, silent, moving at cross purposes. "Moved away. Then, so did I. Just . . . didn't seem much point in being anywhere anymore. Really haven't wanted to settle ever since."

"Oh." Owl rests her elbows on her thighs, processing this. "I'm sorry. That must've hurt."

Slight nod, acknowledging. "It was a few years back."

"You could've just told me."

Ms. Z studies her. "Lesson learned, Rochelle." Gets to her feet. "Ready to go upstairs now?"

Owl's chest feels tight, stomach clenched, but she manages a nod.

"Wonderful. This door locked behind us. We'll have to be buzzed in around front." Ms. Z goes lightly down the steps, pausing to make sure Owl's following.

After a fashion, she is.

LITTLE KIDS WILD on the ride back to North Plover, a roar of indistinguishable noise from the third row, Owl certain of nothing except the rhythm of Micah kicking the seat and a bunny-shaped pencil topper bouncing off her shoulder or head every thirty seconds, which she tosses back again and again.

Aida, rejuvenated by hours of boy watching, first from the project table while Griffin demonstrated the copper mine if someone asked, then during the festivities in the town center, looks at her phone as Mrs. Baptiste guides them through downtown Stokely, halting at a stop sign and saying something quickly that gets even Aida's attention. Owl didn't have a chance to read her lips, is left glancing around at everyone, wondering what's been decided. Expecting Aida might clue her in, but she's right back into her phone again.

Griffin looks at Owl around the side of his seat, earbud wires trailing down, and says, *Doughnuts.* She nods, relaxing.

They go through the Dunkin' Donuts drive-thru in the Shell station, but end up having to park anyway because the younger girls need to use the bathroom, Mrs. Baptiste going inside with them. The car quiet again, Owl pulls the lid off her takeout cup, blowing on her scalding mint hot chocolate, watching the street, her thoughts on what happened in the resource room after she trailed Ms. Z through those double doors into light and activity. The shock of Nia's directness, actually shaking Owl's hand like they were grown-ups; Nia was profoundly Deaf, and didn't speak vocally at all while Owl was there, signing with a purposeful care that Owl knew was for her benefit; Ms. Z must've given them a rundown of Owl's skill level before she came. Owl still fell behind and missed things—she'd never signed a conversation with more than one person before, volleying both ASL and visual contact from speaker to speaker, trying not to drop anything—but after a couple desperate looks at Ms. Z, Nia touched her arm, signing, *Sorry, I'll slow down,* and Owl smiled hesitantly, signed, *Thanks.*

Jamique paired vocalization with sign, just like Owl, asking what it was like to go to such a small school, sparking conversation as they gathered at the round table, Owl not realizing how much she'd settled back into her own skin until it was time to get downstairs with the rest of the schoolhouse kids again. She has Jamique's and Nia's numbers in her phone, made promises to text sometime, Owl still dazed that it happened at all and she was still here—like being hurled from a moving vehicle and standing to find all limbs attached, life more full of promise than it had been minutes before, now that you'd tasted fear and survived.

A black-and-white sheriff's office SUV passes on the street, lights flashing as it flies over the bridge. Micah pops his head between Aida and Owl. "Bus-ted." Grins, mouth ringed with powdered sugar.

Aida pulls a disgusted face. "Yeah, they're called napkins?" Rustles in her paper bag, holds one out. "They gave all of us like fifty."

Micah plucks it, daintily dabs the corners of his mouth— Owl fails at holding back a laugh—as a second patrol car follows the first.

"No sirens," Griffin says, setting his coffee into the cup holder.

Micah thumps forward against the seat. "What's that mean?"

"Not an emergency, I guess, but they still need people to get out of their way."

They see them again in St. Beatrice, along with two more cruisers, an ambulance, and an unmarked van, parked along the stream bank on the opposite side of the small bridge ahead.

Mrs. Baptiste slows, orange detour signs and sawhorses blocking the road home.

A deputy in a neon jacket waves them to the left, pointing to the arrows to the alternate route.

Mrs. Baptiste lifts a hand to him, glancing toward the water as they turn. "Somebody go off the road?" Then, just as quickly, back at the kids, "Don't look."

But they all do, Micah as close to the glass as his seat belt will allow, peering twenty-five feet down at the jigsaw-patterned ice and open water mottling the surface, three more uniformed officers standing together, talking, shoulders huddled against the wind.

# 26

"Heard anything from your dad?"

Later in the afternoon, Cody pulls the skimmer through the boiling sap, snagging some dark bits of leaf or bark from the foam. Owl bends deeply into the storage tank, scrubbing the inner walls, Seth inside the cabin, trusting them with some distance.

"He called here. Seth hung up on him."

Cody taps the steel mesh against the edge of the trash can. "What do you think he wants to say to you so bad?"

Shakes her head, rolling a small screwdriver from the set on the wall back and forth between her hands. "Hurt me back, maybe. Tell me how much he hates me. How I ruined his life."

"Nah. Trust me, rehabbed types are all about forgiveness. It's the last head game they play with you before they cash in their 'fresh start,' you know? You're supposed to say you're okay with the fact they screwed you over, so they can stop feeling guilty. They're counting on that little part of you that doesn't hate them all the way yet."

"Is that what your mom did?" Watching him closely.

Glances back, going to the evaporator again, checking how much syrup has drained down to the draw-off. "You know, not every foster home I got put in sucked. Last one was all right. Janet. She was the mom there." Silence. "She only had three kids staying with her, counting me. I was the oldest, got my own room. Hoop on the garage. Nobody tried being my best friend or anything." Shakes his head slowly. "Then my case-worker comes around, telling me that my mom's out of jail and rehab and wants me back. That we're going to work toward reunification—that's what they call it. Again. Starts with visitations. Mom crying and hugging me and telling me she's got a new job and she's saving toward moving us to a better neighborhood, where it'll be easier for her to stay away from her dealers and loser friends. But she had to hear I forgave her—'You hate me?' she kept saying. And I told her no. Because she's my mom, right? And she's a fuckup. That's who she is." Opens the arch door, puts on the firing gloves to add more wood. "I think about Janet's sometimes—if I'd stayed there. If I put up a big enough fight, they probably would've let me. Shooting hoops after supper with the sun going down. Everybody leaving me the hell alone. Think maybe I could've been okay."

Owl stares at him; he's suddenly totally motionless, none of the restless sharp body language that defines him. "You are okay."

A flicker of a smile—strained, patronizing—there, and then gone, leaves her feeling like some spectator, rows and rows back from him and his life. "Guess I'm saying that sometimes holding on to somebody can be the asshole thing to do." Turns to her the rest of the way. "Think he'd ever come here? Try to see you?"

"No." So quickly she hears her own defensiveness. "He wouldn't dare. Seth would kill him."

"Bet you thought he'd never write or call, either." Looks at her standing there. "Just saying. Might be good to figure out what he wants. Doesn't seem like he's going to give up easy. Even if you hate him, you're still his kid."

"No, I'm not."

Gives her a long knowing look that makes an aggravated flush spread over her neck and cheeks. He comes to her, closest they've been since they last spent the night together. Slides his arms around her waist, hands into her back pockets, getting a grip on her, and she leans into him, shutting her eyes at the reward of touching him again after days of forced distance. "Can't believe he's trusted me out here with you this long." Cody's voice is low, filled with barely contained laughter.

"He's trusting me. They know I snuck out because I wanted to." She presses her forehead into his sternum another long second, then steps back. "We shouldn't get caught again."

Cody watches her, lashes lowered. "Am I really going to have to say goodbye to you in a week?" Voice soft, musing.

Owl gazes at him, the money and the backhanded invitation flickering between them, a sole flame.

Cody glances toward the window then, obviously hearing something; Owl looks, sees Seth coming down the cabin steps, his gaze on the sugarhouse.

They step back. By the time Seth comes in, they're in separate rooms—Cody boiling, Owl bottling—oceans apart.


EARLY EVENING, SUPPER dishes just washed and put away, the three of them in their separate corners, Owl up in the loft, Holly using her laptop on the couch, Seth out in the sugarhouse, the logjam between them still there, not broken by Seth finally speaking to her, merely moved aside so it won't block the flow of the day, of necessity.

Owl looks up from her homework, unable to focus, head a whirl of images: the dual currents of her conversation with Nia and Jamique, lips and hands, Cody's words from earlier— *Might be good to figure out what he wants. Doesn't seem like he's going to give up easy*—scrutinizing the bureau, the letter stashed inside. Goes to it, opens the drawer, looking down into the space as if at a dead mouse responsible for a bad smell.

Smooths out the balled envelope, picturing her dad's hands—create, destroy—bent to give his rage form, articulation. *These are all the ways you ruined my life.* Pressing hard to keep the page steady as he bore down. *Coming for you, Ro.*

269

Sharp intake of breath; stuffs the envelope in her back pocket, dropping the hem of her hoodie over it, then goes downstairs, stopping in front of Holly.

Owl takes a second, gathering herself. "Can I go see Cody? Just for a little while."

"I thought he was done for the day."

"He is."

Holly looks toward the windows, where most of the light has faded from the sky. "Wait until tomorrow, okay?"

"I need to go now." Before the impulse passes and she stuffs that letter into the darkness again. A shifting need so urgent it's bodily, a desperation to get moving. "I only need to talk to him for a few minutes." It wouldn't take long: read the letter together, have him there to help face whatever was inside that envelope and decide what to do next.

"Something you can't say over the phone?"

"He doesn't have one."

Holly frowns, glancing again at the outside. "It's getting dark. I'll drive you, and you can run in, okay?"

"You don't need to. I can snowshoe." Sees her resistance. "I've hiked that trail after dark before. You always let me." Waits. "It's only fifteen minutes before you get to the fork to Wallace's."

Long, tight pause. "Wear your headlamp. Bundle up. And really no more than a few minutes. I'll be counting. If you aren't back here in forty-five minutes, Seth and I are coming to get you." Owl nods quickly as she heads for the coatrack. "Owl?" She turns back, Holly's expression a portrait of misgiving. "Don't make me sorry."

THE BEAM FROM Owl's headlamp rests on the cratered trail ahead, a route she followed through the woods on and off all winter before sugaring began, long weekend solo hikes with a CamelBak, a series of loops that lead close to Wallace's.

She doesn't fear the night here. Worst she could run into is a skunk; bears, coyotes, or fishers seldom come this close to the odor of human.

The impulse to read the letter fuels her pace, getting her there just shy of eight o'clock, according to her phone, full dark outside, light shining from two of the windows of Wallace's little house, shades at half-mast, the corner of a flashing TV screen visible. Two vehicles in the driveway, Wallace's pickup and, farther back, a compact car with one of those WICKED PIS-SAH bumper stickers.

The RV, an old Keystone fifth-wheel sitting propped up on metal legs, is also lit, some of the café-style curtains open, some closed. As she pushes through the dried brambles at the edge of the yard, her ear picks up on something, a constant, featureless sound—a gas generator running, probably powering the RV.

Movement by the nearest window, and she sees him, back to her, in what must be the kitchenette space, and an unconscious smile touches her lips, anticipating what he'll say when she knocks, a few stolen minutes together, maybe even make their way to the bed, though she can't let time get away from her—doesn't want Seth driving down here in the dark, all that mess, more humiliation.

Another person moves past the curtains, Cody turning to

accommodate, and Owl stops, arms still raised to move the thorny branches aside.

The top of the person's head barely clears the ruffle of the curtains, but the cheap fabric lets light through; it's a girl, her curly strawberry-blond hair shoulder-length, a white Sherpa fleece sweatshirt unzipped over her front.

They stand together, talking, and Cody raises a can to his lips—Coors Light, Wallace's beer of choice. Sets it aside, moves closer.

Owl's body cools by ten degrees, all zero at the bone. Switches off her headlamp. Pulled as if by a cord around her middle, she continues toward the camper, drawing close to the windows, the sound of her crunching snowshoes masked by the generator.

The girl looks early twenties, the gap between curtains revealing her tight, hard body, smile generous and wolfish at once. Her cropped T-shirt, gleam of a belly-button ring, and pale skinny jeans give her a summery look, as if she has access to some private sun. Takes a long drink from her can, watching him over the edge of it. Then does a slow, sinuous spin, can held above her head, gazing at him. Because he asked her to do it. Owl doesn't need to see his lips to tell.

Cody reaches, hands sliding around the girl's hips, pulling her in—Owl feels it simultaneously, muscle memory, how often he's done that on her body, her skin—and as they move together down a step to the back of the camper, Owl sees his smile, catches some words, undiscernible, angle all wrong.

Now it's pain, pure self-flagellation, that makes her follow, closer to the next window, where the curtains are partially open. Girl backs herself up to the bed in the yellowed light, smile on the verge of a laugh, unbuttoning her jeans, Cody kneeling down to kiss her neck, the purple V of her nylon underwear appearing as he helps drag her pants down her lean thighs—

Owl tears away, not remembering to switch on her head-lamp until she's forcing her way through the brambles, body propelled forward, no thought, no feeling, just movement.

Running the trail, a bouncing black tunnel broken only by the narrow beam of her light, harsh breathing and rushing blood, everything distorted, mind scrubbed blank, not slow-ing until the distant lights of the sugarhouse and cabin flicker through the trees. She collapses on hands and knees, lungs starving, eyes squeezed shut, sobbing inches from the snow.

# 27

"They pulled a body out of the stream yesterday. Over in St. Beatrice." From the counter, Seth turns down the kitchen radio volume, repeating the report for Owl's benefit in that indirect way they've been speaking to each other, words shearing just off the mark.

Holly sets her toast back on her plate. "God." Her treatment of Seth a bit stiff after arguing the night before. A two-parter: first, when Seth learned where Owl had gone, then later, in their bedroom, after Seth had waited for Owl to come home, watched her hang her hat and coat and then go straight up to the loft without speaking to either of them, her face averted. "Maybe somebody had one too many, went over the side of that little bridge. It's not far to stagger from Houlihan's."

"More'n likely. Could have been a hiker, too, somebody who fell from one of the cliffs and washed down."

274

They watch as Owl, head bowed over cereal, rouses as if from sleep. "I saw that. The sheriff's office had the road blocked off coming back from St. Beatrice yesterday."

She seems to feel the weight of their stares and looks down. Eyes swollen, but no tears, no evidence of whatever last night was about. Seth's got half a mind to call Wallace, get some goddamn answers. Christ, ain't that a laugh.


SOMEHOW THE DAY passes, but in the manner of some inevitable law of physics, gravity dragging a single strand of honey through the octagonal grid of a comb. Owl slides through the hours, serpentine around obstacles—English and math, a few bites of peanut butter and jelly with Aida, more lectures, some quiz. She's a prisoner of memory, of lamplit images she still can hardly believe; spent all night trying to flee through tattered sleep, tearing into wakefulness again and again, where she'd remember.

Early afternoon, Griffin catches her eye, flashes her the *okay* sign, expression questioning. She nods, then makes a side-to-side *so-so* motion, looking away. No reason to fake okayness with him; Griffin wouldn't ask if he didn't really want to know.

Owl has no plans for handling it, for seeing Cody. She just feels the minutes moving toward inevitability cramming in around her, an unstoppable force pushing her to the moment when her feet hit the gravel driveway after stepping out of the Suburban, gaze dead ahead on the sugarhouse, where she knows he is.

Speaks to no one as she goes to the side-by-side after dropping her backpack off inside the cabin, climbing into the passenger seat. Pretends not to feel her uncle's gaze, or notice him leaning against the sugarhouse doorway, watching as they drive away, knowing something isn't right.

She starts to tremble as Cody parks—that face she can't look at, his hand edging into her vision, the lines and shape of his knuckles on the shifter more than she can stand—and she bangs out of the vehicle gracelessly. Can't break it all open with words, shouldn't have to be the one.

Knows he's behind her only in the final seconds—boots crunching snow—his touch on her arm, and she grabs hold of him tightly enough to hurt, flinging his hand down.

"What—?"

Spins, her eyelids skinned back, face drained and flinching. Sees in an instant that there's no confession on his lips, no show of guilt—he's going to play her if he can, forever. Her throat seals so completely she can barely get out, "You know."

"No, I don't. What's the matter with you?"

And she goes for him, an instant of savage drive. He side-steps, catching her arm, and she gives a ragged cry, staggering a few feet before she wheels and comes back at him.

"I *saw* you. I saw what you—" Speech fails, giving way to a guttural sound of pain in her throat, hitting at him, grabbing, anything she can get hold of, when it registers that he's not fighting her, not even yelling at her to stop. She's crushed to him, panting, fists twisted into his clothes, staring up at a face both hard and tolerant, eyes knowing, without a doubt knowing, but he's still going to make her say it. "That *girl*."

He holds her, releases a bit at a time, the two of them standing close enough to share breath. He squints, gives his head a hard shake. "How did you see anything?" As if this were somehow the sticking point.

"I was there."

He's quiet, looking down at the ground as she rips away from him, getting some distance—maybe five feet, the maximum before she starts to lose what someone's saying—and turns back, arms folded tightly, chest shuddering as she fights tears that won't stop coming, slicking her face even as she forces her expression blank.

"Owl . . . you don't need to . . ." He stops, slight wince, swallows as he glances away. "It doesn't matter. Do you get that?"

Shakes her head slowly, voice a husk. "Who is she?"

Scoffs, takes a few steps away, hands going to his pockets. "Hell do I know. Some girl." Looks over at Owl's strangled sound. "I'm not . . . like . . . trying to cover my ass. I don't know her." Stares off into the rows of trees. "She said her name was Kristie, Kirstie, something."

Shuts her eyes against that, a sob ballooning in her throat, torturous pressure. "I don't . . . understand. I thought . . ." Can't continue.

"Look, she hangs around the bar. I ran into her there." Curses, scuffs his hand off the top of his head. "It was just sex. You don't"—searching for words—"have to feel bad."

Near-hysterical laughter escapes. "How can you say that? I didn't give you everything you wanted right away, so you go and—"

"No. It's different with you. I didn't want you to—"

"You never wanted me. You think I'm a kid."

"Stop making shit up. It had nothing to do with you."

"Oh—" Owl's voice fails, but her hands pick up, sweeping the flattened fingers of her right hand beneath her jaw, then shunting both hands down her sides as she walks away from him—suddenly needing more distance, scared not to have it, afraid of what else her hands might do.

"What's that?" He's on her heels. "Some Deaf smack you know I can't read? What're you saying?"

"*Liar.*" She shoves her face in his, voice rough, stare fierce through her tears. "Liar. That's what I said." He's still, gazing back at her as she turns and walks in the direction of the access road.


SETH WATCHES CODY leave at the end of the day, Owl already inside, up in the loft. Seth works at the far edge of the lawn, using the Kubota to clean up some fallen limbs from a dead birch along the tree line—just busywork while he keeps an eye on them. It was impossible to tell a thing from Owl's posture or pace as she walked from sugarhouse to cabin, quick and economical as always, going inside without a glance his way.

Now, Holly comes out, tugging up the zipper on her fleece vest, hustling to her car to get something out of the passenger seat. Seth starts the tractor, drives across the lawn to park under the run-in shed, taking the usual painstaking care getting down so his knee doesn't scream too bad; would have another pill on top of the last one, taken just an hour ago, but he's been trying to put the brakes on.

Holly straightens, watching him approach, folding her arms, some softening in her expression as she waits for him to speak first.

"She okay?" he asks.

Tightening of her lips; this is the subject they've been sparring around for almost a week, sleeping with an invisible wedge between them at night. "As far as I can tell."

"Something's off. She hasn't stayed downstairs with us for more than a minute lately." Looks over at the loft window, shrouded in curtains. "Like she doesn't want us looking too close."

Holly exhales, tips her head back, eyes squeezed shut. "Just leave it."

"Can't do that. I did once, and look what happened to her."

"For god's sake." Cleansing breath, focuses hard on him. "If I'd said she couldn't go see him, it would've just pushed them that much closer together. Them against us, right?" Lowers her voice. "He's out of here in a week. So I said yes, gave her a little trust. Okay?" Picks up the file folders of paperwork from Van's, clutching them to her chest as she slams the car door. "Once you factor in the hike, she couldn't have actually been with him for more than five minutes. I know he's young, but I doubt he's that fast."

"Not funny."

"No shit." She looks at him, and their years are between them, all of them, her expression anguished as she bears down on each word: "This is Owl's *life*. Sooner or later, she

279

was bound to get one of her own, you know? It happens. I get that you feel like you need to carry her every step of the way, but she's not that hurt little girl anymore." Points at him. "You take her choices away, and I promise you, you will lose her." Takes a couple backward steps, shaking her head. "If anybody gets that, it should be us."

"OWL?"

Holly waves her hand through the opening in the curtains, testing.

"Hi." Owl shifts, closing her sketch pad, not wanting to share how little she'd been able to get done on her new drawing, begun after burying her previous work in progress under sheets of blank paper. Now she's starting a fox kit, done mostly from memory and pictures found online, since she'd yet to get a clear pic of them outside the den. Doesn't matter. Whatever oasis her brain finds when she draws is awash in stormwaters, no place she wants to retreat to.

Holly comes in, a quick appreciating look at Owl's other sketches before she holds out a folded envelope. "I found this in your back pocket when I was doing the wash. It almost went through."

The sight of it makes Owl sick, remembering the excitement, terror when she'd finally resolved to read it, face her fear with Cody beside her. Owl stares until Holly makes a move as if to set it on the bureau and leave. "Will you read it with me?" Quietly.

"Are you sure?"

Owl nods, moving her drawing supplies aside to make room for her aunt to sit next to her on the bed. Holly opens the envelope, hesitating. "I can just be with you if you want. I won't look."

Owl shrugs, exhausted by it now, the power this letter holds. "Doesn't matter." She doesn't move to take it, though, letting Holly remove a small sheet of lined paper.

This message is relatively short. A date at the top right, like a school assignment:

Dear Rochelle,
I hope it's OK that I'm writing to you. I should have done it a long time ago. I sent a letter to Seth, but I had some things I wanted to say just to you.

I'm staying at this halfway place now for guys who just got out. They set me up washing dishes at a café I can walk to. Not a bad life for somebody who's done bad things. Anyway I wanted you to know that I'm working.

I'm not the same guy you remember. For a long time I was angry, but the prison has people to talk to and I got to see that I was feeling sorry for myself when you were the one who got hurt so bad. I never wanted to hurt you, Baby Girl. I wanted to take care of you and give you a good life. Seth ended up being the one who did that. I know he did because he always looked out for me growing up when I let him.

I don't blame you if you hate me. I had problems and you're the one who paid for it. It's not fair. But if you want to see me, I'd love to see you and tell you I'm sorry in

*person. You must be so grown up and pretty now like your*
*mom.*

> *Love you forever,*
> *Daddy*

They sit in silence, Owl's gaze raking over the spare words, the halting voice, someone unused to expressing themselves, and she finds herself laughing, some choked version of it, fingers going to her hair. "Pretty?" Digs into the scar, the pink and twisted part that will never heal. "Pretty?"

"Owl." Holly pulls her hand down, holding it tightly in her own. "Stop."

Another snorting burst of laughter-sobs, shaking her head helplessly. "He wants to see me."

"Do you—?"

"No. No, never. I can't look at him." Behind closed lids, child Rochelle is ensconced in the memory of him, held tightly in the crook of his arm, where she once rode, small and high. *Daddy.* All the safety and love and fear and harm in the world right there, in that word, in the twining double helix of their shared DNA. "I loved him so much."

Holly makes a soft, empathetic sound, wraps her arm tightly around Owl's shaking shoulders.

Owl looks up, blinking back tears, which have reached no farther than her lashes. "Do you think . . . my mom . . ." Words she's turned over inside so many times it's laborious to unwind them, locate the beginning and end of her question. "What if he . . . did something to her? And that's the real reason nobody could find her?"

"You mean, like, killed her?" A flinch of affirmation in Owl's shoulders. Holly straightens, staring ahead for a long moment. "No. I really don't think so, hon."

"But . . . I asked Seth, and he said when I was a baby, he saw her hold me so tight." Voice breaks. "Then why—? How could she just . . . ?" Palm drops open to her lap, beseeching, as tears break free, dropping to leave dark spots on her jeans.

Holly holds and shushes, the rhythmic comfort of a lullaby, rubbing Owl's back now and then. When the girl has settled some, Holly gives her a tissue from the box on the nightstand, waiting as she blows her nose. "When Seth said that . . . I know he meant well. And I know—obviously—your dad could be violent. But from what was said about your mom at the time everything happened, she was a runner. She was trying to get away from a bad situation when she met your dad, and then when things went downhill with him, she ran again. It's heartbreaking that she didn't take you with her, but . . . for my own sake, I'm glad she didn't." Returns Owl's stare. "I never thought I wanted to be a parent before I had this chance with you. Afraid I'd turn into my mother, I guess. Seth and I talked about having kids. Talked around it, anyway, but . . ." Shrugs. "Then you came to stay. Got to tell you, for the first couple weeks, I was absolutely terrified."

"You were?"

"Oh, yeah. You couldn't tell? I was convinced I was going to do the wrong thing, say the wrong thing, make everything worse for you. That I couldn't do it, any of it. Couldn't . . . give you the love you needed. But after a couple months, it was like we couldn't remember how we'd ever gotten along without you. We needed you, Owl, not the other way around. You know how they say when one door closes, another opens?" Holly tucks a strand of Owl's hair behind her ear. "I guess, tragic as it was, I'll always owe your mom for closing that door when she did."

Owl rests against her, then hugs impulsively, squeezing tight. Holly strokes Owl's hair smooth again, touch gentle over the scar, reminding Owl so vividly of those late nights, the nightmare images fading from her mind, replaced by the images Holly painted with those creation tales. "You said that the stories you used to tell me were precious. Who told them to you?"

"My grandmother." Holly's smile lingers. "She's a story-teller. Used to travel around the state, performing at schools, festivals, preserving Passamaquoddy culture as much as she could. She and I were close when I was little. The only person who really made me feel special in our family, not like 'the hard one.' She used to call me Kinapesq. Brave Girl." Laughs softly. "She's salty. Hilarious. I miss her."

Owl's quiet. "You should let her know."

"She's not exactly tech-savvy. By choice."

"So go see her. And your little sister. She wouldn't message you like she does if she didn't want you to come back." Pauses. "I just know how much *we* love you. And how awful I'd feel if you left."

Holly looks at her, taken aback, then faces away. "Well . . . maybe. Sometime." Clears her throat. "When I told you those stories, I guess part of me was passing them on to you. Keeping them in our family. Do you remember them well enough to tell?"

Owl nods. "I wouldn't mind hearing 'Glooscap Fights the Water Monster' again."

Holly takes a breath, shakes her hair back, and rests her chin on top of Owl's head a moment. "Okay. Let me think. Begin at the beginning, right? You know Glooscap is a medicine man, a sorcerer. He'll last as long as the world will last. He made all the animals and the humans. And even though sometimes he grows tired of running things and needs to leave us, he can't abandon the people forever . . ."

Owl sits, letting Holly's words sketch, shade, and shadow, until her eyelids grow heavy and she closes them.

When Owl lies down, neither of them notices that the letter wafts to the floor, eventually swept beneath the bed as Holly tucks sleeping Owl beneath the quilt and returns to the downstairs.

# 28

*I brought you something.* Owl makes the sign for *gift*— gesturing toward Ms. Z with both hands, forefingers crooked—then unzips her backpack, bringing out the eight-ounce bottle and setting it on the desk in front of Ms. Z, flushed with the clumsy anticipation of giving.

Her teacher picks up the glass maple leaf, turning it in the daylight filtering through the window. *Beautiful.* The gravity with which she says it completes the ritual, allowing Owl a puppyish squirm of relief, pleasure, before being able to sink into her own skin again.

"You always share your lunch with me, so."

"And you helped make this, is that right? Mr. Duquette mentioned that you lived on a maple farm. You work at it year-round?"

"We tap through late February into March. The rest of the year is filling orders, things like that."

Ms. Z cracks the seal, takes a sniff. "Oh, my goodness." *Amazing.* Moves her spread, slightly bent fingers across her mouth twice. "I've always thought that trees are soulful things. They've got character." Owl nods avidly, never expecting anyone else to appreciate that part of it other than her and Seth. "Thank you, Rochelle. Truly." Puts the bottle into her satchel. "I don't suppose you've reached out to the kids from the Stokely school?"

"We followed each other yesterday."

"Wonderful. You see? Kinder than you expected."

Owl nods, gaze trailing over the homework in front of her, unseeing. "What about the other times? What do you do then?" Meets Ms. Z's eyes. "When somebody isn't who you think. When you trust and they hurt you."

"Well." Ms. Z rests back in her chair, watching the kids at play outside the window, enjoying the mostly clear day before the snow and ice storm predicted for the weekend arrives. "Sometimes it's a matter of them not being who you *wanted* them to be. Maybe they never were that person. Just . . . not capable of giving you what you need." Leans forward on her elbows. "Sometimes the best you can take away from a painful experience is a greater love for the people in your life who hardly ever let you down."

SILENCE FROZEN BETWEEN them, Owl does only what's required to push the sugaring forward, trying to unmake Cody from her vision, her memory, as if she might suddenly look over through the trees and he'll be gone, nothing more than some transient bit of darkness as the sun traveled behind a cloud.

Maybe he's doing the same to her—unthinking her, unknowing her—until they meet at the tank, another awkward dance to avoid each other with pails in hand.

"Let me." Exasperation at her hard look. "It's faster. You're too short."

Handing them over hard enough to slop, sap thicker at the end of the season, running in slow drips down the plastic pail, she stands with arms folded as he empties all the buckets into the tank.

"You never going to talk to me again?" Glances at her, sees she has no intention of speaking. Takes his time gathering the pails by their handles, then meets her gaze, the two of them examining each other warily. He looks worn, shadows dabbed along his inner sockets. "S'fine, I guess. Can't blame you." Doesn't resist when she reaches for her pail. Stops her as she turns away with, "But it's me. Just want you to know that." She looks back. "That's why you're feeling so bad. You're looking at yourself, wondering what you did wrong. Answer's nothing."

Owl doesn't move, expression opaque, waiting.

"This is what I do. Anybody back home could tell you. Get a good thing going, and I wreck it." Falters, an uncertainty she's never seen on him. "I hurt people."

"Girls?" Her voice abrupt, brittle.

"Everybody." Works his lips across his teeth, shrugs. "Seeing you hurt . . . sucked. Can't get rid of it. All I can say is, I never wanted you to find out." Sees the outrage building in her, but his gaze doesn't waver. "Seriously. I never thought you would. I was just, like . . . kicking the shit out of the part of me that liked being with you."

Her voice emerges choked, hoarse: "What's so bad about being with me?"

"Nothing. Jesus. It was like . . . a chance. Or something. Be somebody else. Be better. You're not like anybody I know, and you were trusting me to . . ." Shakes his head as she watches him, arms at her sides, useless.

"I would have done it with you, you know. Eventually. If you hadn't . . ." Shuts her eyes against it, voice vicious with grief: "Why'd you have to *do* it?"

The pause taut with all the potential squandered, everything lost. "It was just a hookup." Each word formed slowly, futilely. "It didn't mean anything. She didn't even want to stay the night with me. She was just a bar slut."

"So are you. From what I saw." Silence. "Why did you say the thing about wanting me to come with you?"

"Because I did. I do."

"But if I did, you'd keep doing this, wouldn't you? Hooking up. Lying, hurting me because you hate yourself." Shakes her head, fighting for control. "Where'd that money really come from?"

"I told you—"

"No, you didn't. You wouldn't be hiding it on our land unless you were scared somebody might come looking for it."

Straightens, staring at him. "Where's your phone?" When he starts to answer: "I know you lied. You had one. Did you drop it in the water up at the Notch?"

"Why are you asking if you already know?" Follows her as she turns in disgust. "Yeah, I tossed it. Now I don't have to hear from back home, everybody telling me I got people looking for me."

"Who's looking for you?"

"The fucking—" Stops. Short exhale. "The guy I took it off of." Brows draw together. "Don't look at me like that—I didn't steal *shit*. That asshole owes me. Owes my mom. So, yeah, I saw my chance to take what I could and got the hell out of there." Insolence, baiting her. "There was more to start with. Lot more. Twenty-five thousand." Owl's eyes widen; Cody's laughter is faint, bitter. "Yeah. Thirteen grand gone, and I guarantee she's already racking it up again." Sharp, dismissive gesture with his hand. "My mom. She had debts."

Owl hesitates. "You stole to pay them off?"

"Nah. Nothin' I'd do." Humorless smile, walking back to lean against the trailer, gazing at her, odd light in his eyes, half-sardonic, half-haunted. "She owed everybody. Dealers give shit out on credit, knowing you can't pay, then they got you. Make you hold for them or sell. This one guy . . . he lets her keep racking up, then comes over, slaps her around. Had her out working for him." Pauses. "Streets. You know."

Owl can't speak, paralyzed while he goes on.

"Those couple nights I spent in juvie lockup . . . I was working as a courier for a dealer I met through Mom." Cody doesn't meet her eyes. "Delivery boy. Cop didn't catch me with much, and he screwed up the arrest somehow—I dunno, stepped on my rights or something—so I didn't get more than probation. Good thing I got charged, though, 'cause if you come off an arrest with no charges, guy above you thinks you rolled on them."

"You helped sell drugs?" Her voice faint, a poor impression of itself.

"Helped transport. Yeah. Don't tell me it was stupid. I know it was stupid. Easy money, and I wanted some. I'd done the joe job thing, and it blows. And anyway, after lockup, I knew I had to get out. I don't do the stuff, so they can't get me hooked that way. I just had to hang in until I saw my chance, you know?" Finally looks at her. "Took almost two years. Ripped off enough to start fresh, buy Mom one last chance to clean up. She's on her own after this." Shrugs. "He'll be looking for me."

"You came here to hide." Under her breath, to herself as much as him.

"Good a place as any. Mom had already set it up, just wasn't supposed to start for a couple more weeks. She wants me out of all of it almost as bad as I do. That's the only reason she started speaking to Wallace again." Nods at the woods. "She always said she grew up in the middle of nowhere. Figured . . . I could earn some extra in the last place anybody'd look, let things cool down. Head up to Canada easy from here. If I wanted." He's getting his smokes out, almost unconsciously, but she's feeling too sideswiped to get on him about it. Around the Newport, the lighter clicking: "Hear about that dead guy?"

Raises her brows. "In the stream. St. Beatrice."

"I knew him." Takes a drag, tucking his chin down into his collar. "Saw on TV. It was Declan. Works down at the bar. We got talking a few times." Blows the smoke to the side, letting the wind take it from them—trick she'd seen him do before, smoker's courtesy. "They're saying somebody shot him. Been in the water a few days."

She registers detached shock, a recollection of Holly being acquainted with the man. "What's that got to do with you?"

He gazes back. "Nothing, maybe. Just weird, is all. Not like you get a lot of murders in a place like this, right?"

Folds her arms, gauging him. "Would this dealer guy really do that?"

"Ballard. Jamie Ballard. You don't know what he's done to people."

"How would he find you?"

"Dunno. Never would've got it out of Mom. She's done a lot of things, but she wouldn't sell me out. Anyway, if it came from her, he'd know right where to go, not have to dick around looking."

Owl takes a step back as Cody gazes at the middle distance. "I don't believe you."

"Wouldn't make it up, would I? And I've got the money."

"No. I don't believe you just came here to hide. You really think somebody bad's coming for you, you could've used the money to run. You could've been out of the state or over the border weeks ago." Spreads her arms, drops them. "So why are you here?"

"Owl." Low, a half note of pleading; she recoils from it, shaking her head like a horse trying to free itself of bridle.

"No. You're still lying." Takes the embankment hard, glad

she's deaf to whatever he says to that. "I don't want to know about any of this. Season's almost up. Seth needs you. I don't."

They split, Owl into the trees on her side of the bush, him standing, watching; sucks quickly from the Newport before pitching it, going his own way.

WALLACE'S PICKUP IS in the driveway when they get back, Cody's gaze finding his grandfather with Seth by the cabin steps as he and Owl pull around and park near the sugar-house, climbing out.

Seth and Wallace stand close; lack of buffer drawing Owl's attention, and their body language—Wallace facing the road like he's been waiting, Seth blocking him, a hand against Wallace's chest. *Don't.* She catches that on Seth's lips as he turns, shoved sideways off-balance by Wallace pushing past, cane the only thing keeping him from spilling over.

*Come 'ere.* Wallace, too far back to hear, but coming at them, eyes red and glazed and fixed on Cody, a yeasty tang of beer washing over Owl before his hand even grabs Cody's upper arm, pointing at Owl with the other, his bellowing slamming into full volume: "—been at her? Have you?" To Owl as Cody pulls free: "Go inside, get yourself in the house." Slams both heavy, arthritic hands into Cody as his grandson tries to move, cramming him against the hood of the side-by-side, fists and collar jammed under his chin. "What you been up to? Huh?"

Owl looks for Seth—he's coming, heaving himself along with the cane, expression wrenched tight—and whips around to see Cody's indignant ferocity, dragging Wallace's hands free, shoving him back, shouting, "What the hell's the matter with you?"

"Think we weren't going to find out? Jesus H. Christ, I gotta hear from neighbors what's really going on here? I put in for you—this how you thank me, you little bastard?" Wallace chokes off in a frustrated snarl, swings, catching Cody at the brow bone before he can dodge. Half spins him into the hood, banging off the steel hard enough to dent it in before it springs back to shape.

"All *right*, Wall." Seth grabs Wallace's shoulders, tries to muscle him back, but Wallace is bigger, out of shape but plenty of bull strength, shrugging Seth off like a coat too hot for the weather; Seth curses, knee going out, staggering back as Owl starts for him, a cry trapped in her throat, vision blocked by Wallace's mass.

Cody's pushed himself up on one arm, covering his eye with his hand, scarlet swelling showing around it as Wallace breathes hard, points at Owl. "Brought you up here to *work*, not be weaseling your way into his little girl's pants! And her, being like she is, somebody oughta string you up by your *balls*." He lunges to grab Cody's arms again.

*Smack*—connection of Cody's fist with Wallace's nose a thick sound, hammer into meat. Blood spurts: The cry of agony from the older man shoots a nauseating bad-tooth jolt through Owl, hand going to her mouth as Cody throws a right cross, which sends Wallace staggering, then down onto the snow.

Cody's face, blanched white but comfortably blank, in his element. Inner time slowing as he drops to his knees over his grandfather, jabs his fist once, twice, Wallace's mouth all blood and Cody's knuckles split open the next time he pulls back—

"*Stop!*" Owl screams it, bent double as she circles around behind him, hardly noticing as Seth comes up behind her, keeping her back. "*Stop it! Cody!*"

At last, her voice seems to penetrate; Cody takes a short breath, straightens up, waiting for Wallace, but the older man lies sprawled on his side, braced on one elbow, face screwed against pain as strings of blood dangle from his mouth to the snow. "Want me to *thank you*?" Cody shouts down at Wallace. "You never fucking cared about us! You never did *anything*!" Swings his foot into Wallace's ribs, the older man's grunt blending with Owl's despairing cry. "Can't believe I ever—" Won't finish, turns sharply away, instantly done with it, wiping sweat and blood spray from his upper lip as his gaze passes over Owl, their eyes connecting without clarity, barely even recognition, before he walks away, a swift and upright pace, almost energized, as he heads toward the road without a backward glance.

"Where are you going?" Owl's call echoes hollowly against the stand of woods, never expecting an answer.

# 29

"Gonna make it, bub?" Seth holds out an ice pack to Wallace, who sits in a kitchen chair, head and hands hanging down. Waits a beat before laying it flat on the table within Wallace's reach, then twists the cap off a Sam Adams instead.

This Wallace takes, not making eye contact, face a swollen mess even after cleaning up in the cabin bathroom, worst Seth's seen since the service, brawls the MPs had to break up, all the blows centered around Wallace's nose and mouth, bruising spreading up around his eyes. No way to sidestep the ugliness of what had just played out. After a long pull, Wallace says, "Not as young as I feel, I guess."

Seth tarries with a beer of his own, knows he shouldn't— the pills, not a good mix—takes the cap off, tosses it to the countertop, so at least Wallace doesn't feel like he's drinking alone. Screw it. Takes a swig, gesturing with the bottle neck. "Maybe get yourself down to the walk-in care in St. Beatrice. Have those ribs looked at. Good chance they're cracked."

"Nah." Sucks half the bottle down, then sets it aside. "I'll wrap 'em. I done it before. Be okay in a couple weeks."

"I tried to tell you. She came clean to us. Said she likes him."

"He took advantage. We both know it. Sorry as hell I ever brought him up here to your place, Seth." Runs a hand through his graying hair, puts his ball cap back on, eases to his feet with a visible wince, bruised fist resting on the tabletop for balance. "I should've taken him in when they asked. Rhetta would've loved it, sick or not. Who am I kiddin' with that? It was me." Takes a halting breath, stops short, lets out a shaky exhalation. "Flesh and blood don't turn each other away."

Seth watches him over the mouth of his bottle, helplessness emerging as exasperation. "It was a tough call. Lots of people would've done the same."

"But not you, right?" Wallace's gaze is long, heavy-lidded.

Seth can't find words. Wallace sniffs, raps his fist softly on the table, then makes his way to his truck at an uneven, considering pace, managing to skew just off the edge of dignity.

OWL'S IN THE sugarhouse. Needs to be free of them, to decide if she's really going to throw up—turns out to be more a case of heartsickness—and to see if the batch, left boiling during the fight, can be saved. She finds the temperature fallen well below 219, the sap overcooked into thick, motionless brown taffy on the bottom of the pans.

Glances back when she sees Seth's reflection grow in the metallic sheen of the evaporator. "It's ruined. We have to dump it."

"Relax. I'm the one who left it." Sees her grabbing the firing gloves so she can pick up the pans, stops her. "We can save it."

"No, we can't." Swears miserably. Silence.

Seth adds firewood, then opens the valve, letting more sap down into the pans, watching as it covers the overcooked batch. "Sorry you had to see all that."

Shrugs, then fixes him with a stare. "You weren't the one who told Wallace?"

Seth shakes his head. "He stopped by the Frankels' this morning. Heard it from Trini. Guess she's got herself all worked up about it." Watches understanding hit Owl, her gaze travel down with a sinking sense of betrayal. "He's been drinking most of the day."

Clenches her teeth together until the words burst free: "Why does it have to . . . matter so much? It's like it's everybody's business but mine if I want to be with Cody." Throws her hands up. "Do you feel like Wallace does? Me 'being like I am,' I don't even know how to say yes or no? And Cody must be some kind of . . . perv if he wants to be with me?"

"You know I don't." Stiffly.

"How? You don't want me around anymore. Ever since you found out that we . . ." Locks up, finds she can't say those words to him, gets even more frustrated with herself, the yawning sense of loss, still largely unconfronted, stretching wider. "I liked him. It felt right. That's what matters." Neither of them notice the past tense.

"Come on, Owl. Look what just happened out there. The kid is damaged and pissed off and wants somebody to hurt."

"Wallace hit him first!"

Bites down on his impulse response, staring hard out the window, reining himself in. "Now I want you to listen to me. What he's been through, I wouldn't wish on anybody. He had a crap childhood, and he's not to blame. But getting ripped away from your mom over and over has got to take a toll—maybe on a boy, especially, when it comes to how he treats the women in his life." Gives a short, harsh sound. "After what you survived, would've figured you'd spot that in a second. Turn around and run the other way. Christ, how many times have we talked about listening to your gut? That your instincts will tell you what's up before anything else." Gestures hard with one hand. "I've got to be able to trust you to be smarter than this."

She could stop now—give up defending Cody, tell Seth it was over between them, practically before it had begun. Tell him all the ways he's right: how there is something broken in Cody that she won't try to fix, that she really does have the basic sense not to funnel her life into someone whose insides will never be full, never quenched by her. But it would open up everything: What Cody confessed about the money. The fracturing scenes in the lamplit camper, Cody's hands on the girl's skin, Owl's memory in abstract patches. Things she can't ever imagine sharing with anyone, let alone Seth. But this discussion is tracing the shape of her own shadow, recognizing shades of herself in everything Seth's said. "What if somebody wrote *me* off like that?" Her voice is quiet. "Damaged?"

"Not the same. You found a safe place. Cody never did."

"And it's not his fault. Like you said."

"No, but you know what? There's got to be a turning point. Eventually, you stop being a kid reacting to what's been done to you and start being a man taking things out on people. Somebody dangerous. Cody's got to make the choice. We all do. Because if he thinks he can keep coasting on the past, he's never going to be any use to anybody." Seth grabs a wooden spoon from the workbench, roughly stirring the two saps into one. "Just another wasted life."

NO ONE SPEAKS much at supper, utensils scraping, occasional "pass the salt," Owl eating because the food's there, no real sense of taste or hunger. She's thinking about tomorrow, what has to be said. And how alone it will make her feel.

Holly presses her fingertip to some crumbs on the tabletop, sprinkles them to her plate, her manner toward Seth abrupt as she asks: "What's happening with the sugaring? What're you going to do?"

Seth gathers his dishes, mug stacked on plate. "I'm calling it for the year. Not much demand for the very dark anyway. We'll make a little less revenue, try to turn it around next season. I'll be on my feet by then." Stands, taking his cane from its leaning position, face trained away from Owl. "I don't expect he'll be back."

Not necessary to say who. She can't imagine Wallace continuing to put him up after today; wonders where Cody will spend the night, if he'll have to walk all the way down the mountain road to the valley, and even then, there are no motels or inns to be had until St. Beatrice. Wonders if she'll hear from him, if she even wants to. Owl's gaze rests on her plate, not sure if it's guilt she's feeling, if the blame lies with her, or Cody, or anyone. It all feels unstoppable now, some landslide coming from a long way off, bound to reach the farm eventually, knock her off her feet, roll her under, tumble her away.

MORNING COMES, PEWTER-GRAY warning light spilling across the granite face of the mountain. Spreading down through the wilds, the entrance to the fox den cast in sharp relief, a hole to the heart of the earth.

The cabin steps come into existence a gradient at a time, the structure itself carved from an uncolored composite of dusk. In a second-floor window, a lamp blinks to life.

AFTER THE USUAL sleepy, sullen a.m. Suburban ride, Owl follows Aida, as lost in her phone as ever. Maybe not lost. More like barricaded—a palm in the face, stopping conversation before it starts.

This time, Owl takes Aida's arm, firmly enough to pull the girl around to face her, her voice low, adamant. "Why did you tell your mom about Cody and me?"

Aida's eyes are slitted against the wind, face expressionless. Her pause is long, Owl recognizing it for what it is, more silent treatment, and beneath that, a resentment she never saw coming, burning through the layered years of Aida's arm holding, whisper sharing, maybe priding herself on her generosity, handing out what Owl wanted so badly, a rare sense of belonging. "You never said it was a secret." Challenging her.

Owl stares, all emotion fading from her face as she allows Aida to extract herself from her grip with obvious deliberateness, then turn and go to the schoolhouse, jogging up the steps, her streaked curls bouncing jauntily against the underside of her flipped-back hood.

For a moment, Owl sees nothing, vision blurred with a brief surge of tears she blinks away, lowering her head.

When she lifts it, Griffin's shape comes into focus, standing several feet off, hands in his pockets, watching. Waiting. Doesn't smile, just observes, brows slightly drawn.

Owl takes a breath, reshoulders her backpack, and walks straight ahead. The two of them fall into step with each other in a natural dovetail, Owl knowing she'll never have the words to show him how much it means, not having to go inside alone.


THAT AFTERNOON, FLURRIES begin lightly, striking the snowpack with the faintest crystalline tick.

Owl begins the task of unhooking the sap buckets, using a crowbar to gently pop the spiles out of the trunks, collecting the last of the sap and all the equipment so it can be soaked in hot water and stored until next year. She volunteered to start it alone, ostensibly to spare Seth's knee, but they both knew she wanted space. Also feels like penance . . . knowing they're losing money partly because of her. Wonders where Cody spent the night. If he had a roof over his head, enough to eat this morning, to put a dent in that endless hunger of his. Everything feels foreign, no sense of his big physical presence beside her, the quiet of the sugarbush immense as snow gathers on her hat. Misses him. Damn him.

A few times, she convinces herself she hears footsteps, turns sharply, searching for Cody coming through the snow, showing up after all, proving them wrong. No sign.

She works until her arms and shoulders ache and her fingers are sore, until the walk from the sugarbush to the access road becomes a blur of blue-shadowed white.

At last, she finds herself leaving the bush, pushing through the trees, searching for the path they followed the day he showed her the money, reaching the clearing and backtracking, looking for the tree with the X carved into it.

What she finds instead are the impressions he made kneeling in the snow, the weight of the bag beside him—not yet covered over with fresh snowfall.

The rope is there, tied tautly to the branch. She angles her head, can see the trash bags up high, white on white.

He's still around.


THE DEN ISN'T far, close enough for a quick visit, but she doesn't hear the strange sound, the strangled barks, until she's nearly there, stopping at the motion through the trees.

It's the vixen—out in the open, jumping back and forth in sharp, compulsive movements near the den, then her head disappears, only shaking hindquarters visible to show that she's digging after something. Reminds Owl of the time with the rabid raccoon, an animal going so far against its nature that something must be frighteningly wrong.

Owl crouches, moving closer, nearly in the clearing before she gets a good view.

The mouth of the den is gone, collapsed snow and soil filling the entrance to the tunnel—given way, maybe from the melting-refreezing action of the past weeks. Owl jerks upright, nerve endings tingling, finally understanding, as the vixen continues her frantic pacing, trying to find a way in. Trying to reach her babies.

Owl doesn't hesitate—no time to think; she runs into the open, sending the vixen scarpering for the bushes, and slams down in front of the embankment, clawing for the kits. Her fingers hook, throwing handfuls of crusted ice sealing off oxygen from their hollow so far below. Breath sobbing out of her, she digs until she can't anymore, until she sees she's getting nowhere, the den too deep, nothing she's capable of reaching, and she weaves back, dropping to the ground, jeans soaking through as she presses her numb, throbbing hands to her face.

# 30

Snowfall is intermittent overnight, leaving little more than a bedsheet's thickness across yard and road, but it's coming down harder by early morning, forecast to dump between seven to ten inches by nightfall.

Holly has her Land Rover warming up outside, plumes of exhaust billowing past the front windows, as she packs a lunch, still wearing her coat. Pausing to cup Owl's cheek, she smells of cold air. "You going to be okay today?" Studies her. "You can come with me if you want. Pull an Aida, hang out in the bear chair." Sees a darkness move across Owl's expression. "Did I say something?"

Owl shakes her head, breaking eye contact, not sure how to talk about this fresh, yet final—no other stamp to put on it—break between her and Aida, this last breach of trust, or how to tell anyone about the tragedy in the clearing yesterday, if she can stand compounding their sadness with her own right now. Flashes a quick *okay* sign.

"All right. Cross your fingers that I can make it home later, if this storm actually does what they're saying. Not really looking forward to spending the night sleeping with my feet up on Van's desk." Flicks her eyes heavenward; monster storms crapping out were common conversation. Weathering it on the mountain is such a point of pride that everyone's equipped with generators and gasoline and stashes of bottled water. "Can't tell if the sky means it or not. We'll see."

DESPITE THE SNOW, Owl drives out to the sugarbush, continuing the job of the final tap while Seth keeps bottling in the sugar kitchen. Today, she's certain Cody will come, that he'll know to find her out here and she'll pick up on his presence before she can hear him. But again and again, she turns to find nothing, no one, just the storm. Somehow, he's the only one she wants to share the loss of the kits with; despite everything, she respects his unsentimental ability to label circumstances as pure shit, no help for it.

Snow thickens, a continuous heavy sheaf. Soon, her hood isn't enough to keep it out of her eyes or from stinging her face, and she gathers her tools, returning once more to check on the bag in the tree.

The rope is still knotted in the same place, still taut, now covered with a coating of frozen snow on one side from the wind last night. Why he hasn't come for it surpasses puzzling, becomes troublesome. He'd never make the trek to Stokely for a bus ticket, then double back for the bag. Thinks of what he told her about the man who was shot, the bartender from Houlihan's, and it provokes in her a desire to finish this, wash Cody's sins from their land, remove one last blight.

Owl shifts, glances around, giving Cody another moment to appear—for a tree shadow to unlimber, take form—then unfolds her knife, mimics what she saw him do, hooking her left arm around a low branch, propping one foot against the trunk to boost herself high enough to hack the rope.

Takes a couple minutes to jerk the bag free of the branches, pull it down to the snow. Stands looking at it, misshapen, swathed in trash bags speckled with ice particles.

She finds herself ripping through the knots to reach black nylon, pulling the zipper down to see the inner bag, bound stacks of bills showing dimly through clear plastic. Opens the Ziploc, leaning close, flipping through grimly rendered dead presidents—same sense of power, revulsion as before, at the thin paper oiled by countless hands, want confused for need, vice versa. Knowing what this money was used for, that Cody got into all that despite what addiction had done to his mom, to his own life. Hesitantly sniffs it again, makes a face, resealing everything before carrying it with her to the side-by-side.

Drives home, bag stuffed down into the leg space beneath the passenger seat, snow billowing out behind the tires in a roiling tempest.


BY NOON, FIVE inches have fallen, hardened by an occasional icy mix, the wind cranking up enough to make the windowpanes shake. Owl sketches in the loft, face solemn, gaze focused, completing the drawing she began some days ago. Below, Seth sits in his chair, a book on Arctic exploration open in his hand, eyelids heavy in the soporific heat of the woodstove.

She slowly flips her art pad shut and goes downstairs, finding him asleep, book in his lap. Watches him, his face lined with chronic pain even in repose, left hand twitching a few times.

Seconds later, Owl's pulling on boots, layering outerwear, balaclava mask beneath hood, leaving only her eyes visible. Dashes out a quick note, left on the kitchen table: *Gone to Wallace's. BRB.*


SHE'D PLANNED ON asking permission—she had—working herself up to it as she finished her drawing, knowing what Seth's response would be when she asked to go to Wallace's one last time to bring Cody the bag of stuff he left behind.

This way, nobody even needs to know, no discussion or arguments. See Cody one last time. Get the money off their property, make it final for both of them that he won't be coming back, put an end to searching for signs of him through the snow. Maybe tell him about the kits.

As she readies herself for the storm, the electricity flickers, goes out; she barely looks up. It's expected. Mountain loses power during any amount of bad weather. Higher snowfall, smallest population: last priority for the power company.

She folds the sheet of paper she tore from her art pad into quarters, slides it into her coat pocket. Adds a couple more logs to the woodstove, shutting the damper partially so the blaze doesn't get out of control while she isn't there to check on it.

Owl sits in an Adirondack to strap on her snowshoes, gather her poles. Hesitates on the front steps, gazing out into the white, guilt a bitter taste. Tells herself Seth will sleep through it all, not be pacing, searching out windows for her while she's gone.

And sets out.

THE STORM DOESN'T seem as bad on the snowshoe trail, enough tree cover to provide shelter from the wind. She wears the backpack, stripped of its protective plastic. Tries to shut out the memories of the last time she went this way: wildly bouncing flashlight beam in the tunnel of dark, seizing lungs, sobbing in the cold, agonized over what she'd seen. What he'd done to them.

Owl reaches the clearing that signals Wallace's place, wades through the brambles, nearly losing her balance a couple times, trying to push the thornbushes back with the frame of her snowshoe.

Wallace's truck isn't in the driveway—a relief—but there is a red-and-black Arctic Cat snowmobile parked near the door, probably one of the many Wallace is constantly tinkering with and reselling.

Her stomach tightens with nerves as she approaches the dark RV, taking her snowshoes off so she can go up the steps to knock. Waits. Knocks again, harder. Nothing.

Owl looks around, not seeing anyone outside. Crosses to the house, steeling herself for dealing with Wallace, wondering if he might not lose it again at the thought of his grandson with the Deaf girl, start another row over something that was none of his business anyway. Maybe not even allow her to see Cody, if he's in there. But how can she just leave the backpack, given what's inside?

Goes to the front door—the walk hasn't been shoveled yet today, and she hopes Wallace isn't sleeping one off. She's about to knock when she sees that the door has been left slightly ajar, tongue out of groove. Looks at it a long moment, taps it with her fingers, watches it swing inward a few feet.

She's been inside a couple times over the years, recognizes the smell of dust, musty paperback westerns piled into haphazard stacks, and the cheap cigars Wallace sometimes smokes. She steps to the threshold, intending to call out, knock on the doorframe, but instead her gaze falls to windowpane rectangles of pallid light stretched across the entryway floor. No lamps on inside, no sound that she can hear. Yet partially melted snow on the mat, just a bit of it.

Owl turns, glancing at the Arctic Cat. One trail of footprints—a man's, no question, both size and weight make it obvious, boots with a commando tread—leading up to the front door in the fresh snow. No trail leading back out.

Now her whole body has gone rigid—*instincts*, Seth said—and she fades back, not caring if she's being silly, if nothing is really wrong, because the least compromised, animal part of her insists that something is.

As her right heel touches down on the snowy step, a flicker of motion from the corridor; she stops. There's a narrow decorative mirror hanging on the hallway wall, reflecting daylight from the room diagonal, what she's fairly sure is Wallace's bedroom.

There's a man in there, not Wallace or Cody, his back to the hallway. Three-quarter-length brown leather coat, a velveteen veneer of ginger hair, short-buzzed; in the light, from her slanted angle, he's like some illustration of a skeleton from an anatomy textbook, the knobs at the base of his skull well defined, and the gradual curve of the vertebrae in his neck where it links to shoulders, spine.

He leans over some piece of furniture in the corner, starts opening drawers—was maybe searching in a closet before, making too much noise to hear her come in, but not enough for Owl to catch from this distance.

She turns and leaves, quickly, lightly, ears full of the scuff of the backpack straps jouncing against her shoulders, horribly loud, checking to see if he's coming, but the partially open doorway remains empty, still.

Reaches the RV steps, jams her feet into her snowshoes, bending to slam the clasps into place, looks at the house one last time—

He's in the doorway now. Hands at his sides, head lowered, slightly angled to watch her.

Owl's breath catches, and she runs, nearly stumbling, rushing for the bramble patch, hearing thorny branches *ziiip* across her coat and jeans as she shoves through.

# 31

Going too fast in the shoes, pushing harder than a brisk walk, will tumble you, but Owl can't slow, putting distance between herself and the man, absurdly hopeful that her gut—this seasick conviction she's stumbled across the path of a hunter—is wrong. His tilted head and sighting eyes, taking in her points; pursuit will follow that look as naturally as moonrise chases dusk.

The money—got to hide it again, get it off her. Doesn't even like the feeling of the bag on her back. If that man is whoever Cody's running from, it's what he's here for.

Snow has changed to sleety, stinging ice by the time she makes it to the farm, occasional pellets striking the rectangle of exposed skin around her eyes. She heads toward the equipment shed—nothing to be done but hide the money the best she can, maybe under a tarp behind the summer tools:

spades and rakes, Weedwacker. Go wake up Seth and tell him everything.

She drags the shed door open against the snow, wedging herself into the dimness, shrugging off the bag. The door jerks open behind her and she jolts violently, spilling into the riding mower.

Cody looks in, sweatshirt hood pulled up over his cap, clothes sodden, snow clinging to the wool of his coat. His left eye is partially bruised down into the corner, swollen from the punch to his brow bone. "What're you doing?" he says.

She shuts her eyes, letting her heart settle before she drags her balaclava off, still breathless. "Where have you been?"

"What do you mean? I was out in the damn woods. I came back for that, and it was gone." Scrutinizing the bag, then her. "Why'd you take it?"

"To give it to you," she says sharply. "Where've you been staying?"

"The RV. Wallace didn't kick me out or anything. He didn't even come back after. I waited." Shrugs, expression remote. "Think he was scared to."

She throws down the corner of the tarp she'd lifted. "There was somebody in Wallace's house. Just now. I was there. Some man—thin, red hair. Searching through things."

Cody doesn't move, watching her narrowly. For a second, she's not even sure if he's heard. "Wallace at home?"

"No."

"This guy see you?" When she nods: "*Shit*. Wearing this?" Slaps the side of the pack. At her second nod, another harsh curse, rubs his neck, looking out at the swirling whiteness

313

before turning back to say, "That's Ballard. The guy I stole from." He presses his scabbed knuckles hard to his lips. "I knew it. Heard about that guy got shot . . ." Deep breath. "Well . . . he doesn't know you. Didn't even see your face."

"All he has to do is follow my snowshoe tracks up the trail. He saw which way I went." Hesitates. "He's got a snowmobile."

Cody immediately checks over his shoulder, then takes Owl's arm in a startling grip, pulling her out of the shed. "We've got to go—now. Where's Seth?"

"Inside."

"Then grab him and let's get the hell out of here." When she balks, yanking free, he leans down in her face: "Ballard's fucking nuts—do you not get that? He's on the stuff he sells half the time. And I took. His. *Money*. Made him look stupid. He's gonna kill me. And he'll kill you because you know." Pauses. "Seth's got guns, doesn't he?"


OWL STOPS IN the kitchen, looking at Seth's empty chair as Cody immediately crosses to the gun cabinet, grabbing the key from the top, where she told him it was kept.

"Seth!" She waits for him to appear from the bedroom, glances toward the loft, though it's no place he'd be. Cody opens the cabinet—two rifles and a shotgun in the barrel rest—grabs a .22 at random, banging it down on the coffee table, then a couple boxes of cartridges.

"Ammo." Comes over and jerks the zipper down on the backpack, jerking Owl around with it.

"I *told* you"—yanks back to look at him—"I don't know how to shoot. We don't hunt—"

"But you've seen Seth use 'em before, right?" Takes her hesitation as a yes, stuffing the boxes into the bottom of the bag. "We'll figure it out. Any idiot can use a gun."

Owl looks at the rifle laid out across the table, swallows dryly, thinking of Seth seeing the gaping cabinet, key still in the lock, rifle missing. Questions if any of this can be real, maybe some dream she's having in the moments before her alarm goes off. "Seth?" If he were here, he would've answered by now—must've gone outside. Please, God, not to follow her to Wallace's.

The CapTel corded phone can call for help even with the power out. She goes to where it sits on the end table, ever since Daddy called.

The end of the cord is snapped, where Seth pulled it free of the wall, raw wire exposed at the end. As she kneels to look at the landline jack, she sees the clear plastic plug still stuck inside.

The windowpanes are getting an all-out assault with sleet, some of it freezing almost instantly to create a pebbled smear of ice running with frigid rain, and she straightens, stares out at the woods, the head of her snowshoe trail. "Cody—"

"We gotta get somewhere with people, somewhere he can't do anything without everybody seeing." Cody's talking to himself, pulling his hood back up. "What's that place with the ice climbers? You said that was right outside of a town, didn't you? Ride the trails there, get a cab to a bus station, blow the fuck outta here." Jagged laughter; shakes the backpack on her shoulder. "Not like we don't got the money."

She's crossed the room halfway at this point, staring straight out the front window, at the world off their deck. "*Cody*. Shut up."

"*What.*"

Maybe he finally hears what she can't—the insectile buzz of an Arctic Cat engine above the clatter of sleet on the metal roof—but coming up close behind her to look out the mottled glass, he definitely sees what she sees: the dark shape of the snowmobile emerging from the trailhead, the driver low over the controls. Slows to a stop, a man's silhouette delivered here, now. Not her father, who she'd feared all along, but a stranger, an unknown quantity.

Owl sees Seth emerge from the sugarhouse, watching from the threshold as Ballard climbs off the seat, then taking a few steps down into the snow, leaning on his cane.

They're speaking to each other, some discussion silent to her, too far away to read, Seth closing the distance between himself and the man as they exchange words. Probably asking if he can help him, maybe thinking Ballard's just a snowmobiler on a day trip who got turned around in the storm.

She goes for the front door, a warning on her lips, but Cody pulls her back, squeezing her shoulders, holding her in place.

The conversation lasts a few agonizing minutes, Seth's new stillness signaling the change in the game, Ballard saying something that reveals what he is. Seth's hands slowly raise. Surrendering. Then he begins walking toward the cabin, with Ballard behind him.

The ginger-haired man takes something from his coat pocket, lifts it—brings the pistol down across the back of Seth's head, dropping him hard to the snow.

"*No!*" Owl yanks against Cody's grip, her gaze riveted to Seth, motionless, Ballard standing over him in contemplation.

"We gotta go. Owl, come *on.*"

"I'm not leaving—"

"You can't help him. *Go.*" Cody dragging her toward the back door, catching the woven strap of the .22 on the way.

A PANIC-BLIND RACE into the woods, Owl stuck on repeat, seeing Seth fall—helpless—and she isn't fighting escape anymore, instead leading the way through the trees, in what time they have before Ballard enters the cabin, realizes they must've fled.

Owl shoves aside branches that slap against Cody, pushes through spindly bushes in the direction of the trails that head toward Lament, on toward Dermott. Their forms thread along not far behind the outbuildings, and she knows there's every chance Ballard hears them crunching through the snow, is maybe watching them flit through the trees from the yard right now. She won't look back.

WITHIN MINUTES, THEIR clothes are soaked, Owl pulling her balaclava on just to ease the frigid beating her skin is taking from the sleet. Beneath his hood, Cody's face looks raw, expression numb, just going, both knowing it won't take long for Ballard to catch up.

She notices him glance back, and then he looks over at her. "I hear his motor. We've got to get to people—which way's fastest?"

Owl swears softly, disbelief blurring her thoughts, hardly able to grasp that this *is* real, they're in this, struggling to sort out routes in her head. "We'll never make it to Dermott. We'll never make it anywhere for help before he does." Bristles at Cody's disgusted look. "He's got an engine. We don't." Shakes her head. "You could leave the bag. Just drop it in the trail behind us, and we'll run."

His laughter is cracked. "Think he might notice it's a little short."

"It's better than getting nothing! Just saying, maybe he'll stop chasing."

"Jesus Christ. People like this don't stop—that's the whole point."

*"Well, why did you steal from him then?"* Shuts her eyes on the last syllable, sucks in air, hating that they're stupid enough to argue right now, with time disappearing. Sees an image of Seth falling, maybe still lying in the snow, body temperature plummeting. Almost certainly losing blood.

Looks at Cody, shifting from foot to foot, rifle over his shoulder. "Then we have to hide. I don't see what else we can do. Up high. Country's too rough for him to drive."

"Yeah, works for you—you know how to climb."

"Beats getting your ass shot off, doesn't it?" Takes his sleeve, pulling him with her. "You'll learn."

THE WAY TO the Notch has snowed in considerably since the last time they were there. The gamble of splitting off from the marked trail maybe bought them some time. Leaving such an obvious set of tracks Ballard can follow, two sets of footprints in fresh, wet snow, haunts Owl, but there's nothing for it—it's too slow going in the trees, wading through drifts; plus Cody's running more ragged than she is, racked with a consumptive sort of cough, spitting a lot, his clothes knockoffs made to a trend, not to resist the weather, like her nylon-lined duck coat and hiking boots.

"I can't hear him anymore. Owl"—Cody touches her shoulder—"I think he's stopped."

"The path's probably gotten too narrow for the sled. The trees and everything." Owl can't help but test to see if she can hear, pulling the balaclava off and stuffing it into her pocket, but there's nothing. "Maybe he's hiking in behind us." Hesitates. "We shouldn't talk unless we have to. It could echo."


THE WATERFALL IS rushing, heavy with sleet and snowmelt, the basin itself swollen, leaden gray, banks clotted with sodden snow and branches that have gone over the falls.

They walk single file now, Owl in front, Cody several feet behind, lagging, fatigue obvious.

"We keep going past the ledge." She glances at him. "Find a hiding spot. Wait him out, then work our way down." Prays Holly makes it home despite the weather, finds Seth in time. But what if Ballard goes back to the cabin, finds them there? A new terror she hadn't considered; she's now sick with it. "Come on."

Grabs his arm, ushering him ahead. "Not much farther." Has no idea if that's true. But they can't go any faster than Cody's pace.

Instead of threading left, onto the ledge, they continue through the boulders, heading up the mountainside, farther than she's ever gone in this direction; the Notch is such a beauty spot that she and Seth and Holly never found a need to hike beyond it. Not much sign that anyone else has, either. There's no real trail anymore—the ground too rocky—just uncertain places to put your feet, broad rock faces with ledges dripping snow or yellowed ice, streams of water leaving dark, circuitous paths down the granite and mica schist. One small good fortune: it's slightly too warm for the sleet to freeze when it hits the ground, instead leaving all surfaces damp, pooling.

There's almost no cover to speak of now, except the occasional spindly dwarf conifer existing in seemingly less soil than it would take to sprout basil in a windowsill pot—not the kind of place someone without climbing experience can navigate, especially in this weather—but Owl guides Cody up, grabbing at him when he loses his footing, both frozen through, exhausted.

There's another waterfall above, smaller than the one in the Notch—a multistep—the water stealing away over a series of rock levels with their own small plunge pools, down the side of the mountain to where it becomes more wooded again, disappearing into the trees.

Cody's hands are on her then, pushing forward, nearly knocking her down—"Go—go, *go*"—and rock explodes in splinters three feet ahead, her own hands flying up to shield her face a second late, in delayed reaction. She jerks her head over and sees the man, visible far below, sighting on them, narrow face lined with anticipation, in his hand the slender black shape of his pistol.

They run, Owl seeing the man start forward just as they reach a rock formation that swells outward, blocking his view.

No time to think, to discuss anything, as the world becomes vertical. It's sheer mountainside higher up—nowhere to go but the falls—and they're reduced to balancing on the edge of their boots in places to avoid losing balance and sliding down the slope.

For a time, they seemed blessed, anointed with adrenaline— they can't fall, meant to make it to the rocky steps, follow the flow of water back into tree cover, get away.

She hears the report of the second shot—small, muffled— screams faintly, and her right foot slips, thin soil crumbling, lands hard on her side, immediately slapping her left hand out for rock, second nature to find a handhold. Feels Cody grab for her, and they both go down, Cody making a harsh cry as he slides below her—his grip releases, and Owl watches in helpless detachment as he begins a descent she's powerless to stop.

Cody skids, gloved hands clawing, trying to dig a heel in to stop himself, but the partially frozen dirt scatters away from rock. Manages to turn halfway as he slams over the shallow ledge below and disappears from sight.

Owl stares, lying on her side, clinging to a handhold, craning her neck to see any sign of Cody—who knows how far he's fallen, if he's even stopped yet.

No sound she can hear but her own breathing; even if Cody were screaming, a broken leg or worse, she'd never know it.

Knows nothing but that Ballard's still coming, gaining, as she lies here in shock.

Digs her knee into the frozen dirt as much as she can and straightens her upper body, glancing back. Still no visual lock on Ballard—maybe hiding, taking potshots, keeping the power by staying out of sight. Gripping rocks and planting her toes in as much as she can, she crabs her way over and down a few feet, teeth gritted, fighting to get eyes on Cody, where he ended up.

No good; the outcropping of rock below must be blocking him, wherever he is. Making a pained face, she edges a little farther.

The rifle. Hung up on some brush about four feet below. Looks back again, searching, then begins inching herself lower, wary of starting a tumble that could turn into a free fall. Battles with herself: How can she leave Cody, not knowing if he's hurt, if Ballard might be right on top of him? How can she waste the time trying to get to him when a third shot could go off any second? And she still wears the backpack on her shoulders.

She hooks a foot through the rifle's strap and lifts the gun, snagging it and throwing it over her shoulder, then, staying low, makes an awkward scramble back up the slope toward the waterfall, where at last she can put her feet on mostly level rock again, at least for the moment. Cody has to be okay. And if he isn't—not much she can do for him now.

She runs across the wet rocks, cold spray splattering her jeans and boots, slips once and drops a leg up to the knee in a pool—frigid shock of ice water—pulls free, gasping, rushes on.

A tier of the falls makes a natural curtain of streaming spray, the only real cover she sees, and she slides into a crag in the rock just off the plunge pool, slamming her tailbone. Teeth chattering, she crouches in the continual mist, pulling the backpack off and digging through the bullets. One box isn't even the correct caliber—.308—but one is marked .22LR, so she fumbles some out into her hands, holding the rifle in a way she's seen Seth do it, stock tucked beneath her right arm.

It's bolt-action—she knows that much, moving the metal bolt handle up and then back to open the breech in front. Seth's religious about cleaning his weapons whether they've been used or not, so the breech is empty, no old rounds—but she has no clue if they slot straight in; she's not interested in guns, because she doesn't want to kill things. Sometimes, Seth puts the ammo in the bottom, up through the stock, but was that this rifle or another?

Curses silently, brass rounds falling from her hands, scattering into the rocks as she tries jamming some into the breech. Cartridges rattle around without sliding home—not sure if they don't want to go in there or if her hands are just too cold and clumsy with fear. Watches with despairing eyes as all but two drop through her legs and roll away.

Motion on her upper left. Someone else reaching the rocks around the falls, rendered a blur through the gushing water above. Could be Cody, could be Ballard.

No time to dig into the box for more cartridges. Owl sucks breath, holds it, cramming the breech shut and locking it, and then presses her back against the rock, feet braced, aiming the gun as she's seen Seth do it, stock between her right shoulder and collarbone, left hand gripping the body, fingers clear of the barrel. And waits.

# 32

The red-haired man steps into view, following the outer
edge of the rocks, an obvious searching quality about
him, his gun out. Hope passes through Owl that he might not
even see her, might go right by and she can double back, find
Cody.

But Ballard's vision strays downward, and he sees her
below, staring at him.

Owl jerks tighter to the rock, legs locked, convulsive trem-
bling taking over, as she hoists the rifle even higher, sighting
down it at him, finger on the trigger.

Ballard squints his right eye slightly—murky green-hazel,
brows near invisible—"Look at you." Voice rough yet papery,
breathless from the hike, hard for her to make out. "We got a
sniper here."

Owl doesn't speak, close to bursting with need to fully

inhale, but hyperventilation is too close, right on the other side of satisfying the starving need for oxygen.

"Where's my boy?" He lowers his gun a few more inches, a semiautomatic similar to the one in Seth's gun cabinet, but it has an additional metallic length attached to the barrel—a homemade silencer, maybe, much like a small, crosshatched flashlight barrel.

She takes air shakily through her clamped teeth, reasserting her rifle position. Ballard must not have seen Cody's fall from wherever he'd been hiding. Can't stand having her back to the rock anymore, snags her foot as she moves, nearly stumbling, but never takes her gaze away.

"Seen him?" He waits, some almost rascally amusement showing through, like fool's gold's shining through silt in a sifter. "You going to kill me with that squirrel shooter?" Sees Owl's gaze go to the pistol in his grip, tips both his hands out, seeming unconcerned with taking his aim off her. "Just want what's mine. Can't blame me. He took from me, and I got to recoup." His gaze settles on the backpack straps over her shoulders. "Looks like he hung it on you."

Owl continues backing up, fumbling behind with one hand to discern the height of the rocks—no use going over on one of the steps—and forces her voice out: "I don't want it. You can have it."

"Oh, I know that." Takes a glance around like someone with dawning awareness of a surprise party, friends hidden behind shapes of shadowy furniture. "Where is he? Really wanted to talk to him. Been trying to get in touch for weeks." Waits for Cody to emerge, looks back at her. "Hiding like a chickenshit, letting you do all the work, huh? Ain't that just like a man." Grin of small teeth, mostly uniform, enamel worn to show yellow dentin like old ivory; then, dismissively: "Put the gun down, honey."

Owl's heart clamors, no idea what to do next, finger adjusting on the trigger, knows she may only have one chance, other rounds wedged into cracks in the rock, sunken into the pool of mineral water. Works her left arm out of the backpack, unwilling to shift the gun by freeing her right. "I'll toss it to you. Take it."

"You think *you're* running things?" Sudden savagery, sprays of crow's feet slicing into the tight flesh across his molded cheekbones: "Get that gun off me. You're not gonna shoot anybody. Probably still got the safety on." Comes toward her, about to boost himself down onto the wet step below him.

"*Stop.*" She braces against the rocks.

He's showing teeth again, still advancing around the pool, gun held up now, as if to cuff her with it. Owl's range of vision shrinks, narrowing to him, air seeming to shimmer because she won't blink, won't lose half a moment's sight as her finger tightens on the trigger, prepared, but also so afraid to squeeze—

Another form enters the frame, unfocused, miragelike, to Ballard's right, stopping several feet back, and Owl's gaze moves there, long enough that Ballard stops and turns, seeing Cody standing on the ledge above at roughly the same time she does.

Cody doesn't speak as he looks down at them, his clothes wet, muddy, a gash across his forehead. Skin pallid, a battered, drained look to him, worsened by the black eye.

326

"Decided to poke your head up, huh?" Big voice on Ballard now, all sarcastic energy, talking loud enough to be heard over the falls. "I was just about to take my money from your girlfriend."

*I spent it. Most of it.* Owl reads it from Cody's lips, the hissing water stealing his sound from this distance.

Ballard rocks back on one heel. "Yeah, I heard—you going around town, paying what Mom owes, helping out my competitors. I known Evie a long time. Not going to amount to a piss in the ocean with her, you got to know that." Another wait. "I worked her over good, trying to get her to tell me where you were. She wouldn't, though, God love her. Wasn't easy finding somebody could tell me where you two hail from. Where you might have people." Shakes his head. "Hope it was worth bringing this shitstorm down on yourself."

*Doubt it.*

"And that's what I couldn't figure about you—you *know* better. You known since you were little how this works. I got to make up my losses. One way or another." Ballard turns to Owl.

*I'll do anything.* Cody takes a step forward, holding up his hands. *I'll do anything. Just . . . leave her.* He makes eye contact with Owl for the first time—unemotive, maybe three seconds, yet something passes between them; Owl pulls in a breath, looks down the sight.

"Can't believe what I'm hearing." Comically overwhelmed. "With all the play you get, you gonna up and get all noble on me?" A slow shift, a stillness coming over him, burlesque humor fading. "Invested a lot of time in you, bud. Years. Then you fuck me over anyway." Levels the gun at him. "Had you figured like my own kid."

*Can't let you hurt her.* Cody starts walking toward Ballard's gun, inviting it.

Ballard's mouth thins, trigger finger moves.

Owl shuts her eyes, squeezes.

Combustion of spark and powder, muzzle flare with an incredible *bang*, mule kick in the shoulder as the rifle recoils. Owl hits the rock. Her eyes snap open in time to see Cody half spin, lose balance, slam onto one knee, then his elbow. Her mouth opens, releasing a soundless cry.

Ballard straightens slowly from a partial crouch, staring at Cody, and Owl flings the gun, not waiting to see what she's done, what's left; just hurls herself at the step above, mantling up, a hard pull and a scrabble of her legs sending her surging into the shallow, rushing water as the world is lost in her scream, Ballard's gun exploding again below.

She crashes onto her knees; not shot, no pain, but mentally crystalized in that moment of Cody going down—her fault, her fault—and then she drives herself on, over the crest of rock and beyond.


AERIAL VIEW: OWL'S a tiny figure racing flat out across great plateaus of rock, all of Waits Mountain's peak above and all of the valley below.

Gasping, weeping, forgotten backpack flapping against her, only one strap on her shoulder. A hollowness in her signals she's reached the limit of escape, run as far as anyone can.

Glances back, sees Ballard appearing over the top of the rocks behind the waterfall, straightening to watch her progress.

A massive face of exfoliating granite lies ahead, as daunting a stop sign as Mother Nature creates. The slope up to it is entirely covered in wet scree—loose, weather-beaten rock chunks shed from the face over time. Owl halts, breath wheezing from her, mind scraped blank, scanning all that lies above.

It's a big wall—multipitch, like nothing she's ever climbed before. And the only way off this shooting gallery. She isn't willing to fold. Knows at once, with grim finality, that she won't surrender to him. To anything. Let this be her last act.


THE SCREE ROLLS beneath her, shifting constantly. Owl uses all fours to claw her way up, dumps over onto her side once, starts a small slide of rock tumbling down to the base that threatens to pull her with it. She cycles her knees and hands madly, not taking a breath until her boots touch solid ground again, launching herself at the wall, knowing Ballard's watching.

She slaps her hands to the rock, running her palms across the surface as she scans the towering wall, assessing, searching for anything, any handhold.

There's a crack running through it, about twenty-five feet in length, widening as it goes up, as if some heavenly axe split into it from above. Barely four uneven feet across at the opening above her.

*Squeeze chimney.* The term rises to the surface of her thoughts. She's seen it done—she, Holly, and Seth once watched a man traverse one in Rumney—a climber wedging himself into a "chimney" in the rock, working his way up. Not done in bouldering—it's real, hard-core mountain climbing, harnesses and ropes—but working herself in is the only chance she has of maybe escaping Ballard's reach.

Owl spots a hand crack right away, and then a foothold to brace the sole of her boot against the opposite side so she can wriggle herself in high and deep before he reaches the wall, hide herself in the womb of the mountain. She falls, she'll have trapped herself—all he'll need to do is aim and fire.

Counterforce. Breath held, she uses the hand crack, boosts from the foothold, pulls herself inside the space.

Pressing both feet against one wall, her back against the other, she assumes a roughly seated position, spanning the chimney with her body as she's seen it done. The rest is strength, consistency, arm locks, jamming her feet for support.

Surrounded by the sound of her own breathing, she pushes herself upward inches at a time, reestablishing hand and foot positions over and over. Now, she closes her eyes, focuses on slowing her breathing and heart rate, not admitting to herself that her quads already feel pumped.

Sleet patters her face when the breeze is right, leaving it dotted with water she doesn't dare wipe away. Doesn't know how many bullets ricochet above until one comes close, spraying shattered rock. She shrieks, nearly slipping.

Shifts her limbs as fast as she dares—she can't let herself fall into the narrow trap of the chimney's base—going deeper, higher, as another bullet pings off the opening of the chimney above.

She sees Ballard below her now. He's not holding the gun—empty, must be—and he stares up the uneven length of the shaft at her, his face twisted and set, before reaching both arms into the space. Pulling himself in.

Owl can't breathe. She fumbles the zipper on her right coat pocket, feels for the shape of her knife. Turns her head, fitting her front tooth into the nail mark to unfold the blade.

Ballard's eyes are like small, heated gems as he boosts himself, climbing into her shadow—his identity erased, unskilled, all predatorial instinct, nearly falling twice—until they both hang there, staggered, between the two walls.

He strains upward, grabbing hold of her lower foot. She swipes down at him with the knife, knowing he's too far to reach—nicks his fingers, making him scream. Blood, scrabbling, then Owl's shriek as Ballard yanks her leg and her knife clatters away.

She lashes out wildly with her foot, heel colliding with his face.

He grunts, jerks—Owl's frantic glance sees his posture loosen, his torso twist as he falls, skidding down, deeper into the crack—two feet, four feet—even below the foothold she used to boost herself in, where he slams into the narrowest point, crying out.

Rage; he jerks his body, trying to lunge up. His left foot is sideways, wedged, shoulder driven flush into the rock.

She watches him awhile, riveted, impervious to his

guttural cursing, his sweeping, flailing hand, until she's certain he really can't follow.

She lifts her head to the section of gray sky above, sees the fault line of another hand crack, widening as it follows the chimney wall. Drives her fist in, skinning her knuckles inside her gloves, grits her teeth as she pulls herself, all upper-body strength, mind already set to making her way back over to the opening of the chimney, one hold at a time, then down to solid ground.

*"Bitch, don't you leave me—"*

But she can no longer hear.

SOME FIFTEEN MINUTES later, Owl collapses at the base of the slope where the scree collects, far away from Ballard. Muscles aching, exhausted, occasional hitching sobs pass through her. She presses her face against her knees, no thought.

She doesn't hear him calling until he's halfway up the scree slope, right arm held against his body, losing his balance and catching himself with his good hand now and then, struggling to reach her. Doesn't register it's Cody even as she lifts her head to his voice, looking straight at him as if he's emerging from some vision, sleeve of his coat torn and black with blood, his lips reading, *Owl, Owl,* a mantra fluid as water spilling down a stone stairway, one level to the next, into tree shadow.

# 33

S pattering of blood; a kill spot in their front yard, shown through a soft fleece of fresh snow.

Owl, running on nothing but the remainders of adrenaline—their descent of the mountain so fast she slipped again and again, afraid she'd get here too late—straightens from the place where Seth fell, scanning the trees, any place he might've gone. Stopped by Cody's call of, "Over here."

Seth made it as far as the cabin entryway; he still lies there, on one side, arm outstretched, feet blocking the door from closing all the way, so that snow has blown and scattered across their kitchen floor, collecting in corners.

"Wake up. *Please*. Wake up." Warming his hand with hers, holding it to her cheek.

Eyelids flutter, a moment's struggle with the hazy allure

of unconsciousness, and then Seth's focusing on her, the now of things falling into place, and his first words are, "You okay?"

SLEET HAS TURNED back to snow by the time Owl and Cody sit together on the couch in the cabin.

Electricity is still out, interior shadowed, but Owl stoked the fire, added logs, and now the flames flicker behind the glass door. It's well past four, the ordeal on the mountain somehow taking only a few hours of their lives. She's just gotten Seth into bed, the wound on the back of his head bandaged as best it could be with gauze and tape; he hasn't seemed drowsy since they woke him—maybe a good sign—but Owl will check him again in a couple minutes, keep watching for signs of concussion. Knows there will probably be messages on their phones from Holly, saying she'll be getting a motel room in St. Beatrice tonight, waiting out the storm. Owl will be heading in that direction soon, to get help. And in time, she'll tell Holly everything.

Cody's stripped out of his wet clothes and put on a dry T-shirt and jeans of Seth's. He watches as Owl cuts open the plastic packaging around a tube of liquid stitches. "This will hurt," she says. "Probably a lot."

Nods slowly. "Bring it." Takes a breath and holds it, watching as she dabs the horizontal slice her bullet made across his right bicep with a towel dipped in water heated in a kettle on the woodstove, then pats it dry. Follows with disinfectant on a piece of gauze, then gingerly pushes the edges of the cut together in a way that makes him inhale sharply through his nose, shutting his eyes.

"Sorry." Squeezes the tube of clear glue from one end of the cut to the other, holds it in place for a count of one minute, like the package says, watching uncertainly after she lets go; it's the first time she's ever used the supplies Seth keeps in their first-aid kit. "Really. I'm sorry I did that to you."

"Not like you meant to." Checks out his arm. "Ballard saw me go down, figured I was pretty much done, so he didn't hang around to finish me off." Swallows. "All this is my fault. I know it. We're lucky we're not dead." Pauses. Maybe waiting for her to speak in the silence, absolve him of this. When she says nothing, he begins shrugging on the chamois shirt she got for him from Seth's closet. "We should leave him up there."

"In this weather, he'd be dead by morning."

Cody gazes back at her. "You don't know what he's done to people."

"Yeah. You said." She confronts the hardness in herself at the thought of Ballard, trapped in the rock, snow sifting down on him, utterly alone. Approaching hypothermia. Difficult to feel for someone who would've left her to a much worse fate—would've reveled in it, in fact. And so easy to see how seamlessly he could be erased. Who would come looking for that man? Who could possibly care that he was missing? And how would they ever know to search here?

She balls up the towels and stands, hesitating by the couch, saying stiffly, "You should go now. Take your money. See how far you get."

"Owl."

"I'm going for help. You can't be here when they come. Or they'll take you away, too." She tries to compose herself, looking down, then back at him. "I know you didn't want any of this to happen. But it did. And it'll keep on happening."

"No. Never again. I'm not—"

"You have a good heart. I know that. But I'm not stupid, either." Tiredness is pressing down on her, but she can't give in, not with so much left to do. "You're going to keep doing things that get people hurt. That hurt you the most, maybe." She studies him, loss a spreading, burgundy-colored blossom in her chest, blood on snow. "You never told me why you really came here. To the mountain, to do the job." Waits. "Was it for Wallace?"

Cody stands, walking over, taking his coat, finding it still soaked. "I just . . . had to know. Who he was. If he was as bad as I always figured. Maybe I thought I'd get back at him or something. I don't know. I mean, he's the only family I got, other than Mom." Looks over as Owl crosses the room, giving him a worn flannel-lined sweatshirt from the rack, taking his coat; he nods. "I used to think about all the stuff that never would've happened if he'd stepped up like he should've." Soft snort, shake of his head, as he pulls up the zipper. "Turns out he's just another sad old drunk. Scared of being alone."

They stand close, close enough for Owl to feel the heat of him. Her voice is a near whisper. "I think you wanted to be wrong about him."

Can feel how badly he wants to touch her. "You don't

know what it's like. When you got nobody. Money's the only thing keeps you safe."

"You're right. I've got people who take care of me. We take care of each other. I guess . . . that's what keeps us safe. As safe anybody can be." Presses her lips together, trying to steady her voice. "I hope you find your place. But it's not here."

The silence goes on, Owl willing the tears from her eyes as Cody looks down at her.

His hand finds her cheek, cups it, warm, familiar. "Don't stop drawing. You're really good at it. I should've told you."

She watches as he pulls his boots on, thinking of the folded sheet of art paper still in her coat pocket. She digs it out—crumpled at the edges, slightly damp. "Here. Don't try to open it until it's dry."

He takes it, turning it over in his hands, watching her return to the couch, her back to him, facing the fire. How still she is, how she probably won't even hear him go out the door, if he chooses this moment to do it.

Instead, he walks past the kitchen table, close enough to say, "Owl." She glances back, her cheeks wet. "Try not to hate me too much. Okay?"

Her gaze, searching, wounded; slight nod, then turns to the stove, huddling her slight frame against the cushions.


WHEN THE DOOR shuts, she feels it. Fists balled in the blanket, face screwed up against the tears, struggling to breathe through it, keep some control.

When enough time's passed, no chance he'd see her, she goes to the front window and looks out.

His footprints leave a winding trail down the center of the driveway, and she sees him at the very end, about to turn onto the road, the light-colored sweatshirt still visible against early dusk. He's flipped the hood up, backpack on his shoulders, head down, shoulders hunched, that fighter's stance as he makes his way off into the storm.

# 34

Mid-April. New life emerges shyly, unfolding in ways unexpected: Buds in trees still skeletal from winter, marsh marigolds lifting yellow heads from drifts of mud and dead leaves. A spider exploring the hilly surface of a residual crust of snow.

OWL'S IN A tree, a big aspen, standing on the second-to-topmost step of her latest project, an eight-foot deer stand, hammering the plywood platform to the frame, nails held in her teeth. She and Griffin found the plans online, and she scrounged all the lumber from Seth's scrap pile; enough room for two camp chairs up here, with height to see the deer path she followed from the sugarbush one day, and to just make out what she thinks is a goshawk's nest in the distance, a dark mass of woven sticks and straw.

Crunch of underbrush, but she doesn't look down, carefully taking the nails from her mouth before she speaks. "You shouldn't be out here."

"I won't say anything if you don't." Raising his voice to compensate for their distance, Seth takes his time checking out the diagonal supports and ladder, knocking on two-by-fours as much to test the sturdiness as get her attention. "Seen much yet?"

"No. And you're going to wear out two knees if you don't take it easy. Holly said."

"If you think I'm going to start knitting pot holders or something, you got a good imagination." His operation almost three weeks ago, Seth's already walking without the cane, returned to whatever dusty closet corner it came from. More pills—different pills—some notion of new taking the place of the old, though no one seemed comfortable saying much about that within Owl's range of hearing. But two days' recovery in the hospital was enough to make Seth determined to set the all-time record for bouncing back; he's full of plans for clearing more of their land, starting some sugar maple saplings on the long road to becoming producers. "Griffin coming over to work on this with you again sometime?"

She looks back to her work. "Maybe."

"Okay." Waits, gives the rail another tap. "Think I could come up there sometime?"

Smiles. "Maybe."

Nodding, he starts slowly back toward the cabin, navigating

the boggy ground with care. A scraping sound stops him—Owl's foot, slipping slightly on the rung.

For a moment, neither of them moves, each waiting to see what the other will do. But Seth sets his sights ahead, using the occasional tree trunk to brace himself as he goes, and Owl chokes up on the hammer, wrapping her left arm more tightly around the rail.

OWL SITS ON the edge of the top deck for a bit, swinging her feet as she gazes out from her new height, then climbs down and heads in the direction of the sugarbush.

She's been this way a few times over the past weeks, usually just walking the rows, but this time she wants to see his mark. Remind herself he was real.

It takes some doing, but she finds it, following the edge of the clearing, not stopping until she spots the X Cody cut into tree bark. No longer green wood but dry, darker, weathered from open air and elements. Healing.

She thinks about him more than she could ever say. Sometimes, it's pain—him with that girl; *Then we won't have to say bye. Ever.* Other times, she dines on anger, a snake-eating-its-own-tail self-fueling cycle of resentment she knows better than to lock into, revisiting the worst times. Then she remembers the closeness, the burnished nights in the sugarhouse, giving herself over to someone so totally, and misses it. *Try not to hate me too much. Okay?* No matter what anyone would think about that.

Wallace's truck was eventually found abandoned in a Greyhound bus station parking lot in Lebanon; amazing Cody was able to make it through the pass at all in that storm, especially in a rust bucket like that. As Wallace told the sheriff's deputies—and anyone else who would listen—he'd been back from Gunnar's place only a few hours, waiting out the storm, when he heard the engine start up. Reached the window just in time to see the taillights bumping off through the snow.

Boy was the only one who knew about the extra key in the shed. Shabby thing, pressing charges against your own grandson, but he wanted the damn truck back, didn't he? Hell, it was the kid brought all that trouble up here, dragged it with him from Manchester.

Seth had said nothing, as usual, when Wallace told him this over coffee in their kitchen, completely unconcerned with the presence of Owl, on the couch, reading every word. Cody wasn't a subject Seth liked to speak on, especially not around her. But the Ram was back, somewhat worse for wear; the police had found it with the keys locked inside and a full tank of gas. *Try not to hate me too much.*

Motion catches Owl's eye, her gaze focusing on something emerging from the brush far beyond the tree.

The vixen appears—unmistakable, Owl would know her markings anywhere.

A few seconds later, impossibly, a kit follows. Just one, grown nearly twice the size she would've been when Owl last saw her. Long black stockings, pert ears, eyes bright, undomesticated energy.

Owl doesn't breathe, doesn't dare, instead watching as the foxes scent on her, vixen stretching her neck, darting her head to get a better look at the human on their hunting ground. The kit is a gift, filling Owl so completely oxygen seems superfluous; little survivor, who maybe hid in the bushes while her mother had tried to reach the others, or found an alternate tunnel to escape the cave-in.

As Owl watches, the vixen turns and flees through the trees, tail a flame trailing behind her, and after a pause, the kit does the same.


BACK AT THE cabin, Owl finds Holly clearing out her little garden by the front steps, turning the soil over with a short-handled pitchfork, hair held back with her bandanna. She glances over, slightly breathless, as Owl hesitates on the steps, asking, "Did you hear back?" Almost afraid to ask, knowing Holly had made a first tentative move with her family, sending her younger sister a long email yesterday, the content Owl isn't sure of. Only knows her aunt sat composing it on the couch for nearly an hour: deleting, rephrasing, sitting for long periods gazing at the screen, lost in thought.

Holly stabs the fork down, leans into the handle, smiling at her. "Feel like taking a trip to Maine?"

"I get to meet them?"

Small toss of her head. "Lottie and Gram, anyway."

Owl nods slowly. "Yeah. That'd be good."

Holly turns over a chunk of sod, sifting with the tines to shake soil from the roots of a big weed before tipping it into the wheelbarrow. "I hope so. You and Gram ought to see eye to eye on a few things, I think." As Owl turns toward the step, Holly puts in shortly, "You're a good girl, Owl," her expression holding a watchful sort of sincerity as her niece looks back at her. Nods slightly. Takes the steps inside at a jog, not wanting to get everyone concerned over some wetness in her eyes.

Owl knows people whisper about her, her part in what happened with Ballard, assigning her a lot more blame than simply being the one who took the Ski-Doo down to the valley to contact the sheriff's department the day of the March blizzard. Ballard's name lies unspoken in the cabin as he awaits trial, recovered from hypothermia, a dislocated shoulder, and various other injuries he'd suffered while trapped in the chimney before New Hampshire Fish and Game was able to reach him and carry him out. Owl will testify—dreading it, won't admit it, not with everyone looking her way in Cody's absence. The police are searching for him. Won't be long before they catch up. Or at least that seems to be the consensus.


NOW, SHE GOES to the loft, sits at her desk, surrounded by her sketches, the fox with the mouse in its jaws, the broken robin's-egg shells. Wonders about when Cody unfolded her portrait of him, rendered from the photo she took on the ghost train; if he opened it while swaying in a Greyhound bus seat down a highway to destination unknown. Someplace right. Someplace that fits.

Owl opens the top drawer and brings out a notebook, flipping to the place she marked with her father's letter. She's already written three false starts, the pages heavily scribbled out in ink, and makes a face now, staring desolately at the lined paper. So strange penning an actual letter; seems impossible to begin, to somehow make herself heard to this man, the distant voice of Rochelle still calling out for Daddy despite the weighty accumulation of years.

Remembers her conversation with Cody that night: *He had his say. Now you get yours.*

*Maybe I don't want a say when it comes to him. Don't need one.*

*Yeah, you do. Everybody does.*

Turns to a fresh sheet, takes pen in hand, releases a tense breath, and begins anew:

*Dear Joel,*
*The first thing you should know is everyone calls me Owl.*

# ACKNOWLEDGMENTS

MY GRATITUDE GOES to Algonquin Young Readers, to Krestyna Lypen, for lending her keen editorial skills to this book, and to my agent, Alice Tasman, for her tireless support of my writing.

I'd also like to thank Dr. Darren J. Ranco, associate professor of anthropology and coordinator of Native American research at the University of Maine, for performing the authenticity reading of this manuscript in its early stages. In addition, the generosity of the Authors Guild provided a safety net that allowed me to complete Owl's journey on a very tight schedule with a baby on the way; thank you.

And lastly, with my whole heart, thank you to my family. You are my happiness, my foundation, and truly what gives my writing wings.